Revenge at Hatchet Creek

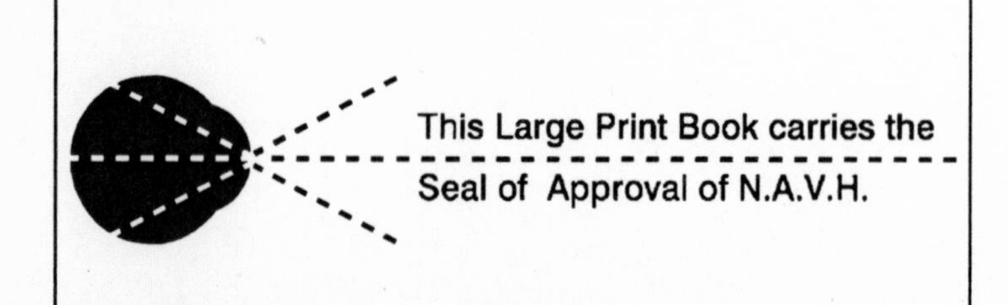
This Large Print Book carries the
Seal of Approval of N.A.V.H.

Revenge at Hatchet Creek

Frank Leslie

WHEELER PUBLISHING
A part of Gale, Cengage Learning

GALE
CENGAGE Learning™

Detroit • New York • San Francisco • New Haven, Conn • Waterville, Maine • London

Wheeler Publishing, a part of Gale, Cengage Learning.

Wheeler Publishing Large Print Western.
The text of this Large Print edition is unabridged.
Other aspects of the book may vary from the original edition.
Set in 16 pt. Plantin.

LIBRARY OF CONGRESS CATALOGING-IN-PUBLICATION DATA

Leslie, Frank, 1963–
Revenge at Hatchet creek / by Frank Leslie. — Large print ed.
p. cm. — (Wheeler Publishing large print western)
ISBN-13: 978-1-4104-4297-0 (pbk.)
ISBN-10: 1-4104-4297-7 (pbk.)
1. Outlaws—Fiction. 2. Large type books. I. Title.
PS3552.R3236R48 2011
813'.54—dc22 2011031781

Published in 2011 by arrangement with NAL Signet, a member of Penguin Group (USA) Inc.

Printed in the United States of America
1 2 3 4 5 15 14 13 12 11

FD301

For the Campfire,
keepers of the flame.

Chapter 1

Yak-yak-yak-yak-yak-yak-yak . . . !

The caterwauling of the Gatling gun seemed to be echoing the first syllable of Yakima Henry's name as the big half-breed himself cranked the handle and stared out over the revolving canister and through the billowing powder smoke. The .45-caliber rounds being slung from the six blazing maws tore the rough-clad posse riders out from behind their covering rocks, and spun them into the spindly Dakota bunch grass like rag dolls caught in a cyclone.

Yakima couldn't help grinning, his green eyes sparking, at the thrill of the kill. This bunch had been dogging him too long, and they'd intended to use the Gatling gun themselves to shoot him off the canyon's north cliff, where they'd had him trapped like a cow-killing wildcat. And they almost had . . . until he'd gotten around them early this morning and taken the gun over for his own retributive purposes. . . .

Yak-yak-yak-yak-yak . . . !

The chest of one of the posse riders opened up like a tomato smashed against a barn door. The man screamed, showing pale yellow teeth beneath his bushy black mustache. He flung his rolling-block Remington rifle over his head and turned a backward somersault over one of the boulders strewn along the shore of Hatchet Creek.

Yakima spied movement to his right and spun the gun toward the ridge. A rifleman had leaped onto a flat-topped boulder sheathed in dry grass and gnarled burr oaks, but before he could raise his Winchester to his shoulder, the Gatling's hot lead puffed dust from his heavy sheepskin coat and blew doggets of blood, flesh, and spine out his back. He screamed as he triggered his rifle into the rock he was standing on, then twisted around and fell back off the rock and out of sight.

Yakima stopped cranking.

He stared out over the red-hot barrel, through the webbing smoke hanging in a heavy, fetid cloud over the back of the buckboard farm wagon in which the Gatling was perched. The wagon sat between the base of the chalky, boulder-strewn ridge and the muddy waters of Hatchet Creek, on the trail that led south from the little town of Wild Rose. Around the wagon, three men lay dead.

They were the first of the seven- or eight-man posse that Yakima, having bided his time over the long, cold night, had taken down when he'd stolen up on the wagon and taken over the Gatling gun. He could see parts of two other dead men peeking out from behind a cottonwood stump on his left, and a boulder about forty yards downstream, along the bank of the creek.

It was just after dawn, and the canyon was all soft gray light and purple shadows. The creek moved darkly in its meandering bank, gurgling softly. The fall yellow leaves of the cottonwoods standing tall along the creek scratched in a rising breeze.

Yakima kept his hand on the Gatling gun's cranking lever. He'd taken down most of the men who'd been hunting him after he'd left Wild Rose like a mule with its tail on fire, but three or four still hadn't been accounted for.

Suddenly, a rifle barrel poked up from behind a boulder on the right side of the trail and about thirty yards beyond the wagon. The entire rifle appeared in a man's gloved hand. The hand waved the rifle slowly from left to right.

"Holy Christ — don't shoot no more, mister," a man yelled. "I give up!"

A man's tan-hatted head appeared from behind a flat-topped boulder halfway up the ridge on Yakima's right. The man's face was a dun oval beneath the hat. A red knit scarf was wrapped around his neck.

"Same here, breed. Hold your fire!"

The Gatling gun's swivel rod squawked as Yakima trained the deadly weapon toward the man on the ridge. "Throw your guns out. Both of you."

Each man tossed a rifle out. The man near the trail tossed out what appeared to be an old cap-and-ball Colt with a wooden handle held together with rawhide. The man on the ridge tossed out two newer-model pistols and a hunting knife. The knife clattered when it hit the gravel and rolled nearly all the way down to the trail.

"That all you got?"

"That's it for me," said the man on the ridge.

"That's all I'm carryin' — right there," said the man nearer the trail.

All night, Yakima had been pinned down about three-quarters of the way up the ridge. From there, he'd seen the posse tether their horses in a cottonwood copse about a hundred yards upstream, toward town, and on the other side of the creek. All the horses were likely still there, though it looked as though all but two wouldn't be bearing riders for a while.

They'd brought the deadly Gatling gun in just after sundown. They'd stood around drinking whiskey and firing at Yakima hunkered behind boulders along the ridge, taking bets on who would kill his wild half-breed ass. Argued over who'd get his long black scalp. They'd been having a real good time.

Not such a good one now. . . .

"You better not have so much as a pocket-knife on you — either of you!" Yakima warned. "Now crawl the hell out of there and vamoose!"

The man nearer the trail rose from behind his rock, hands raised high above his head. He was a stocky, chubby-cheeked man with a black beard. Yakima remembered seeing him spinning the roulette wheel in the Dakota Plains Saloon when the deputy sheriff had slapped iron on Yakima, and Yakima had been forced to dispatch the fool.

"Can we gather our dead?" the chubby-cheeked man asked. "Trail 'em back to town?" He squinted an eye at the sky behind Yakima. "Looks like a storm's buildin'. Don't wanna leave 'em out here to get covered up."

"Go ahead," Yakima growled. "When I'm outta here."

He turned his head to one side, stuck two fingers into his mouth, and whistled for his horse. He hadn't seen the mount since he'd climbed the ridge to try and bushwhack the men who'd chased him out from town but had ended up getting bushwhacked and pinned down himself. Not his best moment. He hadn't expected such a big group to trail him. Especially not one wielding a Gatling gun. The deputy must have had a lot of friends.

Where in the hell had they gotten ahold of a Gatling gun out here in western Dakota Territory, anyway?

Yakima looked at the trail twisting off behind him, following the stream's course. He saw no sign of the horse, but he was sure the black stallion was lurking around here somewhere. Wolf never strayed far without Yakima. They'd been together a long time, been through a lot.

Yakima turned forward, waiting, listening for the horse's thudding hooves. He heard instead the wagon groan slightly, felt it jerk a little.

Something moved behind him. He felt a hot pricking sensation on the right side of his back. He grunted and jerked forward, then turned his head to see the man whom he thought he'd killed when he'd slipped into the wagon — the man who'd been wielding the Gatling gun — scowl at him from about two feet away.

In the man's right hand was a short, bloody knife. The blood on the knife was Yakima's, he realized, as the heavy burning sensation nearly blinded him with scalding fury.

He pivoted, swinging the Gatling gun around, and fired.

Yak-yak-yak-yak-yak!

The .45-caliber rounds, fired from point-blank range, nearly tore the knife-wielding man in two before flipping him back and over the wagon's tailgate. Grinding his molars against the pain in his back, Yakima spun the Gatling back toward the other two men, both of whom jerked with starts when they saw the savage fury in Yakima's eyes.

"Hey!" yelled the man nearest the trail, stumbling back a step but keeping his hands raised as though to grab one of the fast-scudding gray clouds. "Come on, now — that was Raymond Woodyard. Lassiter's cousin. We got no stake in his doin's. We're done, breed!"

Lassiter was the name of the deputy

sheriff whom Yakima had sent to his reward.

The man on the side of the ridge stood where he'd been standing before, also reaching for the sky that was fast darkening with storm clouds. He stared at Yakima, who saw the man's throat move as he swallowed.

Hoof thuds sounded. Yakima looked behind him. His black stallion with four white stockings was galloping toward him from the other side of the creek. The stallion shook its head and snorted, and then crossed the stream in three lunging strides, the reins whipping along behind it. The big, sleek black came up through the cottonwoods, and Yakima released the Gatling gun. He grabbed his Winchester Yellowboy repeater, which he'd emptied along with his horn-gripped Colt .44 when he'd been pinned down on the ridge, and touched his back.

He looked at his hand, saw the thick blood smeared there, and cursed.

He glanced once more at the two surviving members of the posse, then stepped over the tailgate and onto the black. His saddle was loose, but he'd adjust it later. Slipping the Yellowboy into its saddle boot on the horse's right side, Yakima reached for the dangling reins. He turned the horse downstream and touched the heels of his high-topped, fur-trimmed moccasins to the black's flanks. Wolf gave another blow, shook his head, and lunged off down the trail, away from the carnage and the two men who stood staring after him, both still reaching skyward as though in some bizarre religious ritual.

Yakima looked at his bloody hand again and grunted. Goddamn that deputy and the extra jack he'd found in the card deck they'd been using for poker. Or claimed to have found. Yakima knew the man was piss-burned because Yakima had been lying over in Wild Rose for three days and holing up with the soiled dove whom Deputy Lassiter himself had put his stamp on. Besides, the man had obviously been prejudiced against half-breeds. Yakima's green eyes, red-brown skin, and long black hair betrayed his mixed-blood heritage to the unreasoning, knee-jerk disdain of many.

So Lassiter himself had slipped the jack into the deck and accused Yakima himself of the subterfuge.

Yakima had told the man to go fuck himself and then his ugly sister seven ways from sundown. Worse than being called a low-down dirty half-breed, he hated being called a cheat.

Lassiter had given a grim smile and

reached for the big Remington positioned for the cross draw on his left hip.

Yakima had heard Lassiter's reputation for being fast, so Yakima had drilled the deputy from beneath the table — shooting from up through the table and taking the point of the man's chin off. The second shot had drilled him through his heart and left him flopping around on the floor of the Dakota Plains Saloon like a landed fish, the blood pool spreading ever wider and wider across the rough wooden floor.

"Law, law!" the bartender with the west Texas drawl had exclaimed, shaking his head and widening his eyes in horror. "Now you done it, ya crazy half-breed. That's Wes Lassiter you drilled, an' before he's done saddlin' a cloud to ride to the Great Beyond, you're gonna be stretchin' hemp from one of the cottonwoods along Hatchet Creek!"

Now Yakima grimaced as he felt a cold wind blow against him, peppering his face with chill raindrops.

He rode tall in the saddle, refusing to give in to the burning wound in his back. He didn't think the cut was deep — at least, not over five inches, the length of the blade he'd seen in Raymond Woodyard's hand. Of course, he'd have to get the bleeding stopped, but he needed to find shelter first.

Where he'd find that out here, he had no idea.

As he followed the trail up out of the canyon and onto the rolling tableland beyond, all he saw were dun hogbacks turning darker and darker under the darkening sky from which a cold rain was slanting down. The trail rose and fell before him like a thin ribbon of pale string amongst the tawny grass, with not a cabin anywhere in sight.

A lone cottonwood or oak here or there, but those were the only features. All the rest was rolling prairie with its carpeting of autumn brown grama grass and sky.

He was alone out here. As alone as he'd ever been. He could feel his blood leaking from the stab wound and dribbling down under his shirt, turning cold against his skin. He wore a denim jacket over his buckskin shirt, long-handles under the shirt and his buckskin breeches, but he'd need to don his sheepskin coat soon.

The sky for as far as he could see in the east, north, and south was the color of ripe plums. An early-winter snowstorm was blowing across these stark northern plains. It would get cold soon. Freezing cold. The rain would turn to snow, and the snow would get so thick he wouldn't be able to see much farther than his horse's ears.

He knew how it was up here. He'd worked in this country before. He'd tried to stay clear of it since, but a job had brought him back two months ago — a job delivering freight to Winnipeg up in Manitoba — and he hadn't had enough sense to hightail it south as soon as the job was done.

He was in trouble.

Real trouble.

As he rode up and down the hogbacks, letting Wolf follow the trail on his own, Yakima felt himself getting weaker and weaker. The rain turned to snow. It whipped like chunks of ice against his face, clung to his brows and the long hair falling down to his shoulders and curling around his bear-claw necklace. He paused to don his coat and to tie a scarf under his hat, to keep his ears from freezing, and then he continued riding, hoping that soon the trail would lead to a farm or a ranch or possibly a roadhouse — anywhere he could get warm and get someone to patch his wound before he bled dry.

The horse stopped.

Yakima lifted his head. He hadn't realized he'd slept. He stared out over Wolf's twitching ears and into a vast canyon filled with a wide black stretch of flat water. The Missouri River. Had to be. There was no other watercourse that large and imposing out here.

Shit, he'd come to the end of the line. There was no way across the Big Muddy, especially not now when the water temperature was likely near freezing.

Yakima had barely noted the passage of such troubled thoughts across his brain before his heavy lids closed down over his eyes. His hands released the saddle horn, which they'd been clinging to for the past two hours, and he fell down the side of his horse and into the heavy, damp snow that was piled as high as Wolf's hocks.

The snow drifted heavier and heavier as the wind whipped it sideways on its descent from the nightlike, storm-tossed Dakota sky.

Chapter 2

Aubrey Coffin pulled her rabbit-skin hat down tighter on her head and, taking Hannibal's reins in her teeth, quickly retied the earflaps tight beneath her chin. The Canadian clipper was settling in hard and fast, and the wind was kicking up the wet snow and basting her face with it. She felt the chill chipping at her bones like a dull knife.

Taking the reins in her hands again, she gave them a shake over Hannibal's broad back. The mule gave an indignant bray and, lowering his head against the wind and the snow that had turned his coat color from dun brown to woolly white, lurched into a shambling trot. The wagon rattled along behind him, and he seemed to be sticking to the trail, though Aubrey could see only the trace's dimmest outline under the thickening blanket of white.

The sky was dark, but the rolling hills around her were white and getting whiter.

She could see little farther than maybe fifty or sixty yards before her. Having lived out here in the high plains most of her life, Aubrey had sensed a storm was on the way even before she'd left her farm to head to town for supplies early that morning. She should have stayed home, but she'd been getting down to her last scoop of coffee beans, and her larder had been entirely gleaned of sugar and flour when she'd made her last dried apricot pie — a rare indulgence for the woman, who lived alone and tried to make do with the bare necessities.

It had been a long winter, however, and better to indulge a little now and again than to go insane, like Mrs. Angus Johnston on the other side of the Missouri River. The poor woman had gotten up one cold winter morning a month ago, leaving her husband and four young daughters in the house asleep, and hanged herself in the barn.

Angus had found her later that morning, hanging nude from the rafters — not a stitch on her frail, pale body.

If only she could have held out till spring . . .

Aubrey snorted at the thought, glancing once more at the gunmetal blue sky hovering low over the wagon, and at the snow-covered land. Spring was a long ways away.

They had the winter to get through before they'd see the robins again, or the Canada geese winging back northward as they followed the broad, deep bed of the Upper Missouri River.

Aubrey hauled back on Hannibal's reins suddenly.

The mule stopped, glancing back over his shoulder at the woman, likely wondering why she'd stopped when they were less than a mile from the warm barn, a crib of fresh hay, and a bait of oats or even the more warming corn. Aubrey sat squinting her eyes against the spitball-sized snowflakes as she looked around, her snow-rimmed dark brown brows furled.

She'd heard something beneath the squawk of the wagon's wheels and the moaning wind and the ticking snow. Or, she thought she'd heard something. Wait — there it was again. A horse's shrill whinny. She shuttled her gaze to the east.

The sound had come from the direction of the river, though she didn't know anyone to be grazing horses out that way. Old Man Driscoll had once let his Percherons pasture out there, after the Mirren family had abandoned their claim, realizing that the railroad companies had lied to them about this being the Promised Land of knee-high grass and year-long balmy weather, and headed back to Chicago.

But Old Man Driscoll was in his cups most of the time now, and his son, Cal, had sold both Percherons and started using mules to plow his fields with. And Aubrey had never known Cal to use that range out that way. No one did, especially not this time of the year when winter was capable of striking early and fiercely. Except for the large ranchers like Ma Lassiter and the Fury clan from the next county — whom Ma was always at war with — most were still keeping their stock closer to home; if the weather didn't get them, the small packs of Sioux who still roamed the western Dakota prairies and badlands even in the wake of the Custer battle would.

The whinny rose again, tossed and torn on the wind. It was a frightened, angry scream.

Whatever horse was out that way was obviously in trouble. The storm was raging harder and harder, but Aubrey couldn't leave a horse out there in distress. She'd never get a moment's rest for thinking about the poor, miserable beast.

"Come on, Hannibal!" she yelled above the moaning wind, flicking the reins over the mule's broad back and turning him off the trail's right side. They'd cut cross-country and, risking losing a wheel rim or felloe to a snow-covered boulder or pothole, head straight for the continuing pleas of the obviously terror-stricken horse.

Hannibal was reluctant to head anywhere but home, but finally Aubrey had him trotting through a crease in the hills that angled gradually down toward the broad, deep canyon through which the Missouri traveled. Aubrey had to be careful here — because of the near-whiteout conditions, there was a risk of her and Hannibal continuing right over the lip of the canyon and into the river. Such had been the end of more than a couple of travelers over the winters that Aubrey had lived out here.

She followed the horse's screams up and out of the crease, and jerked back on Hannibal's reins again suddenly. Ahead, near the lip of the canyon, a black horse was in a frantic struggle with three gray wolves whose coats were ugly and patchy as they replaced their sleek summer pelts with the thicker, bushier coats of winter.

The horse was running back and forth in front of the canyon, trying to run off one wolf and then another. When a third one tried to work around behind the stallion, the black wheeled and tried to flog that wolf with its front hooves. It wheeled once more when one of the other wolves, flanking it, rushed in with jaws snapping hungrily.

Obviously, the savage game of cat and mouse had been going on for a spell. Even through the slanting snow, Aubrey could see several bloody patches on the horse's hips, hocks, and cannons, where the wolves had lurched in with their sharp, scissoring teeth.

The black wore a saddle and bridle — fully rigged. It was a tall, finely muscled, and broad-barreled riding horse with a white blaze on its face and three white socks. Where it had come from, Aubrey had no idea, as no one around here owned a horse of that quality, though it had obviously been ridden recently.

Where was the rider?

It was obvious from the stallion's lunging, heavy-footed gait that the horse was tiring. Soon, the wolves would have it down, and that would be the bitter end of the beautiful stallion.

Fury surged through Aubrey. She had the frontiers-woman's disdain for the opportunistic wolf that, while only trying to survive and feed its own family, were merciless animals that hunted in packs, outnumbering their prey and often wearing it out or hamstringing it before actually killing it. There were enough deer to hunt around the river. They wouldn't get the black if Aubrey had anything to say about it.

Setting the wagon's brake and ignoring Hannibal's disgruntled brays — the only predators a mule hated worse than wolves were mountain lions — Aubrey reached into the tarpaulin-covered wagon box behind her and pulled out her double-barreled shotgun. She reached under the seat, flipping the hinged cover on a box of tools she kept there, and plucked out a handful of twelve-gauge wads.

A woman alone, she always kept the barn-blaster fully loaded, so there was no point in wasting time breaching the weapon. Carefully, she climbed down from the driver's box, the wind blowing her petticoats and skirt up around her waist, beneath the hem of her heavy, quilted coat she'd sewn herself from fleece and deer hides from game she also had brought down herself, and stepped out around the fearfully braying mule.

"Shut up, Hannibal," she said, mostly to hear the comfort of her own calm voice as she moved down the slight grade toward where the three wolves were still harassing the black.

Her voice belied her fear, however. This was likely crazy. She'd probably get herself and Hannibal killed, but she couldn't abandon such a magnificent beast to these three rapacious killers.

She bit off her right deerskin mitten and shoved it into her coat pocket. She needed her trigger finger free. The cold and wet snow bit her hand. Forcing herself to keep from shaking, however, she thumbed both rabbit-ear hammers back to full cock and raised the shotgun to her right shoulder. She shoved her index finger into the trigger guard and touched one of the icy, curved triggers as she continued to move toward the lip of the canyon.

The black now stood forty feet in front of her, head down, front legs splayed. The horse's eyes were white-ringed, and Aubrey could hear the labored breaths rasping in and out of the horse's expanding and contracting nostrils. Its sides heaved.

One of the wolves had seen Aubrey, and stood regarding her, tongue drooping down across its lower jaw. The other two wolves were both barking and yipping in front of the black, likely trying to drive it back over the lip of the canyon. If they followed through with their amazingly pragmatic intentions, they could scramble down the ridge and dine on the horse's warm flesh along the frigid waters of the Big Muddy.

"Get away!" Aubrey shouted, her voice sounding like a crow's last dying gasp against the sighing, growling wind. "Get away from that horse, damn you!"

The other two wolves wheeled toward Aubrey. The wind was slicing in from over the river, so they hadn't scented her yet. But as they saw her now, they edged off away from the horse, twitching their ears and mewling in wary frustration.

Their demeanors seemed to say: "Who the hell is this crazy woman, interrupting our dinner plans on such a stormy afternoon?" They thought they'd had the black all to themselves, probably thought Aubrey was trying to horn in to enjoy a horse feast of her own.

All three predators now glared, red-eyed as the mythical wolves in fairy tales, at the interloper with the long stick in her hands. Their hackles stood straight up, and their tails were arched. The one to Aubrey's right showed its teeth, the razor-edged canines curving savagely down from its upper jaw. It made lewd chewing, snapping motions, making its teeth clatter as it started moving toward Aubrey and the wagon, keeping its head and back down as though preparing for an easier dash.

Aubrey felt her mouth go dry. Her knees quaked inside her swishing skirts, petticoat, and pantaloons.

She had only two wads. Two wads and three wolves. What the hell was she doing out here? Had she gone as suicidal crazy as Lizzy Johnston? The thought had no sooner swept through her fear-racked brain than the wolf on the right lunged toward her, stretching its legs out and arching over the freshly fallen snow.

Aubrey gritted her teeth and trained both barrels on the approaching, snarling beast.

Boom!

The blast was swallowed by the wind and caterwauling snow. The twelve-gauge buck tore through the wolf's blue-brown fur around its right shoulder, and it gave a fierce yip as it flew sideways, hit the snow on its other side, and rolled once before coming to rest in a drift that half buried it. Before the shotgun's kick had finished reverberating through Aubrey's shoulder, one of the other two wolves made a leap toward her. She swung the gun hard left and tripped the second trigger.

Another blast was swallowed by the wind. The wolf gave a sharp yowl as it, too, was dispatched to the snow, which darkened with its blood.

The mule brayed loudly. Aubrey could vaguely hear it stomping one of its front hooves. A sick feeling filled the woman as quickly, but clumsily — her right hand felt nearly frozen — she breached the double-bore. She was too scared to look up at the third wolf. It was likely lunging toward her at this very moment. Plucking a wad from her coat pocket, she dropped it, watched it disappear into the snow.

Aubrey cursed loudly, then began to pray as, keeping her eye on the gun and the gun only, she dug into her coat pocket for another shell. She managed to wrap her fingers around two. She pulled both out, nearly had one in the shotgun's right barrel before it caught on the edge of the barrel opening and flipped off into the snow.

Continuing to move her lips as she prayed and willing her mind to stay focused on the task at hand, Aubrey slipped the second wad into the shotgun's right-side barrel. She grunted, relieved, and clicked the gun closed and locked it.

She raised the shotgun to her side, aiming in the general direction she figured the wolf to be, and ratcheted the right hammer back. She frowned as she looked around. The wolf wasn't there.

There was only the black stallion standing splay-footed, head down, through the veil of falling snow. Movement to her left, and she turned to see the wolf galloping up a low knoll — a gray-brown blur in the storm. The wolf reached the top of the knoll and disappeared down the other side.

Aubrey released a long, raspy sigh. Her knees buckled with relief, and she dropped to the ground, suddenly dizzy as her heart began slowing after hammering so hard against her breastbone. She looked at the two dead wolves before her, then slowly gained her feet once more and, looking around cautiously to make sure no more predators were in the vicinity, she then depressed the shotgun's hammers, walked back to the wagon, and slid the big barn-blaster into the driver's box, on the floor beneath the seat. Ignoring Hannibal's angry, frustrated brays, she walked around the mule toward the black, who hadn't moved.

Was he too exhausted to run off now even though he could?

Aubrey walked up to within twenty feet of the stallion and stopped, regarding the horse warily, hoping that he could sense that she was here to help and not harm him. She'd always loved horses, but most of the ones she had known were dubious animals whose trust had been hard won and easily lost. Would this horse trust her now that she'd killed two of its attackers, or had the shotgun caused her to remain an object of suspicion and fear?

She stared into the black's eyes. He stared back at her. It was hard to read the animal's gaze. Definitely, the horse was tired. Exhausted. The saddle and bridle indicated he had a rider somewhere. Had the horse — possibly having been frightened by the storm — thrown the man and run off?

Or was the rider out here somewhere, too?

If he was, the man was in trouble. Probably a line rider for one of the two area ranchers. Possibly a drifter. God knew, they got plenty of those through here — grubline riders, they called them — though mostly only in the summer and early fall. Not this late in the season. If he was one of Ma Lassiter's pistol-savvy hellions, Aubrey wanted nothing to do with him. Ma was known for hiring the coldest, meanest men in the territory, and keeping them on all winter long, to not only fight for land against the Furys, but to keep nesters off her own graze, as well as Indians and rustlers.

Northern Dakota was still a hard, untamed frontier.

Wherever the horse's owner was, Aubrey needed to get the stallion back to her farm, get him warm, watered, and fed, and make him feel secure enough to sleep so he could get his strength back. Those bite wounds needed tending, as well. There was a point past which a horse rarely recovered its strength, Aubrey knew. Their heart and lungs gave out, and they either died or had to be put down.

Her barn was rickety, but it would suffice. That's where Hannibal and the milk cow, Old Sarah, as well as two pugnacious geese sheltered winter nights. When the storm passed, Aubrey would ride out to the Furys' Box Diamond and to Ma Lassiter's Coyote Ridge spread and see about finding the horse's rider. She didn't want to be mistaken for a horse thief, as horse thieves were hanged out here pronto — women as well as men.

Slowly, holding both her hands out in supplication, Aubrey moved toward the black. The horse did not try to move away from her. It stood there, head down, regarding her with that oblique, weary stare.

"Easy, boy," Aubrey said softly, just loudly enough for the horse to hear her above the wind. "Easy, now — I won't hurt you. Gotta get you back to the farm, all right?"

The horse blew loudly, its leathery nostrils expanding and contracting and blowing steam. It rippled both withers and nodded its head. Not in agreement with her wishes, though. No — he seemed frustrated, angry . . . maybe worried?

"What's the matter, boy?"

Aubrey stopped four feet away from the beast and stretched her hand out toward the horse's long, fine snout. "The wolves are dead. They can't hurt you now." Gently, she raked her fingers across the top of the beast's expanding and contracting nose from which a thick vapor cloud lifted with every labored breath.

The horse whinnied and shook its head so hard that it almost shed its concho-trimmed, braided rawhide bridle.

"What is it?" Aubrey asked. "What's the matter, fella? What are you trying to tell me?"

A man grunted. It was a disembodied groan, like a hiccup in the wind. A startling, ghostlike voice.

Aubrey gasped and jerked her head around.

Her gaze lit on the sprawled, man-shaped figure buried in the snow beside the horse. She took a startled step backward, tripped over a rock, and fell in an icy drift.

Chapter 3

Aubrey found herself cursing like an Irish mule-skinner before she finally managed to back-and-belly the big man into her wagon box and get him arranged amongst the dry goods she'd purchased at Latham's Mercantile in Wild Rose.

She doubted she'd have been able to manage if he hadn't come around some, just enough to help her a little by putting some weight on his own feet and keeping an arm wrapped around her neck while she'd led him to the wagon. When she had him secured between flour sacks, his head resting on a horse blanket she'd always kept back there in case she ever got stranded herself, she drew the tarpaulin over the box and secured it. The tarp would protect him from the weather without compromising his air.

The black stallion had followed her and his injured rider over to the wagon, and he stood there now — a big black sentinel, hanging his head over the tarpaulin-covered box and twitching his ears while his tail blew up over his hindquarters in the wind. Aubrey doubted she needed to tie the horse to the wagon. She had a feeling, after seeing how the horse fought off the wolves, she couldn't have separated the horse from the man if she'd wanted to. He'd follow her and his injured rider back to the farm, all right.

She reached under the horse's belly to loosen the latigo straps. No telling how long the horse had been saddled, and after his struggle against the wolves, he needed all the air he could get. He'd been bitten several times, but none of the puncture wounds appeared deep. Some of the horse's own urine, kerosene, and balsam root powder all worked into a single compress should tend him.

Noting that the horse seemed to trust her instinctively and was only waiting patiently for his rider to be taken to safety, Aubrey climbed back into the wagon. The wind hammered her, whipped her hair out from under her hat and scarf, and blew it around her head.

The cold was like sand raked across her cheeks though she'd lost most of the feeling in her exposed skin. It would be damn nice to get home and to get a fire roaring in her field-rock hearth. Hang a pot of water for tea over the flames.

Releasing the brake, she swung Hannibal around and headed back out to the main trail, the mule braying as though in competition with the wind. As she turned Hannibal onto the main trail, she shuttled a glance over her shoulder. The black was following close behind the wagon, snorting and shaking its head at the snow and the wind. Aubrey turned her own head forward and shook it.

She'd never seen the like — a horse following its master like a loyal dog.

That put Aubrey's mind somewhat at ease. The man she'd found in the snow had a pistol on his hip. She'd seen a bowie knife on a belt sheath beneath his sheepskin coat, and she was certain she'd felt another weapon, probably a knife, sheathed between his shoulder blades, under his coat and shirt. A Winchester rifle jutted from the horse's saddle sheath.

Most men went armed out here, as this neck of the frontier was slow in settling and even slower in settling down. But the number of weapons this man was carrying bespoke a possible hard case. Maybe even a regulator hired by one of the larger ranches to keep rustlers or the smaller settlers at bay.

Ma Lassiter or the Furys, Aubrey figured.

Aubrey lived alone, and the last thing she wanted was to find herself trapped in a cabin with a human bobcat. The love that the black obviously felt for the man, however, told Aubrey that despite his many armaments, he had to have some tenderness in him. Certainly compassion for his horse, at least. She knew from her own experience that animals were the best judges of human character.

The mule started braying again when they climbed to the top of the last hill, and started down into the hollow in which Aubrey's farm sat — gray and quiet and lonely-looking in the fresh coating of snow. Hannibal had trouble with some of the four- and five-foot drifts that had already piled up just a few yards down the farm-side of the hill, and for a moment Aubrey thought he was going to give out on her. Hannibal must have smelled the fresh hay in the barn, however — Aubrey had contracted a fresh supply last fall from her neighbor, Cal — and with another weary bray the mule high-stepped out of the drift and down the hill and into the yard.

Aubrey angled the mule past her two

holding corrals and the barn on the yard's right side, to the little cabin sheltered by a low ridge on the left. The wind blasted the weathered gray, sod-roofed log structure, making the roof timbers creak. The yellow weeds on the roof just showed above the snow. Aubrey stopped the mule, who shook his head in frustration. He wanted to get to the barn, and the woman didn't blame him, but she had to get the man into the cabin before tending the stock.

"Hold on, Hannibal," she scolded, the wind sucking her breath from her lungs as she set the brake and started down from the driver's box. "You'll have your supper in a minute!"

Aubrey removed the tarp from the box, lowered the tailgate, and climbed up to where the man lay on one side, legs drawn toward his chest. He was breathing hard, his chest and shoulders rising and falling sharply. The flat, rugged planes of his dark-skinned face, surely betraying Indian blood, were etched with pain. His jaws and lips moved as he shivered.

Aubrey touched his shoulder. He jerked his eyes open and his head up, and his right hand closed over the horn grips of the Colt jutting from the worn leather holster thonged midway down his right, buckskin-clad thigh. Aubrey pulled back slightly, heart quickening. She stared at the gloved hand on the revolver's handle, and felt the taut muscles in her back ease slightly when the hand loosened its grip and did not pull the gun from the holster.

The man's eyes were on her — green eyes set deep in dark red sockets beneath sleek black brows. The hardness left his stare, and he removed his hand from the gun.

"I'm gonna take you inside my cabin," Aubrey said. "But not with that gun. You understand, mister?"

The man looked up at her, snow catching on his long eyelashes and brows as it swirled over the sides of the wagon. He nodded, and with his thumb he flipped the leather strap over the Colt's hammer free, pulled the pistol from the holster, and set it on the crate of dried peaches beside him. He couldn't quite lift it that high, and the Colt fell to the bottom of the wagon. Groaning, he dropped his arm as though his hand weighed a ton.

That'll do for a start, Aubrey thought, closing her hands around his arm.

"Can you help me?" she said against the wind, shivering herself now from the penetrating cold. "You're too big for me to handle alone."

The man started to push up off his hip, and, with him putting some weight on his legs and Aubrey tugging on his arm, she got him to the end of the wagon and then down to the ground. He tried to stand, but he fell back against the wagon, so Aubrey pulled one of his arms across her shoulders and sort of half dragged, half carried him onto the snow-laden stoop.

She grunted beneath his weight — he had to weigh close to two hundred pounds though he didn't seem to have any spare flesh on him. He groaned as he dragged his boot toes; several times they nearly fell together. She had her hand around his back, and she could feel a greasy wetness on his coat. Blood, most likely. He might have been thrown from his horse onto something sharp, but she had a feeling it was worse than that.

Finally, she got the cabin door open and helped him inside, where he fairly collapsed into a chair by the kitchen table. The chair creaked beneath his weight till she thought the back would break off, as it had done before and she'd had to repair it with rawhide and nails.

Her late husband, Joe, had bought the chair though Aubrey had warned him that store-bought furniture was no good. Since

Joe's passing, she'd never bought anything she could grow or build herself.

Shivering, Aubrey leaned close to the man, who sat back in the chair, chin dipped toward his chest. "Can you sit there a minute? I'm going to get a fire going in the bedroom."

Keeping his eyes closed, he nodded. Vapor jetted from his nostrils. The cabin was like an icehouse, and as dark as deep-winter dusk. Aubrey looked at the open door. It was probably only around three — she'd headed for town at 10:00 a.m. and started back to the farm around two, when the rain had started — but it indeed looked like dusk out there, as well. A stormy dusk. Fortunately, she'd laid in a good load of wood last fall and had been splitting most of it all herself, though Cal Driscoll had ridden over a few times, against her protestations, and split for her, as well.

She passed through the doorway in the kitchen's back wall, covered by a bearskin curtain, and got a fire going in the cabin's single bedroom. When she went back into the kitchen, she found the stranger sitting as before, chin dipped nearly to his chest.

"Gotta get you into the other room, into bed," Aubrey said, shaking his arm, worried he'd fallen into a sound sleep and she'd never get him into her bed. "I have a fire in there. Gotta get you in there — you hear? — get your clothes off, and thaw you out."

The man opened his eyes and looked up at her, and the skin above the bridge of his nose wrinkled slightly. She flushed. Had he thought she had less than respectable intentions? You never knew about men. Even wounded and half dead, they could be stirred by physical hungers. . . .

"All right," he rasped, lifting his left arm to the top of the table and heaving himself up.

Aubrey draped his right arm across her shoulders and guided him unsteadily, both staggering like a couple of drunks leaving a saloon on a hopping Saturday night in Wild Rose, through the curtained doorway and into her small but tidy bedroom. When she had him sitting at the foot of the bed that was covered with several quilts, including a marriage quilt — a wedding present from one of Joe's aunts — on top, she drew the bedcovers down.

Holding the injured man's arm to keep him upright, she looked at the back of his coat. The sheepskin wore a large patch of crusty blood. She fingered the hole in the middle of the stain. A slit, rather. The kind of cut a knife would make.

Turning her mouth corners down in disgust, Aubrey began peeling the coat down the stranger's heavy shoulders. "Gotta get this coat off you and get something under you. Don't want you staining up my bed. These are the only quilts and sheets I have."

She felt a little guilty at the hardness of her voice, but she'd seen too many like this man to feel much sympathy. She'd do her best to keep him alive, but if she had to keep alive every hard case who got himself shot up or stabbed out here, she wouldn't have time to go about the hard business of keeping herself on this side of the sod.

He helped as much as he could, mostly just shifting his weight, as she pulled his bloody coat off and tossed it onto the floor between the braided hemp rug and the whitewashed log wall. When she had his shirt off, she spread an old, moth-chewed wool blanket onto the bed and eased him onto it, on his side, as the other side was probably too tender to lie on.

She lifted his legs onto the bed, then removed his cartridge belt and bowie knife and looped them over a chair back. She removed the rawhide sheath containing a savage-looking little knife from around his neck. Also from around his neck she removed a leather strand of bear claws, glancing at the ornament with vague interest before looping it also over the chair.

Standing before him then, she looked down at him, rubbing her hands on the front of her own quilted leather coat. She felt a little self-conscious about undressing him further, and delayed the job by adding more wood to the fire in the creaking, cracking sheet-iron stove. She stoked the fire, relieved to feel the warmth pressing against her, then closed the door with the poker, set the poker in the wood crate beside the stove, and turned back to her charge.

He had his eyes partway open. The pale light from the open doorway behind Aubrey made them glow like narrow chips of jade set in dark red sandstone. They were spoked with pain lines. Strands of his long black hair were splayed across the large, nearly square cheekbones that tapered down to his broad mouth, heavy jaw, and strong chin that bore a faint white scar. Probably a knife scar. Or could it be from the point of a spur rowel?

His chapped lips moved, and with effort he said, "S-sorry about this."

A knifepoint of guilt prodded her loins. He had likely sensed her brooding indignation.

"You tended the stock yet?"

She looked at him.

"You go ahead and put the animals in the barn," he said, swallowing and resting his head on his crooked arm. "Do what you have to do. I'll keep."

He closed his eyes. Instantly, his broad chest rose and fell beneath the sweaty buckskin shirt that clung to him like a second skin. The arm curled across his belly was broad and corded, fine black hair curling against the red-brown skin. The biceps bulged like a wheel hub.

Aubrey turned away from him quickly, a little desperately, she vaguely thought. "All right." She passed through the doorway and drew the robe tightly across it, to keep the heat in.

Purposely switching her thoughts from the stranger, she closed the front door, noting that the snow had already formed a small drift on the inside of the jamb, and set about building a fire in the field-rock hearth set against the front wall, left of the door. When the flames leaped and cracked, a good foot or so high, she tied her hat back tight on her head, feeling a little chagrined for wondering how ridiculous she must look in the homemade rabbit skin she'd sewn herself from two rabbit pelts, then went outside, climbed into the wagon, and swung Hannibal toward the barn. The black, who'd been standing near the wagon and was now, like Hannibal, nearly coated in white, followed haltingly, as though reluctant to leave its owner.

"It's all right, Black," Aubrey shouted. "I'll take good care of him." She climbed down from the wagon and opened one of the two large doors, putting her shoulder into it and heaving against the snow piled up in front of the barn. "Come on in here and get yourself warm."

She didn't have to invite Hannibal. The doors were barely open before the mule pulled the wagon into the barn and stopped about halfway down the narrow alley, heehawing for hay and oats. Ignoring the mule for now, Aubrey went back out to grab the black's reins, which she'd tied around its saddle horn, and lead the big, beautiful but shamble-footed horse into the barn.

When she had the doors closed, she quickly got to work, unsaddling the stallion and hanging the tack on a stall partition near where Old Sarah eyed her from the nightlike shadows, mooing her complaints about the storm as well as the unexpected guest. The two snow-white geese that Aubrey had wintered over for the past two years and had become like family to her fluttered like large white angels down from the hayloft. Once in the alley near Aubrey they squawked and flapped their broad, clublike wings, jutting their hooked, orange beaks, and lifted a din like demons loosed from hell.

The stallion, obviously not used to geese, snorted and sidled away, white ringing its eyes as the two geese stood up and flapped their wings in the characteristic anger and discontent of their breed.

"Shut up, you two banshees!" Aubrey scolded, kicking one of her high-topped fur boots at the geese. "Can't you see we got company?"

They kept coming at her, stretching their necks out and shoving their beaks close as though to nip her legs, until she gave one a swift kick. Both birds leaped and fluttered away though they continued to harp at Aubrey from the shadows as she led the black into its own private stall — one of four in the small barn. Hannibal added his own voice to the birds' and the cow's din, and the stallion shook its head in disgust.

"Sorry, Black," Aubrey said as she threw several heavy wool blankets over the cold, exhausted horse's back from which steam rose in tendrils. She patted the long, sleek neck to which ice still clung. “If you stayed here long enough — which I hope you don’t, you understand — you’d get used to it.”

Chapter 4

Sheriff Rance Hagan reined his copper-bottom gelding to a halt at the top of a high bluff and looked westward down the other side of the hill, where the little Dakota cow town of Wild Rose — originally a hiders' camp named after a whore, it was said — nestled along the snowy banks of Hatchet Creek.

Wild Rose wasn't much of a town — only about four square blocks with big, barrack-like, false-fronted structures serving as the business district. Whores' cribs flanked these, and beyond the cribs, a dozen or so sod-and-brick shacks, with here and there a humble but tidy frame house, were arranged willy-nilly — back doors facing front doors, privies between shacks and stables or vice versa, and fenced pastures so close to some houses that horses had worn the siding boards to a dull yellow. There were chicken coops and cow pens, and goats and pigs had the run of the town until someone complained or shot a particularly pesky beast.

The last Indian attack, four years ago, had wiped out half the settlement. The half-burned hovels still sat amongst the dry brush and chokecherry shrubs, all of which glistened now under the fresh coating of yesterday's snow. The cemetery that sprawled across another bluff to the north had more gravestones than the town currently had living citizens.

The sun glistened so brightly off the snow that Hagan's eyes felt as though javelins had been driven through them. He should have been used to such light by now, having spent nearly fifteen winters up here, first as a trapper, then as an Indian-fighting cavalry sergeant stationed at Fort Totten. Chickenpox had saved him from a grisly death along with the rest of his platoon in the Kildeer Mountains. After he'd retired from the army, he'd run a woodcutting camp to service riverboats along the Upper Missouri River. Now, for some reason that he couldn't even quite remember — though it seemed to have had something to do with the territorial governor getting him drunk and pinning a sheriff's badge on his shirt down in Yankton, during a Fourth of July rodeo two years ago — he was sheriff of Brule County.

Christ, what a place to have found himself in. And for the long haul, it appeared . . .

Hagan gave an angry grunt and heeled the copper on down the hill and into the town, noting that only a couple of sets of wagon tracks and a few sets of horse tracks etched the snow in the broad main street that twisted around a big cottonwood before continuing west. Smoke puffed from chimney pipes and rock hearths. Only a few people out. Aaron Latham, the lanky, handlebar-mustached former cowboy who ran Latham's Mercantile, paused on his high loading dock from which he was sweeping the fresh snow, to squint against the sun and give Hagan a peculiar stare.

Hagan pulled back on the copper's reins, frowning up at Latham. "What?"

"Huh?"

"Why're you lookin' at me like that?" Hagan growled. "I done paid you for that case of whiskey last week."

"I know you did." Latham shook his head covered in a ratty fur hat. He wore no coat, only an apron over his shabby striped shirt and broadcloth trousers. No gloves, either — his hands horny-callused and red. He glanced westward along the street. "You got a little surprise waitin' for ya yonder. And here you damn near got through the whole year with the same deputy."

Latham shook his head and continued sweeping.

Hagan leaned out to the left of his horse, looking around the slight hitch in the street that generally followed the course of Hatchet Creek to the south of it. The undertaker's little shop was directly across the street from the sheriff's office about two blocks west. Hagan saw that a casket was leaning up against the front of the long, low structure that doubled as a furniture shop though the Swede who ran it had pretty much given up building furniture for drinking whiskey. But he still built coffins and buried the dearly departed citizens of Wild Rose for what some considered the ghastly sum of three dollars a head. More for those too big to fit his prebuilt standard-sized coffins.

Milford Hansen was out in front of his shop, working on whomever he had in the casket while his pet crow, whom he called Bill, perched on the peak of the building directly above the undertaker and the casket. Hansen's breath puffed in the air around his head on which he wore a battered canvas hat tied down with a cream scarf.

Hagan narrowed an eye at Latham, who

continued sweeping, then touched spurs to his copper gelding, and, his cheeks above his sweeping salt-and-pepper mustache growing hard, his eyes fateful, headed on up around the hitch in the main drag. He reined up in front of Hansen and blew out a long sigh as he stared down at his deputy, Wesley Lassiter, propped inside the box, the box itself leaning against the door of the Swede's shop. The box was a little too narrow for Lassiter, who was tall and broad, and his shoulders looked uncomfortably hunched, his head bent to one side.

The hunched look didn't matter much, given Lassiter's otherwise less than pleasing visage. Half his nose was gone. Although the Swede had obviously cleaned up the blood, Lassiter's face had what appeared a chunk of half-cooked meat dead in the center of it. A ragged crater. That and the fact that the Swede had combed his longish yellow blond hair neatly with a middle part and dressed him in a nice shirt and string tie, made him look about the most bizarre thing Hagan had ever seen.

The Swede wasn't finished with his work. He was currently sewing Lassiter's left eye closed while the right one stared in mute horror at the scrawny, little, hawk-nosed man doing the sewing.

On an upright log beside Hansen was a small canvas sewing kit and an uncorked bottle of forty-rod. Hansen poked the needle through Lassiter's left eyelid and, sticking his own tongue out of his mouth in deep concentration, drew the thread through the lid before poking the needle through the skin of Lassiter's cheek, just below the eye.

"You're a thorough son of a bitch. I'll give you that, Hansen."

The undertaker glanced up at Hagan sitting the copper-bottom gelding just beside and behind him. "Ma might wanna see him. Some folks don't like to lift the lid off a coffin and see two eyes starin' up at 'em." Hansen wheezed a slow laugh, making his shoulders jerk. "Makes 'em soil their drawers."

The crow on the peak of the shack's roof gave a caw and stretched one wing out to the side, preening.

"Who do I have to thank for making me shorthanded?" Hagan asked. "And now with winter settlin' in and me wantin' to go to bed and stay there for the next four months."

"That half-breed."

"Who?"

"The breed that was here, last few days.

Till last night." Hansen grabbed the bottle off the log and glanced up at Hagan. "The one that was holed up over at the Dakota Plains."

"What happened?"

Hansen lifted the bottle to his thin lips and took a quick drink. "Wesley accused him of slipping an extra jack in the card deck they was playin' poker with."

"He didn't."

"Sure he did." Hansen set the bottle back on the log and resumed his work, crouching over the open coffin.

Hagan cursed and looked around, his own breath puffing in the sun-bright air over the copper's head. "I told him before I rode out yesterday to stay away from that breed. That breed was holin' up with the redheaded whore — what's her name? Over at the Dakota Plains . . . ?"

"Wynona somethin' or other. Don't know her last na—"

"That's the one." Hagan glared down at Lassiter, who was staring with that one open eye at the copper's left wither. "Wesley didn't like it. He figured the redhead was his. Wanted permission from me to order the breed out of town. I told him I wasn't in the business of ordering anyone not immediately breaking the laws of this town or county to do anything — even a fiddle-footed, grub-line-ridin' half-breed."

Hansen hiked a shoulder as he poked the needle through Wesley Lassiter's eyelid and cheek once more, then drew the thread taut and reached for the scissors. Hagan looked back the way he'd come, toward the Dakota Plains Saloon he'd passed a half block to the east and before which one saddle horse stood, stretching its neck to nibble its hip. The Indian cook, Horace Burnt Bear, sat on a stool on the saloon's broad front gallery, peeling potatoes.

"He still over there?" Hagan asked.

"Huh?"

"I said, is he still over there. You deaf?"

"Oh, no."

"Oh, no — you're not deaf? Or oh, no — he ain't over there?"

"They run him out of town yesterday." Hansen cut the thread from the needle, then took another swig from his bottle. "Ran him out and followed him out, shootin' like they was after Red Cloud himself. Havin' a real good time."

"Who did this?"

"Who do you think — Trace Early, Galvin Creed, and Luther One-Eye. Led a whole posse out — musta been ten men of our finest citizens. Figured Ma Lassiter would reward 'em well for bringin' the breed back to town so's Ma herself could take her satisfaction." Hansen took another swig and grinned, his brown eyes glowing in the sunlight. "Didn't quite work out that way, though. They pinned the breed on a ridge over Cottonwood Canyon. Couldn't get him out for nothin'. So Luther One-Eye and Galvin come to town for the Gatling gun."

Sheriff Hagan narrowed a hard blue eye at the undertaker. "Swede, if you're jerkin' my dick . . ."

"No, sir. I wouldn't do that. They come ridin' back, madder'n ole wet hens, for the Gatling gun. Put it and a case of beer and whiskey in a wagon and headed back out to Cottonwood Canyon."

"They're still out there?"

"As far as I know . . ." Hansen let his voice trail off as he turned to look westward up the street, thin lips stretching back from his false teeth. "Oh, no, they're not."

Hagan turned to follow the undertaker's gaze. A string of horses led by two horseback riders was crossing the wooden bridge over Hatchet Creek. The lead rider, bundled against the cold, with a red muffler wrapped around his neck, hunched low in his saddle, his face a grim brown blur beneath the crown of his soiled Stetson. He was leading two horses while the man behind him was leading three more, the hooves of the mounts clomping dully against the wooden boards of the bridge.

That the led horses were carrying dead men was obvious by the blanket-wrapped, man-shaped bodies tied across their saddles. Hands dangled out from the blankets on one side of the horses, a few pairs of boots from the other side.

Hagan felt a burning in his belly as he watched the lead rider turn under the big, skeletal cottonwood on the creek's north side and gig his horse on into the town, heading toward where the sheriff and the undertaker stood watching.

"Gonna be a busy day, looks like," said the Swede. "Looks like I'll be able to afford a new load of firewood, after all. Maggie'll be right happy about that."

"Hansen, do me a favor, will you?"

"Sure."

"Shut up."

The undertaker gave an indignant grunt, then tipped his bottle back for another drink. In the meantime, Hagan stared at the two strings of horses clomping toward him, snow rising around their hocks, the lead rider whom the sheriff recognized as Bill Anderson heading directly toward him.

Anderson's face was a stony mask, the man's weathered cheeks mottled white from frostbite.

Hagan raked his gaze across the bloody blankets and poked his hat back off his forehead. "What in holy hell happened, Bill?"

Anderson stopped his horse in front of Hagan while the other man, Galvin Creed, came up behind him. "You know that breed that come into town two, three days back and holed up in the Dakota Plai— ?"

"Yeah, I know, I know," Hagan said, impatient, bile burning up from his belly and into his throat. He canted his head toward his dead deputy. "I've done seen the work he done on my deputy here. Are you gonna tell me he killed all these men, too?"

Hagan moved to the first horse standing hang-headed behind Anderson, who hipped around in his saddle to follow the sheriff with his dull, pale blue gaze. As Hagan lifted the blanket over the head of the first dead man, recognizing Boone Dodge, Wild Rose's sole blacksmith, Anderson said with a customary dull-witted grunt, "Uh . . . yep."

"Uh, yep," the sheriff mocked, glancing up at Galvin Creed bringing his black-and-white pinto to a stop off Anderson's left flank.

Hagan snapped the blanket back down over Dodge's head and strode to the next horse in Anderson's string. He pitched his voice with sarcasm. "Well, good morning there, Galvin. How're you this morning?"

"Not so good, I reckon, Sheriff," said Creed darkly, running a hide mitten across his red, runny nose.

"Not so good, huh?" Hagan jerked the blanket up from the shaggy head of the second dead man in Anderson's string. "Why's that — 'cause you're so damn heartsick over losin' half your friends, including Halvorssen's dunderheaded son, Melvin, here?"

Halvorssen ran the Union Saloon. His now-deceased son, Melvin, had worked in the watering hole and took on sundry odd jobs around the town for the old folks and widows, including splitting wood, hauling water, and cleaning game. Now they'd have to split their own wood and clean their own game. Melvin was going into one of the Swede's pine boxes.

"Wasn't our fault, Hagan," Anderson said as the sheriff walked over to inspect the dead men that Creed was hauling. "That breed's smarter than he looks. We had him stuck halfway up a ridge in Cottonwood Canyon, but he snuck down like the damn sneaky savage he is and took over the Gatling gun."

"Yeah, I heard about the Gatling gun," Hagan said in disgust, releasing a handful of Tomas de la Garza's thick black hair and letting the Mexican's head flop down against his stirrup fender.

Anderson, still hipped around in his saddle, slid his apprehensive gaze to Creed, whose mouth corners curved down with chagrin.

"That was Luther's idea," Creed muttered, looking sheepishly away. "He said the town done had it, so why not use it? The Injuns ain't a threat no more. At least, none besides the breed his own self."

"We needed something to get him out of those rocks," Anderson chimed in, his tone defensive. "Hell, why not use the Gatling gun? The army left it, and the ammo for it was just rustin' away in Luther's livery stable. . . ."

"The army left it for us to use against the Sioux." Hagan didn't bother inspecting the other two dead men. He knew the town well enough to know who the other two men would be — Bob "Hackamore" Harris and the saloon bouncer, Stan Lewinsky. "They should have come and retrieved it, though I figure they must have forgot about it.

Should have sent it back myself. I knew Luther had fallen in love with the damn thing, was hopin' someday to haul it out of his livery barn and put it to good use."

Hagan looked around at the bundles of dead men lying across their saddles. "Well, he finally did, didn't he?"

Anderson and Creed looked at each other, then away.

"Where's the breed?" Hagan asked.

"Dead, most likely," Creed said. "Luther stuck him with that toothpick of his . . . before the breed done chopped him to pieces with the Gatling."

"You leave the gun out there?"

Anderson nodded. "The mule for the wagon had done got loose, and there was a storm on the way. Couldn't take time to run it down."

"So you just left the gun out there in Cottonwood Canyon?" Hagan was getting more and more exasperated, as townsfolk who'd seen the string of horses pull into town were now bleeding out of their shops and houses and spilling into the street, heading toward Hagan, Creed, Anderson, and the dead men.

All of whom had friends and family here in Wild Rose.

They, like old Ma Lassiter, were going to

demand action for this massacre, the likes of which Hagan hadn't seen since the last Sioux scare.

He just hoped to God Creed was right, and the breed was dead.

Chapter 5

Yakima Henry opened his eyes and saw the woman. She sat on the edge of his bed, and she was holding a spoon of steaming broth in front of him.

"Please," she urged. "You have to eat something."

She'd placed two pillows under his head, propping him partly up. Yakima looked around the room. The windows showed a little lilac light behind their drawn curtains. The wind was moaning under the eaves and making the timbers creak. A fire ticked in the stove against the wall to Yakima's left. The room was warm. More firelight danced beyond the doorway over which the bearskin curtain was partly drawn.

"Just a couple of spoonfuls," the woman said. Her brown eyes bored into his. She wasn't what a man would call pretty, but she was even-featured, with tapering cheeks and fair skin that had not been hidden away from the weather. Somewhere on the lee side of thirty, Yakima guessed, opening his mouth so she could slide the spoon between his lips.

Her hands were strong, callused from work.

He closed his lips on the spoon, and the warm, salty liquid washing over his tongue made his stomach rumble for more. It had a few flecks of meat in it and a slightly gamey taste.

"Venison," she said. "A mite old. I had a haunch left in the cellar. Intend to shoot a few rabbits tomorrow if this wind lets up. Really blowing out there. Kicking up a ground blizzard. All day long."

She spooned more broth up and slipped it into his mouth.

"Usually happens after a storm. The sky clears for a day, and you think the fall's returning with Indian summer. Then the wind kicks up and makes it look like January all over again."

The broth was so good that Yakima wanted to crawl down inside the bowl and drown in it.

"How long I been here?" he asked as the salty, gamey brew hit his stomach once more, instantly nourishing and making him want more. "By the way my ass . . . pardon . . . my butt aches, I figure a couple weeks."

She lowered her head toward the bowl in her hand, dipping up more of the broth and shaking her head so that her long, straight brown hair shifted across the planes of her face. No, not a pretty face by most men's standards — nose a little too long, lips a little too thin — but a nice face just the same. Her long hair was rather limp, not much substance to it, and a few strands were edging toward gray.

"Only a day. After I got you into bed, you went right to sleep. Woke a couple of times, just barely. I could tell you were coming around a few minutes ago, though, so I heated some of this broth." She deposited more of the broth onto his tongue and pulled the spoon back out of his mouth. "You lost a lot of blood, judging by the stains on your shirt and coat. Need food to build you back up again, get you back in the saddle."

Yakima glanced at the double bed and its four log posters. There was a curtained closet on the room's right side, a wardrobe, a tin-topped washstand. A few tintypes of formally attired men and women — the woman's family, most likely. Maybe even the woman herself. The room was too dark for Yakima to see anything clearly except the firelight dancing in her brown eyes like small, umber chips at the bottom of a forge.

"I'm taking up your room, aren't I?" Yakima smiled as another spoonful of the satisfying broth met his tongue. He swallowed. "Your only bed."

"The sofa is right comfortable. And I keep a fire going in there."

Yakima waved off another spoonful of the broth. "You're keeping two fires going? So you're going through twice as much wood?" He wasn't sure why, but he sensed there was no man around the place. "I'll lay in a good store before I go."

"No need. I have plenty of wood. I split it myself, and I have a neighbor who splits it for me whether I want him to or not." She raised the spoon higher, and Yakima shook his head.

"I've had enough."

"There's plenty."

"It's mighty good, but my bucket's full." While the first few spoonfuls had soothed and nourished him, his stomach was starting to rebel.

She emptied the spoon into the bowl and set the bowl on her knee. "Best not to push it, I reckon."

Yakima laid his head back against the pillow. Weakness and nausea caused the room to pitch slightly. He could tell that she'd bandaged the knife cut in his back, but he could feel the tender rawness of the wound. It seemed to penetrate all the way to the back side of his belly.

No telling when he'd be ready to ride again. He felt bad that he had so little money with which to pay the woman, but he'd find a way to compensate her for her help. His presence here could mean trouble for her, and she didn't deserve that.

His eyelids grew heavy.

"I'll let you sleep."

Yakima nodded. He watched her move to the door. She wore a simple wool skirt and a man's heavy flannel plaid work shirt with the tails untucked. On her feet were square-toed stockmen's boots. His natural male curiosity caused his eyes to take their automatic appraisal, and he judged her a nicely built female — round, firm rump, long, strong legs and arms, well-shaped breasts though the shirt and several layers of underclothing did all they could to conceal the fact.

"Not to be forward, but . . . haven't heard you mention a name. Mine's Yakima Henry."

She stopped before the bearskin curtain

and turned back to him. "Aubrey." Her voice was soft, her eyes only flickering toward him, too shy to hold his gaze. A country shyness. "Aubrey Coffin."

"Is it Mrs. Coffin?"

She dropped her chin slightly, let her gaze glide over to the ticking, dully snapping woodstove. "Yes. But he's not alive. I'm a widow." She started to turn away but then turned back to him once more. "You don't have to tell me, of course, but I can't help being curious. That wound . . . that knife wound . . ."

Yakima drew a deep breath and felt his belly rumble now from a little too much of the broth, as well as dread. He might still be alive, but he was far from out of the mess he'd gotten himself into in Wild Rose.

"I killed a deputy sheriff, Mrs. Coffin. A posse came after me, tried to kill me."

Her eyes found his now suddenly. They were sharp with incredulity.

"No. Deputy Lassiter?"

"That's right."

Aubrey Coffin stared at him for a time, and fear slowly edged away the skepticism in her gaze. "I'd heard there was trouble, but I didn't know what kind."

"I'll be leaving just as soon as I'm able, Mrs. Coffin."

She nodded slowly, then turned to the door, putting a little edge in her voice as she said quietly, "Yes, I'll be looking forward to that, Mr. Henry."

In his sleep, Yakima could hear wolves howling beneath the wind.

Faraway sounds.

There was also the ticking of blown snow against the cozy little cabin's log walls. Several times during the night he rose from his deep unconsciousness to hear the woodstove door squawk open and the muffled thuds of wood being dropped inside. The fire gave a little whoosh as it consumed the added fuel, and then the door squawked again as the woman closed it. There was the low metallic rasp of the latching lever.

Twice he felt her hand on his forehead and the rough caress of a cold cloth. He felt himself shivering against his own inner chill and the uncomfortable sensation of his own cold sweat.

The wolves continued to howl and the wind continued to blow.

He was glad when he opened his eyes and saw the pearl wash of light through the windows. The wind had stopped. The cabin was silent except for the quiet shuffling of feet in the other room and the sounds of opening and closing cabinet doors. He touched his forehead, ran his thumb across his chest.

Dry.

The fever had broken.

He swept the bedcovers back and lifted his head from his pillow, dropping one foot to the floor. Too fast. The room spun. His vision dimmed. He sagged backward, caught himself, then slowly dropped his other foot to the floor and sat there at the edge of the bed, letting his blood flow through his veins, sending oxygen throughout his body's extremities.

When the room stopped spinning, he rose slowly from the bed.

The woman had apparently washed his clothes, because they were neatly piled on a chair, his capote hanging from a hook nearby. The stove was stoked, but the cold air pushed against his naked body. He moved closer to the heat, until he was only inches away from the ticking iron. Enjoying the warmth that leached soothingly all the way to his bones, he reached behind with one hand to touch the fresh gauze bandage the woman had applied late last night, just before she'd retired for the evening, he'd assumed. She'd changed the bandage twice, and both times the whiskey she'd apparently soaked it with had felt like a rabid rat burrowing deep into his back from the right side and giving the back side of his heart a nip with sharp teeth.

But the whiskey would keep the infection out and speed up the healing.

He lifted his arms slowly, attempting a much needed stretch, but the wound pulled at him, and he winced against the sudden, hot stab of pain and finally lowered his arms halfway to run his hands through his long black hair, yawning and groaning.

"Mr. Henry?"

The bearskin curtain was thrust aside, and the woman stepped into the room. Yakima swung his head toward her with a start.

"Oh," she said, and he watched her eyes widen as they dropped down from his face and naked chest to his belly and beyond, quickly taking him all in and blushing, for he wasn't wearing a stitch. She'd removed the clothes herself, trying not to admire the amazing specimen of male he was.

She turned away, and while it was too dark for him to see the flush in her cheeks, he knew it was there. He'd been naked around too many women for it to bother him much.

"I'm sorry — I heard you stirring, and. . . ." She stopped halfway through the doorway, holding the curtain aside with a shoulder.

"I'm gonna ride out today," Yakima grunted, seeing no reason to mention his nakedness and prolong the moment's awkwardness. "I've taken up your bed long enough."

She turned her head to one side. "If you think you're ready, Mr. Henry . . ."

Then she continued on out the door, letting the curtain swing back into place behind her.

Yakima winced as he reached for his clothes, forgetting that he had to take it easy on his right side, try to do as much with his left as he could for a while. But he also had to remember that men — probably plenty more where the Wild Rose posse had come from — would be coming after him. He sure needed the use of his right hand — his gun. When he got out away from the woman's farm, he'd draw a few times, see how it went. He could shoot left-handed but he couldn't hit much unless he was right up on his target.

Maybe he could beat a path the hell out of Brule County before anyone caught up to him.

As he dressed he gave a wry chuff and shook his head. Of all the lousy luck. Not only had he killed a deputy sheriff with a large passel of friends, but now he'd killed most of those friends. The two men who'd led the dead men's horses into town from the canyon in which they'd pinned Yakima down had likely spread the grim news, and a fresh, enraged posse was likely arming itself and saddling its horses — if they weren't already scouring the countryside for him, that is.

Yakima had to get out of here. He couldn't involve the woman in any of this. Every minute he lingered here he was endangering Mrs. Coffin. If the posse knew she'd given him shelter and doctored his wound, it likely wouldn't go well for her.

As he tucked his shirt into his pants, then buttoned his fly, he ducked his head to look out the window left of the woodstove. The day was overcast, and it looked cold. The snow hadn't melted. Judging by the texture of the woman's tracks in the yard angling around the cabin to a roofed pole shed housing logs for firewood, the wind had given the snow a crusty cover.

Yakima cursed as he went over to a washbowl and tipped water into the bowl from a porcelain pitcher. Because of that crusty snow and the cold, he'd be giving a posse plenty of tracks to follow.

He had to beat a trail south as fast as ole Wolf could haul his, Yakima's, stupid ass.

Never should have spent so much time in Wild Rose. Not with that deputy giving him the evil eye. Trouble was, Yakima had never held with being hazed out of town by some prejudiced local — even if said local was toting a tin star. No, his inbred stubbornness had forced him to stay and hole up with the pretty redhead, Miss Wynona Dupree, even though she'd tended to jabber too much and really wasn't all that adept at her job.

Well, he was paying for that stubborn stupidity of his now. . . .

He wrapped his cartridge belt around his waist, noting that all the ammo loops were empty and remembering with a sinking, hollow feeling that he had no more cartridges for either his Colt or his Yellowboy repeater in his saddlebags or war sack. Which meant that if anyone came for him, he was wolf bait.

As he went out into the main part of the cabin, he vaguely wondered if the woman had any ammunition, then nixed the idea of asking her. He could ask her for nothing more, especially ammo with which he could kill more men. She'd likely see it as blood on her own hands, and she had every right to see it that way.

She was poking something around in a

pan at the black range — side pork or bacon, by the smell, which made his mouth water and his stomach rumble. He saw her cast him a quick, furtive glance over her shoulder as he went over to the door, where his saddlebags, canvas war sack, and rifle leaned against the front wall. He pulled his coat on slowly.

"I'm cooking breakfast, Mr. Henry. You'd better eat a bite before you go."

As hollowed out as he felt, he couldn't turn her down. He glanced out the window right of the door, scrutinizing the snow-covered yard under a broad sky gray with high, flat, gunmetal gray clouds, the eastern edges of which were touched with the umber light of morning. Nothing out there but the barn to the right, a few purple tracks in the snow, and shadows.

"I'd be obliged."

He pulled out a chair and sat down, and indulged in a look at the woman who had her back to him. She was dressed in baggy dungarees and the same shirt she'd worn yesterday. Her hair no longer hung in a dull, loose mass, but it seemed to have more of a shine to it, and she'd drawn it into a ponytail secured with a beaded rawhide thong at the nape of her neck. He let his gaze begin dropping down her slender back.

Suddenly, she turned toward him, her eyes brushing his. She'd caught him appraising her, and the nubs of her cheeks paled as she lowered her eyes quickly and hauled a pan over to the table. Yakima felt his ears warm, and he dropped his own gaze as she forked pancakes and bacon onto his plate. She did so wordlessly, keeping her hard, disapproving gaze away from his.

"Smells good," he said by way of conversation, rolling his shirtsleeves up his forearms, trying to add some levity to the grim cabin. "Looks even better."

When Mrs. Coffin had filled her own plate and filled both their stone coffee mugs with piping-hot brew from a large blue-speckled pot, she set the pot on a wooden trivet on the table, then sat down and drew her chair forward, keeping her cool eyes on her own side of the table.

Yakima sat with his hands in his lap. Some folks enjoyed a table prayer before setting down to the business of eating. She merely cleared her throat, picked up her knife, and slathered some whipped butter onto her saucer-sized griddlecakes before topping both with honey. There was no syrup — not this time of the year, anyway. Probably rarely out this far. Pondering that got Yakima wondering how she made out, likely being a good hour, hour and a half from town, and all alone.

She'd mentioned a husband. What had happened to him? Must get awful lonely out here for a woman. Yakima had gotten used to tramping around by himself. But it seemed unusual for a woman to live alone. Especially hard out here, with few frills. Just the hard business of getting by, one day to the next. . . .

The food was good, and by the time he'd finished, Yakima felt strong and ready to ride. He threw back the last of his second cup of coffee and set his mug down on the table. He was about to excuse himself when he saw the brown eyes boring into him from the other side of the table, through the steam lifting from the cup she held up close to her chin in her two slim, strong hands.

"Before you go, you must tell me, Mr. Henry, because I'll always wonder . . ." Mrs. Coffin let her voice trail off as though she wasn't quite sure how to continue.

"Tell you what?"

"Are you a desperado?" She set her cup on the table in front of her empty plate. "You said you killed the deputy, and . . . there's plenty of desperadoes in this Upper Missouri country. My husband used to say there was a little outlaw ranch in every creek and ravine along the Big Muddy." She paused. "Are you one of them?"

"I reckon I've been desperate enough times, Mrs. Coffin. But I'm no desperado." Yakima felt a little miffed as he slid his chair back and rose to his feet, wincing at the hitch in the lower right side of his back. "Just wore out my welcome in Wild Rose, I reckon. In all of Brule County, most like." He went to the door and donned his hat. "I'll be riding on."

"Not just yet."

Yakima turned to her. She sat where she'd been sitting before, staring out the sashed window left of the door, a perplexed expression on her suntanned face. Her voice was grim.

"Looks like I have another visitor."

Chapter 6

Rance Hagan held the bottle up to the gray light filtering through the frosty window, and squinted one painful eye to gauge the level of remaining forty-rod. The otherwise dull light reflected sharply off the bottle. It drilled his open eye and continued on into his brain, spitting fire.

The Brule County sheriff squeezed the eye closed and sucked a sharp breath through his teeth.

Beside him in his bed in the Brule Hotel in Wild Rose, June Trevelyan gave a moan. She rolled onto her back, lifting her arms to her shoulders, stretching. The bedcovers slipped halfway down her breasts, and Hagan dropped his head between the two pillowy mounds, seeking tenderness and solace from the devilish little men hammering at his brain with small but savage ball-peen hammers. He wriggled his nose down into the deep cleft between the schoolteacher's breasts and sniffed. He could smell the cherry fragrance of June's toilet water tainted with the smell of cheap tobacco and June's favorite drink — straight rye whiskey, known locally by the Canadians as Ole Pap.

"God, it's morning already?" June groaned.

Hagan grunted and sniffed, nuzzling the side of the teacher's right breast. She'd come here from Grand Forks farther east in the Territory, Canada before that. Born in Winnipeg. She'd followed her brother here, but he'd drowned in the Big Muddy while trying to tie up a sternwheeler that had pulled toward shore to take on fresh wood for its boilers. Hagan didn't think she'd ever married, but they didn't talk much about their pasts. Not doing so just made everything easier.

She ran her hands through Hagan's close-cropped, gray-flecked dark brown hair. "Anything left in the bottle?"

Keeping his face buried in June's breasts, Hagan lifted the bottle in his left hand. She took it from him and she lifted her head and shoulders as she took a long pull, the rye sloshing around in the half-empty jug. Whiskey trickled down her lips, chin, and neck. It dribbled toward Hagan's head and he shifted his face slightly to lick up the little rivulet. He followed it up to the woman's neck and then over her chin, and she tilted her head back, squirming around beneath him and giggling.

"Don't get any ideas," she said. "Time to rise an' shine. I got school. Don't you have something to do today, too, Rance — seein' as how you're a mite shorthanded of a sudden?"

Hagan had felt the old carnal pull in his loins, but that pull had released its grip on him, and he lifted his face to the woman's, scowling. "Goddamn it, June. You have to remind me of that?"

"Sorry, honey." She tugged on one of Hagan's ears and chuckled drily. "But when you lose a deputy and half the men in the town under the age of forty, you've bit off a sizeable problem, as my old man used to say."

"I know that."

June was about to tip the Ole Pap to her lips once more. Hagan grabbed it out of her hand and, looking away from the light's reflection off the bottle, took a long pull of his own, causing the bubble to jerk back and forth twice before he lowered the bottle once more and raked a sleeve of his grimy underwear shirt across his lips and mustache.

June beetled her brows at him, grabbed the bottle back. "We could pull out."

"Huh?"

"Today. We could do it, Rance. Just you an' me. Head down to Bismarck, play a little stud and blackjack, rake up enough cash for a ticket on one of the riverboats headed for St. Louis."

Hagan stared at her. She took a pull from the bottle, smacked her lips, and set a hand on the side of his face, caressing his cheek with her thumb. She'd once been a pretty woman, but too many hard years out here had lined and pitted her features somewhat. Oh, she was still one of the best-looking women in town, with her full lips, expressive hazel eyes, and pert nose, but she was looking her age — nearing thirty. Fine strands of silver streaked her long cherry red hair. With her knowledge of books, she was too smart for these parts. Too smart for Hagan. But she'd found no one around she could talk to, so she'd settled for the sheriff, as even a schoolteacher needed someone to haul her ashes from time to time, make her feel like a woman.

Hagan felt sorry for her. Sorry that she'd found no one better than him — an illiterate, broken-down sheriff of a backwater

Dakota county given to tanglefoot and cards.

"Don't you tempt me, now," Hagan said, rolling off the woman and dropping his feet over the edge of the bed.

"I'm serious, Rance." She sat up and hooked an arm around his neck, pressing a breast against his back. "Why not go? We're not getting any younger. How long's it been since you've seen anything but this godforsaken prairie and all those desperadoes along Hatchet Creek and the river?"

He turned his head to look at her over his left shoulder, but he didn't say anything. He didn't like the worn, tired, cowardly way he was feeling these days. The reason he was feeling that way was that he was actually considering June's suggestion. As he sat there staring at her, mindless of the chill in the room — the fire had died in the stove long ago — her lips spread slowly, their corners edging up into her morning-gaunt cheeks.

Outside, a dog barked and a wagon clattered. A woman yelled something in a deep, mannish voice. The sounds jerked Sheriff Hagan out of his reverie. He was glad to be jerked out of it, because he'd found himself drawing a breath to speak, and he was suddenly afraid of what he was going to say.

As the dog continued barking and the woman continued yelling, the sounds growing louder, he turned to look at the hotel room's single window.

"What the hell is that?"

Hagan stood too quickly. His gut and his head rebelled, the room pitching this way and that, and he grabbed a brass bedpost to steady himself as he made his way around the foot of the bed and tramped barefoot to the window. Sliding the curtain aside, he looked down into the street. The pearl light of dawn seared his eyes like the desert sun at high noon, but it was what he saw down there and not the misery the light caused his brain that caused him to mutter "Oh, shit."

"What is it?" June asked from the bed.

Hagan stared through slitted eyes, pressing the fingers of one hand to his temple. The red farm wagon had pulled up to the front of the Brule House Hotel and Saloon, directly below the window of the room Hagan had rented for nearly two years. In the back of the wagon was a coffin, and it was at the coffin that the dog was barking — the big yellow mutt that Hagan recognized as belonging to the dead blacksmith, Boone Dodge. Hagan also recognized the five riders flanking the wagon as well as the wagon itself.

They all belonged to the Coyote Ridge crew run by the notorious mother of Hagan's dearly departed deputy sheriff, Wesley Lassiter. And the beefy, skirted beast just now crawling down from the wagon's driver's boot was none other than Ma Lassiter herself. Hagan couldn't see the woman's face, but he could see the messy tumble of curly gray-brown hair spilling across the shoulders of her ankle-length buffalo coat that looked so old and gamey that he imagined he could smell it from here. Ma's hat, too, was notorious — a battered opera hat with a ratty feather protruding from the braided rawhide band around the crown.

The woman was yelling at the dog. As she set both feet on the snowy street, she reached for the big pistol holstered on her rotund waist, on the outside of her coat. The dog was standing up with its front paws on the wagon's tailgate, barking and snarling at the pine box inside the wagon, its tail whipping crazily.

That dog never had liked Wesley Lassiter, Hagan reflected.

"Goddamn it!" Ma Lassiter roared in her malelike baritone. "I done told you to *git* away from there an' leave my boy *alone!*"

She cocked her pistol and aimed from her

right shoulder.

Hagan closed his eyes and gritted his teeth as the gun roared twice. The dog yipped. Hagan figured that when he opened his eyes again he'd see the dog lying in a pile of its own bloody entrails. But no — Dodge's mutt was merely loping off across the street, unscathed but thoroughly hanging its head and tail, where it soon disappeared into a gap between the hardware store and the unpainted and now-defunct HERMAN & ROTHSCHILD'S STAPLE AND FANCY DRY GOODS shop.

That was Ma Lassiter, Hagan thought. Famous for having a soft spot for horses and dogs. It was men, including her own son, she was so quick to draw down on.

Grimly, Hagan said, "It's her."

"Who?"

Hagan watched with a dreadful expression as the stocky woman holstered her pistol and then, as the men around her swung down from their saddles, strode toward the hotel. She mounted the porch steps and disappeared beneath the shake-shingled roof.

The sheriff ran his hands through his hair, pulling at it. "Ma."

June sat bolt upright, eyes wide. "She's not coming up here, is she?"

"Oh, I suppose she is."

"Oh, my God! I have to get out of here, Rance!"

Hagan walked back around the bed and scooped the bottle off the floor. "Why's that?"

He could hear Ma Lassiter's voice echoing downstairs as he held the bottle up once more — only a quarter of the Canadian forty-rod left, damn it — then took another, more conservative pull. Meanwhile, June scrambled off the bed and began to gather her clothes, which she and Hagan had flung around the room in their drunken, ribald haste earlier that morning, after they'd finished playing poker at Woody's Inn tucked discreetly away in Davidson Gulch, not far from the river.

"I don't want her to see me here, for chrissakes. I'm the damn schoolteacher!"

Hagan snorted as he set the bottle on the room's only dresser. That was June — always trying to keep up appearances despite that during the summer when school was out she often took to less than respectable endeavors to pay for a two-week sojourn to St. Louis. "Hell, June, all of Brule County knows we're together!"

"Yeah, but they've never actually *seen* us together. A teacher needs to be respected."

Clad in only her camisole, June shook her dress out, then stopped and turned to the sheriff as he picked his patched denims off the floor near the washstand. "Unless you're willing to pull out, Rance. You an' me? Hightail it for Bismarck before the river freezes up solid?"

Hagan didn't say anything, just stepped into his jeans as several pairs of boots clomped up the stairs. The sounds were nearly as loud as rifle blasts. Hagan ground his molars as he buttoned his denims, then found his shirt poking out from under the bed. He shook the dirt and cobwebs from the shirt. As the footsteps grew louder, June gave up on trying to get dressed before Ma reached the room.

Cursing, she crawled back into bed, pulling the covers up over her head.

Hagan looked at the quivering lump under the bedcovers and chuckled.

The quilts and wool blankets came down and June lifted her head, her eyes wide with beseeching. "Please, Rance — think about it?"

Someone pounded on the door. June gasped and pulled the covers back over her head. Hagan set his jaw and balled his cheeks against the onslaught.

"Sheriff, you in there?" Folks who didn't

know any better would bet the seed bull that a man owned that voice. And not an attractive man, either.

"Yeah, I'm in here, Mrs. Lassiter. Just hold on."

Hagan scooped up his socks, then stumbled around the end of the bed, pulling them on.

"Don't tell me to hold on, Sheriff!" Ma's fist hammered the door three more times, causing Hagan to wheeze and groan as he pulled his second sock on his foot. "My only son has been murdered — gunned down in his prime — and I'm here to find out what you been doin' about it!"

Chapter 7

Sheriff Hagan gave up on tucking his shirttails into his pants or on getting his boots on. Screw it. In his stocking feet, shirt untucked, he turned the key in the lock and drew the door open.

Ma Lassiter, a little fireplug of a woman, stood beneath her high-crowned, feather-trimmed opera hat just outside Hagan's room, her bushy brows beetled and mantling her deep-set eyes the color of cold dishwater. She had a square, mannish face with thin lips and several moles. Moles were beauty marks on some women. On Ma Lassiter, they were moles.

"You gonna invite me in, Sheriff? I reckon we got somethin' to discuss, you an' me."

Hagan threw the door wide and stepped back. The woman came in, followed by a motley contingent of her infamous ranch hands, all dressed in heavy coats and smelling like the crisp air and wood smoke, thumping the handles of their holstered pistols against the doorframe as they jostled around. Their cheeks were red from the cold, and they held their gloves in their left hands — the mark of gunmen. Their boots thumps and their spurs *ching*ed. They sniffed and snorted as they all gathered in a loose clump behind the woman. One incredibly tall man, the Coyote Ridge foreman, Blaze Westin, closed the door. He dwarfed the others in the room, including Hagan, who was nearly six feet.

"Guess who I have in my wagon out yonder." Ma tossed a gloved hand toward the stairs.

"My deputy?"

"Some green-eyed half-breed killed him, they say."

Hagan nodded.

"Santee Sioux, most likely. Never did care for that bunch of savages." Ma paused, staring grimly at Hagan. "Did you see it?"

"I was out of town, chasing whiskey runners out of the county. When I got back, I saw Wesley in his coffin. Then Anderson and Creed rode back with the others."

"You know where this breed is, Sheriff?"

Hagan leaned against the brass bedpost, vaguely wondering if any of this sullen bunch had noticed June cowering beneath the covers behind him. "No, I don't. I rode out yesterday to Cottonwood Canyon, where they had him pinned down, but the snow covered all sign. I brought the Gatling gun back to town, and by then it was cold and dark. I figure I'll ride out for another look around today."

He hadn't really been planning on doing that, but it sounded right, now that the mother of his dead deputy was here with five gun-handy range riders. "Creed said Luther One-Eye knifed the breed in the back. Likely he's dead out there somewhere. Dead and covered up by the snow."

"Them breeds is tough. I heard what he done to those men that went after him. Indian tough, he is. Wild. Mean."

Ma Lassiter looked around Hagan at the bed. She returned her gaze to Lassiter — a dubious look that bit the sheriff in the balls. Finally, the ranch woman reached up and removed her hat, then stepped around Hagan to sag down in a chair by the wash-stand. She hiked a boot on a knee, then leaned back in the chair, hooking her hat on her upraised knee and propping an elbow on the stand to her left.

Hagan watched her warily, his stony expression belying the hammering in his head. He couldn't smell it, but he supposed the room smelled like Ole Sap. And sex. The chill in the room might have dulled the stench some.

"That boy out there," Ma Lassiter said in a low, grim tone, glancing toward the window, "he's my last one. His father done run off when Wesley stood no higher than a pump handle. His brother, James Daniel, was killed by horse thieves on American Creek. He was the good one, the sound one. Wes — he sprung up tall and handsome, but he wasn't much good. As you know, he was given to runnin' with bad men."

Hagan dropped his gaze and nodded.

"That's why I sent him to you," Ma Lassiter continued. "Hoped maybe wearin' a badge would straighten his spine, firm up his belly. Temper that colicky nature he was born with . . . like his father, Ephraim Lassiter."

"It's a shame this happened," Hagan said. "He was a good deputy. Would have gotten better with time."

When he was sober, Hagen did not add aloud. And when he wasn't feeling "colicky" over some girl he'd staked his claim on. But Hagan had trusted him to keep the peace around town when Hagan had had to ride out after rustlers or roving bands of thieving Indians. And Wesley would take his turns around town of a night when another man would balk at such late hours, given the low pay. The badge had given him a sense of pride. He had, honestly, tried to be a good man, a good deputy, and Hagan had wanted him to succeed. He knew why Ma had wrangled the job for him — she'd wanted him to succeed Hagan, and then she'd have a good grip on the law in Brule County and could run the Furys out, or kill them all, and not be called a criminal for it.

That had been fine with Hagan. He didn't care who ran the county. Hell, he didn't care who lived or died. He just knew he was ready to retire, and who else would have taken the miserable job up here on this canker on the devil's ass if Wesley Lassiter hadn't wanted it?

"Yes, it is a shame." Ma Lassiter spoke in a sad, lonely tone, causing the hard-faced, unshaven gun slicks around her to fidget around uncomfortably. A couple removed their hats and held them over their bellies, fingering the brims. "It's a damn shame, Hagan. All he needed was some responsibility. To get some years behind him. And he would have turned out all right. I ain't gettin' any younger, and I'd have been proud to turn Coyote Ridge over to him in a few years."

"He'd have been ready for it, ma'am. I'm sure of it."

"Now I got him lyin' out in that crude box the drunken Swede nailed together." She turned bitter eyes from the window to Hagan. Her lips were set in a hard white line. "I want the man that done this brought to me alive, Sheriff. I want you to find him, if he's out there, and bring him back to me so that I can hang him myself."

Hagan drew a slow, deep breath. His mouth was dry, and it tasted as if he'd chewed up a dead frog. He wanted this woman here, and to be in this situation, about as badly as he wanted to be stretched out naked over a low Sioux fire with hungry curs feeding on his privates. He met the woman's hard stare, felt the eyes of her five riders searing the left side of his unshaven face.

"Look, Mrs. Lassiter. That . . . that ain't the way the law works."

"The hell it don't. That's the way it works around here."

She rose slowly, slowly donned her ridiculous hat, and unbuttoned the top two buttons of her coat. She reached into her coat, dug around her opulent bosom for a bit, then pulled a wad of rolled greenbacks secured with a rawhide thong. She held the wad out to Hagan, who accepted them automatically, without thinking.

"There's five hundred dollars, Sheriff. You do your job now, like we elected you to do. You bring me that breed, and you'll get another five hundred."

As Hagan stared down at the roll of worn greenbacks in his hand, he heard an almost inaudible gasp beneath the bedcovers. If Ma or her men had heard it, they didn't let on. Ma gave her chin a resolute dip, keeping her washed-out eyes on the sheriff. They were ever-so-slightly red-rimmed and tear glazed, betraying the emotion that fairly boiled behind them.

"You consider that a bonus, above your regular pay. I'd send my own men but we're havin' problems with wolves out to Coyote Ridge, and some nesters who figured on settin' up along American Creek for the winter. Besides, this is your job, Sheriff Hagan. Now you do it."

Hagan turned the roll in his hand. "What . . . what if he's dead?"

"Then you bring me his body and keep that five hundred. Bring him to me kicking and howlin', and you'll get the rest of what I promised." She narrowed one eye at Hagan, who felt his heart shrink up and his throat grow tight. The woman's jowls quivered. "If he's rode on out of the county, you find him. If he's rode on out of the territory, you find him. Whatever you do, Sheriff — alive or dead — you find him and bring him to me."

She gave her chin another dreaded dip, then slid her gaze to the bed behind Hagan. "Good day, Miss Trevelyan."

Ma Lassiter turned and, her group of men parting for her as the Red Sea had parted for Moses, their boots thudding and spurs ringing, headed for the door. She opened the door and went out. Donning their hats and casting cold glances at Hagan over their shoulders, her men followed like a gaggle of ragged geese.

The door closed, and they were gone.

June poked her head above the bedcovers, her eyes bright, fervent. She looked at the money in Hagan's hand and came slowly to a sitting position.

"A thousand dollars," she rasped, letting the sheets and quilts fall down beneath her pendulous breasts. "Imagine that."

Yakima swung toward the window faster than he should have.

The muscles drew taut across his back, jerking at the knife wound in his back, and he felt a sharp pain very much akin to the original stabbing. His lights dimmed, and he pressed a hand flat against the door to steady himself before stumbling over to the window left of the cabin's main entrance.

As he doffed his hat and edged a look around the frame, Mrs. Coffin rose from her place at the table and walked over to the window, sliding the curtain aside with the back of her hand.

Yakima picked out the rider approaching the farm from a crease in the hills about two hundred yards away. The man wore a buffalo coat and a Stetson, and he seemed to be following a horse trail down out of the hills, the meandering line of which Yakima could make out faintly through the snow.

"My neighbor."

Yakima looked at Mrs. Coffin frowning through the window. "He rides over now and then, just checking on me."

"Could you get him to check on you later, after I've gone?"

She nodded, obviously not opposed to getting rid of the man. As she moved past Yakima and over to the door, Yakima touched the grips of his .44, forgetting for a moment that the gun was empty and that he was without cartridges. Mrs. Coffin must have seen the move, because she stopped at the door, her hand on the handle, and gave him a dark, reproving look.

"There'll be no need for that, Mr. Henry. Just keep out of sight, and I'll tell you when the coast is clear."

With that, Aubrey Coffin grabbed her quilted coat and stepped out of the cabin onto the front gallery from which she'd swept the recent snow. She shrugged into the coat, then pulled her gloves out of the pockets and drew them on, walking up to the edge of the porch and hunching her shoulders against the cold. Cal Driscoll rode toward her, reaching the base of the hills now and putting his steeldust mare into a trot, moving through the thin stand of cottonwoods that, only last week, had finished turning yellow. Now the storm's winds had torn off the yellow leaves, and the snow and the cold foretold another long, lingering winter. Just like the winter before and the winter before that.

Aubrey wasn't sure why, but looking at those trees and the high, flat, iron gray clouds, she felt a wave of loneliness rush through her. It was nearly as poignant as the one that she'd felt after she'd buried Joe, only two years after they'd married and proved up their farming claim and built the barn.

"Good morning!" Cal Driscoll hailed

from the edge of the yard, heeling the mare into a lope and waving his arm.

Aubrey smiled and tried to put some cheer into her voice as her neighbor reined up about ten yards from the cabin. "Good morning, Cal. Cold one to be out riding, isn't it?"

"If a man stayed home every cold day in Dakota, he'd never leave home." Cal Driscoll smiled, his pale blue eyes sparkling beneath the brim of his soiled cream hat. He was a tall, broad-shouldered man with a rugged face, and Aubrey supposed he was handsome, but there was a hardness in his eyes that had always left her cold in spite of his fawning. "Just rode over to see how you made out during the storm. Would have rode over yesterday, but that wind kicked up."

"It was awful windy."

"How's your wood holding up?"

"Just fine, Cal. Thank you."

Driscoll looked around, and Aubrey knew he was waiting for her to invite him to light. She wanted to send him on his way, but he'd been a good neighbor to her, and she didn't want to offend him or to seem ungrateful for all he'd done even though she'd prefer he left her alone.

He turned to her, and smiled. "I sure

would admire a cup of your coffee, Aubrey." He started to swing down from the mare, but he stopped and frowned when she held out a waylaying hand.

"Oh, I'm so sorry, Cal, but I just have a ton of work today!" Aubrey flushed at the urgency with which she'd spoken, and Cal flushed a little, too, beetling his sandy brows. "I mean, I'm letting the fire die in the stove, and I'm about to head to town to lay in supplies. Fresh out of coffee, I'm afraid."

She smiled but she thought her face would crack with the artificial force of it.

"Well, that's all right," Driscoll said, irritation in his voice as he swung stubbornly down from his saddle. "Since I'm here, I'll lay in a fresh supply of split wood for you, anyways. It's no bother. I'm happy to do it."

Grinning, he wrapped his reins over the hitch rack fronting the gallery.

Chapter 8

Yakima's pulse quickened as he pressed his back against the cabin's front wall, between the door and the window.

He wasn't sure what he was going to do if Mrs. Coffin couldn't get rid of her neighbor — hide under the bed like a damn fool? — but he knew what the consequences would be once word had spread that Aubrey was harboring a fugitive. He wasn't so much worried about himself. He could take care of himself — once he got his hands on some .44 shells, anyway — but he didn't want the woman caught in the center of this powder keg.

Several options were running through Yakima's head when he heard through the door Mrs. Coffin pipe up with "Cal Driscoll, I am no shrinking violet. I was out here early this morning splitting my own damn wood. Now, I'm getting ready to head to town, so will you please stop wasting time out here and go on back home to your ranch? I'm sure your father would say you have plenty enough chores around home without worrying about mine."

Silence.

Driscoll chuckled, and Yakima could tell from the sound that the man was facing the door. He edged a look around the side of the window frame as the man standing in front of the hitch rack shook his head and said, "Aubrey, I don't think I've ever known a more independent, mule-headed woman in my life!"

"That's how we all survive out here, isn't it?" Aubrey removed the reins of her visitor's horse from the hitch rack and extended them to him. "I do appreciate your help, of course," she said with a disarming smile, the likes of which Yakima hadn't yet seen on the woman's face and which shaved a good five or six years off her age. "But your running over here every two or three days is silly. Joe may not have been much, but his weaknesses did oblige me to take charge. Besides, I feel guilty, pulling you away from your old father and all the work you have to do around your own spread."

"You wouldn't be pulling me away from my own spread, Aubrey," the man said, taking his reins and moving up close to her, dipping his chin to look down at her, "if you'd finally say yes. Then my spread would be our spread. Both these places would, and our lives would be a whole lot easier — mine an' yours."

Yakima pulled his head back against the wall, suddenly feeling like a voyeur. He couldn't help wondering how long Driscoll had been asking for the woman's hand. He certainly was a persistent bastard — Yakima would give him that.

"I've done told you, Cal," Aubrey retorted in a buoyant but chiding tone, "I will not be rushed. Now, you go on home before your father comes over and gives me a tongue-lashing for taking you from your work."

Again chuckling without mirth, Driscoll swung up onto his mare's back — Yakima could hear the squawk of saddle leather. "All right, Miss Aubrey. You go on and get to town, fill your larder. I'll be back for coffee by the end of the week."

There was a jangle of bridle chains. Hoof thuds dwindled. Yakima edged another look around the window to see Mrs. Coffin standing in front of the porch, facing Driscoll, who was riding back the way he'd come at a spanking trot. When the neighbor was at the edge of the yard and continuing to diminish into the distance, Yakima went to the door and pulled it open. The woman stopped in front of it, casting a quick glance over her shoulder.

"He won't be out of sight for a while." She stepped in and closed the door. "Best sit for a spell, have another cup of coffee."

When she'd hung her coat on a hook by the door and refilled each of their coffee cups, Yakima moved to the table. "I'm sorry if I got between you. He's obviously . . . interested."

"Yes, but I'm sorry to say I'm not all that interested in him. Cal's a good man, but he was a friend of my husband's — and it just doesn't seem right somehow." She sank into her chair and wrapped her hands around her cup. "I guess it would if everything else about him did, but it doesn't. I reckon I'm just not attracted to the man." She sipped her coffee and set her cup back down on the table.

Yakima glanced out the window. Driscoll was about halfway up the line of hills, his horse trudging through the snow, and likely wouldn't be completely out of sight for another five minutes. Yakima sat down, sipped his coffee. Something was troubling him. It must have been obvious by his expression, because the woman was staring across the table at him, curious.

"Just so you know," Yakima said, "I'm not a hard case or a shootist or any of the like. True, trouble does tend to follow me, and I reckon trouble does tend to follow those who court it . . ."

He let his voice trail off, not sure why he felt compelled to justify himself to Mrs. Coffin. She stared at him, brows furled, waiting.

"What I'm sayin' is Lassiter drew first. He made up that business about the jack in the card deck because I was spending too much time with a sporting girl he'd put his stamp on, and he wanted an excuse to run me out of town or kill me."

"I don't doubt that, Mr. Henry."

"I should have left when I first sensed trouble, but I didn't. That's what I meant by courting it. But if I let everyone run me out of town who wants to . . ."

"I understand, Mr Henry." Aubrey Coffin looked down at her coffee cup with a thoughtful expression that was hard to read. When she lifted her head again, she glanced out the window flanking Yakima, and said, "He's over the ridge now."

Yakima took another sip of the coffee, then slid his chair back and gained his feet.

"Are you sure you can ride? You lost quite a bit of blood, and not much time has passed."

"I can ride just fine, ma'am." Yakima grabbed his gear off the floor with a grunt, draping his saddlebags and war bag over one shoulder, resting his rifle over the other one. He turned and gave the woman a nod. "Much obliged, Mrs. Coffin. Luck to you."

"The same to you, Mr. Henry."

Yakima pulled the door open a crack and looked out cautiously. Seeing no one around, and noting that Driscoll's tracks led back up and over the southern ridge, the half-breed stepped out onto the front porch and pulled the door closed behind him. He headed off the porch, and, noting the hard chill in the air, he strode across the yard to the barn and pulled one of the big doors open.

He hadn't closed the door again before he heard Wolf blow and nicker an eager, restless welcome. Hearing the geese squawking around in the loft and the milk cow mooing curiously, Yakima set to work saddling the black, moving as slowly and easily as he could, because he could feel the tearing sensations in his lower right back.

Irritating the still-tender wound made him feel sick to his stomach. Lying low another day would have been wise, but he simply couldn't afford it. A posse looking for the man who'd killed the deputy and another six men in Cottonwood Canyon would likely appear soon, and he couldn't endanger the woman.

Besides, without shells for his guns, he was defenseless. A posse finding him out here would likely hang him from the nearest sturdy tree. He knew from experience that courts of law were mostly reserved for white men, excluding damn near everyone else.

When he had the saddle on the fidgety black and had tightened the latigo strap, he tossed the saddlebags over Wolf's hindquarters, behind the saddle, then hung his war bag by its lanyard from his saddle horn. He was leading the black out of its stall when one of the double doors swung open, stretching a trapezoid of gray-blue light onto the barn's straw-flecked earthen floor.

Yakima's right hand went automatically to its holster, but he quickly removed the hand from his pistol's stag-horn grips when he saw the woman step into the barn's shadows, holding a burlap sack by its neck, which she'd tied closed with a rope.

"I packed you a lunch," she said, stopping a few feet inside the door. "Some venison and biscuits, a can of sliced peaches. It's not much, but . . ."

"I'm obliged." Yakima led the horse down the short, narrow alley.

He'd lifted his left hand to reach for the sack the woman was holding out to him, when the barn floor rose abruptly before him. He tried to grab his saddle horn, but his right hand only grazed it, and then the floor came up sharply on his left to smack his left shoulder so hard that for a moment he thought he'd separated it.

"Yakima!"

She set the sack down and knelt beside him, but he was already pushing himself back up to one knee, cursing softly under his breath. "Christ . . . musta stumbled."

"I should say you didn't. Your knees buckled." She twisted around to reach a hand up beneath the back of his coat. He felt her hand close over the bandaged wound. She made a face. "You've opened up that cut. You're not going anywhere, I'm afraid, Yakima. You can't ride. Hell, can't you see that merely saddling your horse about did you in?"

She tugged on his arm. "You'll have to come back inside. Back to bed, I'm afraid."

Yakima shook his head. "No, no . . ."

"You wouldn't make it to the edge of the yard," she said with disgust.

But when he glanced at her, he thought

he saw more genuine concern in her eyes than disgust. And he knew she was right.

Christ. He was like a winged duck on a millpond out here.

"Can you stand?"

"Yeah, I can stand."

Aubrey stretched his arm around her neck and helped him to his feet. He was weak-kneed and he felt nauseated, as though he might throw up, but he was able to make it back out the barn door mostly on his own, with the woman only balancing him.

"My horse," he said as they tramped through the snow toward the cabin.

"I'll unsaddle him, bring your gear back in. You're gonna be here for a few days, I think. That's all right — I've patched up the black, but he could use a rest, same as you."

"Nah, we'll be good to ride tomorrow."

"I don't think so," she said. "You'd better get used to the idea."

He glanced at her, her face only inches from his. "What about you?"

She returned the glance. "I can handle whatever comes."

Cal Driscoll drew his mare to a halt, his sandy brows bulging over his eyes. He ran a gloved hand across his nose in frustration and glanced back toward the hill rising between him and the Coffin farm.

He'd given up awfully fast, he told himself. Maybe too fast. Aubrey had seemed sincere in turning down his request for help today, but maybe what the woman really wanted was for Cal to show a little more determination.

After all, Aubrey was a strong woman.

Maybe she was holding out for a man she could plainly see was equally as strong as she was, and would not turn tail at her own hard-edged words mostly uttered out of politeness. There was also the possibility that Aubrey didn't know her own mind, as was the problem with women, more given to emotion than reason.

Didn't she realize how much better her life could be if she had a man to do the heavy lifting around her spread and to drive her to town when the weather was bad? A man who could take charge and keep her own, simpler, more sensitive mind clear for the business of hauling water, washing clothes, keeping house, and, yes — bearing and raising kids.

Neither Driscoll nor Aubrey was getting any younger. Of course, he'd heard the rumors — likely spread by her deceased husband, Joe — that she was barren. But Aubrey appeared too ripe and rosy-cheeked to be unable to conceive. Everyone in the county knew that Joe had been a bad drunk. Maybe he'd been the one unable to get the seed growing. . . .

Didn't Aubrey realize these things?

And what better man to be the man Aubrey needed than Cal Driscoll himself? Hell, there was no man more available than he in the entire county, and here he lived only three miles away!

Deciding that he should have insisted on driving the woman to town today — that's probably all she'd really wanted, for him to show enough pluck to make up her own mind for her and take the decision out of her hands — Cal Driscoll turned the mare around and booted it back up the path climbing the snow-crusted hill.

He was feeling light in his chest, happy, even hearing wedding bells tolling in his head and imagining how it would be, his and Aubrey's first night together, when he reached the top of the ridge and started down the other side. The mare's hooves thudded along the trail, snow crunching and squawking, the horse blowing vapor up around her ears.

"Whoa!" Driscoll said, drawing back on the reins again suddenly.

The mare stopped and gave its head a

hard, incredulous shake as though wondering why the man couldn't make up his pea-picking mind.

Driscoll's eye sockets spoked as he stared down the hill and into the Coffin farmyard, where the cabin spewed smoke from its large rock chimney and the tin chimney pipe venting the range. But his eyes were not on the cabin. They were on the barn. Or, more specifically, on the two figures just now staggering out from the one open barn door and into the yard, tracing a serpentine path toward the cabin.

Two figures. One plainly being Aubrey herself.

The other a tall man with long black hair spilling down from the brim of his flat-brimmed hat. The man wore a three-point buckskin capote, buckskin breeches, and a holster thonged low on his right thigh, hanging down beneath the hem of his coat.

Silently booting the mare back up and over the ridge crest, Driscoll stopped the horse once more, swung down from the saddle, and stole up to the crest of the ridge for another look.

Who in the hell . . . ?

Chapter 9

Cal Driscoll could see his and his father's small spread in the distance — little more than a brown blotch on the rolling white prairie — when he came to where the trail to Wild Rose intersected with the horse trail he'd been following. There were two shabby signs, one pointing toward MISSOURI R., the other toward WILD ROSE and announcing 3 Mi.

Driscoll studied the sign indicating town, his brooding eyes sunk deep in their sockets. He looked straight out over the mare's head toward his ranch. His old man would be there, forgetful as ever and asking the same questions over and over again. His old man's squaw would be there, too, skulking around and working in her sullen way, sweeping and cleaning and dressing deer carcasses. Limon Hendricks would be there, as well, skidding wood out of the near ravines to cut up for wood to sell to the last steamboats paddling on up the Missouri before the final freeze-up. A couple had already made their final journeys downstream, hauling Montana miners on out of the cold country till spring.

That's how the Driscolls made their living — running a few head of beef that managed to tough it through the Dakota winters, and selling wood to the riverboats. Driscoll had grown up out here, with his father and the old man's several wives, most of them squaws, and he sometimes swore that if he ever saw another cow or another stick of firewood, he'd run off and drown himself in the river.

He'd been married once, but she'd died after a load of logs had fallen on her. She hadn't been much of a wife, anyway — always wanting to go to town and always begging Driscoll to hop aboard one of the passing riverboats and light out for Montana and a change of scenery. She'd been notional and fickle, and the old man hadn't liked her despite their shared love of drink.

Driscoll had thought Aubrey was different. And maybe she still was different, but who in the hell had been that gent with the long hair she'd been helping to her cabin? Why hadn't she mentioned her visitor to Driscoll?

Of course, there could be only one reason for that. She hadn't wanted Driscoll to know the man was there. There could only be one reason for that, too. And that thought filled Driscoll's belly with hot bile that oozed up his throat like liquid fire. It made his ears ring and tears varnish his eyes with raw emotion.

The last thing he wanted to do right now was head back to the ranch and listen to his father's endless questions, and Limon Hendricks's stupid jokes while he sawed wood and smoked. Driscoll was heading to town, and he'd stay there till he was good and drunk and could figure out what in the hell he was going to do about Aubrey Coffin and the man she had at her place.

Driscoll swung the mare hard left and booted the old beast northwest up the snow-crusted trail. While he rode, he thought. He thought hard, and the harder he thought the angrier he became.

She'd lied to him.

Aubrey had lied to him.

She'd told him she was going to town, when what she was really doing was making time with that dark, long-haired stranger she'd had in her barn . . . Good Lord, she could have at least had the decency to tell him she'd taken up with someone else, not play him for a damn fool, keep him riding over there to beg her to let him help her out.

By the time Wild Rose came into view, sitting along a broad horseshoe in Hatchet Creek, smoke unfurling toward the leaden sky from its chimney pipes and stone hearths, Driscoll was so blistering mad he thought the top of his head would pop like the cork on a bottle of homemade beer. Not only mad. Hurt. He'd be damned if he wasn't in love with the gal, and had worked hard for her.

And look what she'd gone and done to repay him for his kindness.

As mad as he was, however, part of Driscoll would not let himself believe she was really two-timing him. There had to be another explanation. He'd like to know what that was, and it certainly didn't look good from where he was standing, but he dearly did want to get to the bottom of this thing and find out who she had out there.

Driscoll pulled up in front of the watering hole he usually frequented whenever he was in Wild Rose — the Union Saloon. It was run by his old friend, Stamp Halvorssen. Stamp served the best ale in the county, and he could make a good hot toddy, too, when a man needed something to thaw his bones and soothe his soul.

As Driscoll moved the mare up between two other saddle horses, both geldings that he recognized, a crow cawed from atop the broad log building's false facade. Driscoll looked up at the crow sitting there all by itself. You didn't see many crows lighting solo, as they were social birds. Unless this one was Bill — pet crow of the Wild Rose undertaker, Milford Hansen, known by most as "the Swede."

Driscoll doubted he was looking at Bill, however. Bill wouldn't be here unless the Swede was, and the Swede's broad-bottomed wife, Maggie, rarely allowed him to visit saloons and bawdy houses. She wanted him home working and not out spending money, especially on tanglefoot, as he'd been known to nearly literally drink him and Maggie out of house and home.

The crow cawed and shifted its weight from one spidery foot to the other, looking down at Driscoll as though awaiting a handout, which was something Bill would do.

"That can't be you — can it, Bill?" Driscoll asked the bird, squinting one eye at it, wondering how you could tell one crow from another, as he stomped up the Union Saloon's front gallery.

The crow gave another demanding caw.

Driscoll shook his head and opened one of the Union's two split-log doors and stepped into the warm shadows, instantly feeling better as the aromas of liquor and tobacco swept against him. He couldn't drink at home, because his old man had a weakness for it and it didn't help his memory any, and, anyway, Driscoll preferred to drink in town among friends.

As he removed his gloves, he blinked against the pleasantly dim light and looked around. There were several men in the place, including, sure enough, the Swede, sitting in a ladder-back chair to the left of the big, roaring, bullet-shaped stove in the room's dead center. Hansen straddled his chair backward, holding a beer in one hand, with two empty shot glasses perched on the vacant chair beside him and from the back of which hung the undertaker's old blanket coat. He had a watch cap on backward. He turned his head toward the newcomer, and his eyes catching the light from the front windows were glassy and shrewd.

Driscoll headed toward the bar on the room's left side. "Well, I'll be damned," he said, chuckling wryly. "Swede, how'd you get Maggie to spring you from your cage — someone die?"

None of the six or seven men in the room said anything as Driscoll walked over to the bar, boots thudding on the puncheons, spurs *ching*ing. In the back-bar mirror, Driscoll saw the undertaker merely sip from his beer glass, his cheeks coloring. The bartender and the Union's sole owner, Stamp Halvorssen, gave Driscoll the evil eye.

"As a matter of fact they did, Cal," the barman said. He was a tall, thin man with pasty, pockmarked cheeks, oily black hair, and a handlebar mustache with waxed ends. "Ain't you heard?"

"I ain't heard nothin'." Driscoll set his gloves atop the bar and glanced over his shoulder at the Swede. "What'd I miss?"

Had Maggie died? If so, he'd put his foot in his mouth, hadn't he?

"Melvin, for one," Halvorssen grunted, setting both his pale, freckled fists against the bar and leaning into them.

"Your son?"

Halvorssen nodded grimly. His eyes were red-rimmed.

Bill Anderson and Galvin Creed were playing cards at a small table beyond the woodstove. Nearby, Halvorssen's Indian whore, Verna, sat looking bored in her skimpy black-and-red bodice and fishnet stockings, black feathers in her hair. She had a ratty blanket thrown over her shoulders.

"And a whole lot more," said Anderson, perusing the cards fanned out in his hand. "Damn near half the able-bodied men in this burg."

Driscoll frowned as he set an elbow atop the bar. "Who? What happened? Fire?"

Fires were the plague of settlements all across the frontier. Over the past couple of years, they'd become more deadly than the Sioux, who had mostly been cowed in the wake of the Custer debacle at the Little Bighorn.

Galvin Creed spoke grimly around the half-smoked cigar smoldering out from one corner of his mouth. "Wes Lassiter first. Then, hell, Trace Early, Luther One-Eye, Dodge, Hackamore Harris, that bean-eater who made saddles . . ."

"De la Garza," said Halvorssen.

"Boomin' business for the Swede," said a man sitting at a table with two others on the far side of the room, beneath an antelope trophy and near the now-silent player piano. This was "English" Charlie Waters, a woodcutter who'd lost his right arm to gangrene after another man had laid it open with a double-bitted axe during a brawl in their camp along Hatchet Creek. He wasn't fit for work much anymore, so he mainly drifted from camp to camp and town to town, drinking and gambling and begging for easy work.

"Look at him, sittin' there," said English in his heavy accent, jutting his chin at the Swede. "Happy as a fat tabby cat in a barn full of mice!"

English Charlie gave a dry chuckle. The others scowled at Hansen, who lowered his gaze like a shamed dog, and buried his snoot in his beer mug.

"Christ, that's a lot of men dead," said Driscoll, still trying to work his mind around all that he'd heard, the faces of the dead parading behind his eyes. "I'm sorry about Mel, Stamp," he said to the bartender, who was still scowling across the bar at the drunk undertaker. "That's hard — losin' a son."

"He was a good boy," growled Halvorssen.

"Wes Lassiter, too?"

"He was the first one the breed killed."

"Huh?"

"The breed that was holed up over to the Dakota Plains. You prob'ly never seen him." Halvorssen plucked a dimpled schooner off a shelf on the back bar and filled it from the beer spigot, tipping it to dislodge the frothing tan head into the wooden pail below the spout. "Lassiter started the whole damn thing, I hear. Had his neck humped over that redheaded doxie. She was holed up with the breed, prob'ly just tryin' to make ole Wes jealous as she's liable to do."

"Well, she did," said Bill Anderson.

"In spades," added his poker partner, Galvin Creed.

"Believe it was a jack of hearts he said the breed had buried in their poker deck," piped up the Englishman playing stud with two other men — a livery barn swamper and Aaron Latham, the lanky ex-cowboy who ran the mercantile.

"Fitting," Latham said around the briar pipe in his teeth and snapping a card onto his and English Charlie's table with a flourish.

"Yeah, well, whatever the hell card it was, my boy's dead on account of it. Same with a half dozen other good men."

"Including my brother-in-law," said Anderson, whose sister had been married to the freighter and sometime stage driver, Trace Early. "Now I got Mavis and her two screamin' brats holed up over at mine and Eva's place. I tell you fellas, if you wanna know what hell is like, it can't be no worse than livin' with two women and five kids under the same fuckin' roof!"

Driscoll sipped his beer thoughtfully, feeling a witch's cold fingers caressing the back of his neck.

"Half-breed, you say?" he asked Halvorssen. Then, in a hopeful tone: "He dead?"

"Probably," grunted Anderson.

Driscoll looked at the man in the backbar mirror. "What do you mean — probably?"

"Luther stabbed him in the back," Creed said. "Last thing ole One-Eye ever done, before the breed swung the Gatling gun on him."

Halvorssen answered Driscoll's questioning look with "Anderson, Creed, and the others all went out after the breed after he done shot Lassiter. Got good and drunk and decided that since the sheriff was out of town chasin' whiskey runners, they'd go breed-huntin', maybe get a nice reward from ole Ma Lassiter herself. Mostly, the fools were just wantin' to break up the boredom, knowin' another long winter was on the way."

"Ah, hell," Anderson said, turning an angry look on the barman. "The man killed the deputy sheriff. He'd have been halfway to Deadwood by now if we hadn't lit out after him."

Creed bit his cigar as he perused his cards. "Can't have strangers ridin' in, killin' your deputy sheriff."

Halvorssen held his tongue. The bereaved father of the town idiot odd-jobber merely shook his head in disgust and brushed invisible dust or crumbs off the top of the bar fronting Driscoll.

Driscoll looked at Anderson and Creed again in the mirror, again feeling the cold fingers massaging the back of his neck. "Where is this kill-crazy half-breed? He dead or isn't he?"

"Who knows?" Halvorssen grumbled. "Sheriff Hagan went out to see if he could find some sign of him. Ma was in town here a while ago, and she was madder'n an old wet hen, as you can imagine."

"He probably dragged his sorry carcass off into a canyon," English Charlie said. "Died there, most like. Latham, are you in or out? Kindly make up your mind. If you're out, I'd like to clean the table off and buy me a poke from Verna."

"Verna don't fuck one-armed Englishmen," said Creed, not looking at English Charlie but lifting his mouth corners faintly with devilish satisfaction.

"Oh, yeah?" English Charlie said, cocking

an eyebrow at Creed. "How many one-armed Englishmen has Verna known?"

The Indian whore sat where she'd been sitting before, one bare foot hiked on her knee as she crouched to inspect her big toe, the blanket hanging off her shoulders.

"Just one," drawled Anderson, looking across the table at his stud partner, Creed. "And I reckon that's where she made up her rule — didn't you, Verna?"

Verna only yawned and dropped her foot down to the floor.

"Oh, go up and have you a poke," said Halvorssen, not too heartbroken over his dead son to have stopped thinking about income. "And you pay me, not Verna — you got that, English?"

Cal Driscoll only vaguely heard. He was leaning against the bar, staring into his beer and remembering the man with the long black hair whom Aubrey Coffin had been helping from her barn to her cabin.

CHAPTER 10

Aubrey Coffin poured tea from her china pot into a chipped stone mug and took the mug to the doorway covered by the bearskin curtain. She tapped her knuckles lightly against the doorframe. Getting no response, she slid the bearskin aside with the back of her hand and peered into the bedroom.

The man called Yakima lay in the bed unmoving except for the slow rise and fall of his chest. She moved slowly into the room, letting the bearskin slide back into place behind her. Stopping beside the bed, she opened her mouth to speak, to tell him that the tea she'd promised was ready — how surprised she'd been to learn he drank green tea whenever he could get it — but let her lips draw together. He was dead asleep. Tired from the strain of earlier that morning, when he'd tried to leave, as well as the blood loss. She'd reheat the tea for him later.

She continued to stand beside the bed, eyeing the man with the dark Indian features — the high-boned cheeks, deep-set eyes in weathered-stone sockets, and long black hair fanned across the pillow behind his head. The rawhide necklace of bear claws rested against the dark red skin of his stout neck.

His own long-handles had been badly bloodstained, so she'd given him a pair of Joe's that she'd found at the bottom of her steamer trunk. She'd kept very few of Joe's possessions, but the long-handles she could wear herself in a pinch. But she'd given them to Yakima. As he was taller and broader than Joe had been, the top of the wash-worn garment was drawn so taut across his chest that the V neck was stretched open across his chest, revealing a good bit of his pectorals and the deep cleft between, as hard and rippled as a steel file.

Aubrey's throat tightened as she found herself staring at the man. Openly admiring the ruggedness, the maleness.

He smelled slightly of leather, horses, and the soap she'd given him to wash with. His arms were thick and bulging, the forearms rippled with ropelike cords. His leathery brown hands, crossed atop the bedcovers over his belly, were large, thick, and heavily callused. They, like his chest — she remembered this from his first day here, when she'd sponged his naked body with cold water to bring the fever down — were etched with both large and small white scars.

Rope scars on his hands and forearms. Knife and bullet scars on his chest. Which meant he was a fighting man. A man accustomed to trouble whether he instigated it or found himself fated for it. But she no longer felt afraid, as she had felt. It wasn't so much what he'd told her about himself — men said a lot of things to women — but it was what his eyes told her.

Eyes rarely lied. Not even men's eyes.

This man's eyes told her that he was strong and had had a hard life, and was good with a knife and gun and horses. And that he'd killed many men, including, as she knew, the deputy sheriff of Brule County.

But he had a good heart.

And the raw maleness of him, his big hands and broad shoulders, sent little shock waves of desire deep into her womb. She could admit that to herself now. She hadn't before, when she'd bathed him from head to toe, but she could now because there was no longer the fear. Only a desire to feel his hands on her, to feel his fingers caressing her cheeks, his lips pressing against her neck, his breath pushing against her skin like the breeze on a hot prairie night in August . . .

As though slapped by the unexpected onslaught of her own lusty thoughts, Aubrey Coffin stepped back suddenly. Some of the tea slopped over the sides of the cup, burning her hands. She hissed at the pain. Yakima's eyelids fluttered, opened. The green eyes stared up at her through red lids, from behind a veil of confusion.

"I'm sorry." Aubrey felt her cheeks warm. "I made you some tea. Guess you fell asleep."

The man continued to stare up at her, directly into her eyes, his expression oblique, his eyes narrowed, the small vertical lines cutting into the brown skin above his nose.

"I'll set it here," she said, setting the cup down on the small, doily-covered table beside the bed. "If you don't want it now, I'll heat it later."

" 'Preciate it."

She set the cup down awkwardly, trying not to burn herself and feeling self-conscious with those jade eyes on her, as if he could read what she'd been thinking, able to sense her own inner hungers. How long had it been since she'd lain with a man? Over two years now. She didn't realize how lonely she'd been until now. A rare wave of self-pity swept over her as she turned quickly away and headed toward the door.

Over two years.

Only now did she realize how long that had been, how badly she needed someone. How desperately her body was crying out to be touched. . . .

She passed through the doorway without looking back at the bed, knowing his eyes were still on her, and let the bearskin curtain flutter back into place behind her. She stopped at the end of the table. The cabin was warm, a fire popping in the hearth, but the afternoon was waning and she could feel the evening chill pressing through the chinking between the logs.

She crossed her arms on her breasts, closed her hands over her arms.

As she looked around the cabin, everything suddenly looked strange to her. As though she found herself in someone else's home — the home of a much older woman who'd lived alone too long but had been making do and keeping busy and content the best she could, by sweeping the hard-packed earthen floor until it looked hard and clean as Paris concrete, the logs whitewashed and spotless, pictures and animal hides hung just so. She'd kept the place so neat and tidy that it almost looked as though no one had been living here at all.

As though it had been scoured and then abandoned by someone who'd never returned.

Aubrey shuddered. She bit her lower lip and looked outside. The light was fading, the clouds darkening, the crusty snow turning moth-wing gray. Shadows angled out from the barn, the corral, the springhouse, and the windmill whose blades she could hear squawking in the chill, rising breeze.

Suddenly, the geese began barking like angry dogs. Frowning, Aubrey moved to the window beside the door and saw both white, yellow-beaked birds moving out from behind the windmill's stone water tank to stretch their necks belligerently toward the main trail curving into the yard from the west. Aubrey's breath caught in her throat when she saw the horseback rider trotting across the western flat between the sparse rows of cottonwoods lining the trail, heading for the yard.

On the rider's black-and-white wool coat, a badge flashed in the dim light.

Sheriff Hagan.

Aubrey froze as she stared at the man

riding toward her astride the copper-bottom gelding, the man's breath and the horse's breath frosting in the chill air that was growing even colder now as the sun fell behind the gray clouds in the west. What the sheriff was doing out here was obvious. He was looking for the man Aubrey had holed up in her bedroom.

What would Aubrey say when Hagan asked her about the man? Lying would make her a lawbreaker, wouldn't it?

Her heart fluttered. Her stomach grew hot and heavy, her knees weak.

She looked around as though searching for a place to hide. But of course there was nowhere for her to run. She had to face up to the sheriff's questions, and she had to make a decision about what she would tell him.

Of course, telling him that the man who had killed Hagan's deputy was in her bed would mean a death sentence for Yakima.

The white geese squawked and closed on horse and rider as they entered the yard. Hagan muttered something to the pugnacious water fowl as he rode on past the geese. The birds scrambled dramatically out of the copper bottom's way, flapping their wings and raising an even louder din. Aubrey stepped back away from the window and moved to the door. She could hear the horse's hoof thuds through the door as she stood staring down at her hand on the metal latch, taking deep breaths and slowing her thoughts, composing herself.

"Mrs. Coffin?" the sheriff called.

Aubrey forced a smile to her lips and drew the door open. "Why, Sheriff Hagan," she said with forced cheer. "What on earth are you doing way out here this late in the day?"

She hated the phoniness in her voice but maintained the smile on her lips as she stepped outside and drew the door closed behind her to keep the heat in the cabin. Her stomach rolled when she saw Hagan looking off to his left, toward the barn, his eyes beneath the brim of his Stetson scouring the ground between his horse and the barn. There were several sets of tracks there, meandering between the cabin and the barn — Aubrey's own tracks, and Yakima's tracks.

Was the sheriff appraising the two?

"Evenin', Mrs. Coffin." Hagan turned toward the woman and pinched his hat brim. He looked worn out, unshaven, long lines spoking out from his eye sockets. "How's everything been out this way of late?"

Aubrey stepped out to the edge of the porch, shivering against the cold and her own trepidation, crossing her arms on her chest. "Well, I was beginning to think Indian summer would hold, what with the warm weather into October. Now . . ." She glanced at the hard crust of gray snow in her yard, piled up against the base of the barn and the other outstructures, and shook her head. "Now I reckon winter's reared its toothy head."

"We'll have another bait of fall. Give it another week or two, and we'll see the sun again."

"I sure hope so. It's too early for winter."

"Yes, ma'am, it is." There was a sadness in Hagan's voice.

Aubrey lifted her gaze to the man atop the horse, forced herself to meet his eyes.

Hagan poked his hat back off his forehead and looked around once more, causing Aubrey to tighten her stomach. "Lookin' for a man, Mrs. Coffin. A half-breed who goes by the name of Yakima Henry. He killed my deputy, Wes Lassister —"

"I'm sorry to hear that, Sheriff."

"Killed Lassiter and nearly the whole posse that went out after him. The posse was mostly made up of troublemakers, and they had no business takin' the law into their own hands like they did — not to mention confiscating my Gatling gun. Not that

that's any trouble o' yours. But . . ." He seemed to be scouring the tracks leading from the house to the barn more closely. ". . . it's my job to run the half-breed down and take him to town for a court trial."

Aubrey took a deep breath as she ripped her own eyes from the man-sized footprints in the snow. "What makes you think he stopped here, Sheriff?"

Hagan looked at her blankly for a time. He had a long nose and close-set eyes. His jaw was blue with two-day beard stubble, and his salt-and-pepper mustache was shaggy. Slowly, he let his thin, wind-chapped lips form an easy smile beneath it. "Why, I don't reckon he'd have stopped here, Mrs. Coffin. I was just wondering if you mighta seen him around. He was injured — wounded — back in Cottonwood Canyon, along Hatchet Creek. And since he did have a horse, there's really no tellin' how far he would have made it from there. Could be around here somewhere, or he might be down in the southern part of the territory by now. Could be dead, even. In fact, he's *probably* dead and covered in the snow along the river. But he killed my deputy . . ."

Hagan let his voice trail off as he turned his head to inspect the opposite side of the yard from the barn. The windmill blades continued to creak and groan. The geese were pulling at the yellow weeds poking through the snow around the holding corral.

"Yes," Aubrey said. "He killed Ma Lassiter's son — didn't he, Sheriff?"

She was surprised by the disdain she'd heard in her voice. But she knew Wesley Lassiter. Well, not *knew* him. But knew enough *about* him to have tried to skirt him whenever she'd ridden to town for supplies.

Still, nearly every trip, she'd felt the man's shrewd eyes on her, and the leering smile on his lips. He'd been a hard case, and Aubrey suspected that Hagan had hired him because Ma Lassiter, the owner of the largest spread in the county, had pressured him to. Probably as added leverage against the other big spread owned by the Fury clan. And possibly to make a man out of the young firebrand. Though Aubrey doubted that an evil-eyed man-child such as Wesley Lassiter would ever make much of a real man.

Certainly never a good man.

"Yeah, well," Hagan said, "that does sort of complicate matters."

He was studying the tracks again between the cabin and the barn.

"If you're wondering, Sheriff," Aubrey

said, letting her lips go ahead and tremble, and her bones quake, from the cold, "the only man through here lately was Cal Driscoll."

She left it that. She didn't know for sure, but she suspected that Driscoll had let his interest in her be known around the county. It was hard for men to keep their mouths shut about things like that. Even about love, if you could call Cal's interest in her love.

Hagan nodded. "Well, if you do see a dark-haired man around here, with Injun features, whatever you do don't let him inside. Not that you would, but . . ."

And he let what he had to say go at that.

"No," Aubrey said. "I wouldn't do that, Sheriff."

"All right, then." Hagan reined the copper away from the cabin and pinched his hat brim.

"Good evening, Sheriff."

"Good evening, Mrs. Coffin. Better get on back inside and get yourself warm."

Hagan rode away. Aubrey stared after him for a time, shuddering.

Then she went inside the cabin and dropped the locking bar into its brackets across the door.

CHAPTER 11

Yakima woke to singing.

He opened his eyes and looked around the near-dark room. The little stove to the left of the bed ticked and sighed. Beyond, the bearskin hung over the door, in black contrast to the neatly whitewashed log walls to either side of it. Around the edges of the rug, red firelight pulsated.

And the woman continued to sing softly. So softly that Yakima couldn't make out the words, but the tone was sweet and light, almost happy. It was accompanied by the sounds of splashing water. The woman was bathing — probably just a sponge bath at the kitchen table, judging by the pitch of the water in the shallow vessel. While she bathed, she sang and hummed.

Yakima felt a smile shape itself on his face. He rested his head back against the pillow. The woman's contentment was catching, and he felt a peacefulness settle deep in his bones, relaxing all of his muscles as well as his mind.

Outside, the breeze brushed the cabin's walls, and the windmill squawked. But above the breeze and the rusty windmill blades, the woman was singing as she bathed.

He closed his eyes and didn't blame himself for imagining her standing out there naked or clad in only a light shift as she ran a sponge up and down her arms and legs and across her breasts. It was a pleasant, homey image. He hadn't had a home now in a long while. Nor a woman except for the occasional whore for satisfying his natural and undeniable male urges.

When the singing stopped and Yakima heard Mrs. Coffin open the cabin door and pitch her wash water outside, he looked at the tea mug on the table beside the bed. The mug was still full of tea, and likely cold as bone.

Well, it was time for him to get up, anyway. He was weak, but there was no need for the woman to continue serving him. He wasn't that weak, and, besides, the best way to get himself strong again was to get up and move around. He'd dress and then he'd reheat the tea himself and drink it out in the main part of the cabin, maybe visit with Aubrey

Coffin for a while.

She was no raving beauty, but he'd found himself liking the easy, honest way about her.

He grunted and groaned as he gained his feet and began gathering his clothes and dressing. When, tea mug in hand, he passed through the doorway, he saw the woman standing at the hearth left of the door. Her back was facing Yakima as she crouched over a Dutch oven suspended above the flames, holding a wooden spoon to her mouth.

Her hair was down again, glistening like burned copper in the firelight. She wore a different dress from before — a tan and cream frock that hugged her slender waist and her rich, full hips and long legs. The collar and sleeves were lace-edged. It was a simple dress, one she'd probably sewn herself, and it wasn't new, but she wore it well.

Yakima cleared his throat to alert her to his presence. She glanced at him over her shoulder, and her eyes shone with a smile, lips parting to reveal the whiteness of her teeth.

"Why, you're up."

Yakima felt a little uneasy — why, he wasn't sure. He glanced at the mug in his hand. "Thought I'd heat the tea. Nodded off, didn't get a chance to drink it."

"I can do that." She set the wooden spoon down on the hearth and picked up the Dutch oven's lid with a heavy swatch of antelope hide.

"I can manage," Yakima said as he turned to the range on his right, on his side of the freshly scrubbed kitchen table. There was a damp spot on the floor near the table, he noticed, where she'd stood as she'd bathed.

He was about to take an empty pot off the rack atop the stove when the woman moved up in front of him, a look of beseeching adding color to her cheeks. "Please, Yakima — I have a pot on the stove with tea in it, and I can add what you have here to the rest."

Yakima saw the black iron teakettle with its weathered wooden handle, and nodded. He let her have the mug and hiked a shoulder. "Just gravels me to have you servin' me, Mrs. Coffin. You've done enough."

"I don't mind," she said as she poured his tea back into the pot, her back facing him now, the small of her back flaring to full, inviting hips.

There was a different sense about her. It went with the flush in her cheeks and the sheen in her hair and eyes. It made him want to put his hands on her, but he resisted the urge and went around to the far side of the table, pulled a chair out, and sat down.

"I would appreciate it if you'd call me Aubrey."

He looked up from the table. The teapot was chugging behind her. She had her arms crossed on her belly, and her eyes were on the floor between her and the table. He could smell the fresh aroma of her — something she'd put in her bathwater, he thought.

He didn't say anything, and she didn't, either. But she must have felt his heated gaze on her, because she dropped her arms suddenly and turned away without so much as glancing at him and walked across the room to the hearth. Although she'd already checked the stew, she removed the lid to check it again.

When she had the cover back on the stew pot, the teapot was whistling, and she came back into the kitchen and filled his mug and one for herself. Her hands shook slightly, and some dribbled down over the sides of the cup.

She brought his mug around the table to stand beside him. She set the mug on the table and stood there, pressing her hands against her skirt, smoothing it against her thighs. Yakima looked up at her standing over him. Her eyes were on his tea mug. The top two buttons of her dress were undone, revealing the very beginning of her cleavage. Her full breasts rose and fell heavily as she breathed.

Yakima's loins surged. He could smell the want in her, the desperation that made her timid eyes glow.

He stood abruptly and lifted his hands. She gave a shocked gasp, and her eyes brightened as she stepped back away from him. Yakima grabbed her shoulders and pulled her toward him. She stared up at him, her face tight, fear in her eyes. He took her hair in his hands, slid it back behind her shoulders, slowly leaned forward, and kissed her. Her lips were stiff. He pulled away from her, eased his hold on her. She stepped into him and pulled his head down to hers once more, kissing him hungrily.

He wrapped his arms around her, and she slid her own hands up his back, avoiding the bandaged wound. Her lips were warm and pliant, and after they'd kissed for a while, she groaned and stepped farther into him, pressing her heaving bosom against his chest.

He pulled his head away from hers, looking down at her, a question in his eyes. His blood was surging hotly through his veins, but he wasn't going to do anything she didn't want him to do. Seeming to sense that, she nodded slowly. He took her hand and began to lead her toward the bearskin curtain.

"No."

He looked at her.

"In front of the fire." Quickly, her breath rasping in and out of her lungs, she took the bearskin down from the nails that held it over the bedroom door, and spread it on the floor in front of the hearth. There was already a braided hemp rug down there, but this would pad it further. When she had it neatly arranged, she looked up at him from her knees. He stared down at her, his broad chest rising and falling, his temples hammering, his cheeks and ears branded by his own barely bridled lust.

She wrapped her arms around his legs and pressed her face against him. He nearly groaned as desire stabbed through his belly like a freshly forged steel blade, and it continued stabbing him as she pressed her hot cheek against his swelling groin.

After a time, she pulled her head away, staring at his crotch, then lifted her hands and began unbuttoning the bodice of her frock. Yakima quickly removed his shirt. He kicked out of his boots and shucked out of his buckskin trousers, tossing it all on the floor near the table. He'd finished undressing before she did, and as she stood before him, clad in only her camisole, the rest tossed away with his own clothes, he walked to her, placed his hands on her breasts through the camisole's thin fabric. Her nipples jutted like acorns.

She sucked a deep breath and closed her eyes, tipped her head back. He kissed her, and then he lifted the camisole up and over her head, and he laid her down upon the bearskin, mounting her quickly, answering her urgent need. . . .

She groaned and dug her fingers and heels into his back.

When they finished, they lay together in front of the fire, Aubrey on her back, Yakima on his side, facing her and the fire. They sipped their tea, which she'd reheated and to which she'd added a liberal jigger of whiskey from her late husband's cache. The stew pot dribbled and smoked as the flames licked up around it.

They stared into the fire for a time, both naked and bathed in the fire's heat. Aubrey lifted her head to sip her tea, and when she rested it back down upon the bearskin, she lifted her eyes to his, caressing his arm with the back of her hand.

"Where will you go when you leave here?"

"Haven't figured that out yet." Caressing one of her breasts with his left hand, he leaned down to nuzzle her neck. "I reckon I'll know when I get there."

"Fiddle-footed, are you?"

"I reckon." He used his nose to slide her hair back behind her ear, then kissed her earlobe, giving it a nibble. "You pretty rooted here?"

She groaned and smiled, her eyes lightly closed, as he continued to nuzzle her ear and finger her nipple. "I don't have anywhere else to go. Since Joe died, it's just been me. Till tonight, I reckon I thought I was used to living alone. Living with Joe was sort of like bein' alone, as after our first few months together he was in town most nights. Had the bottle fever. That's how he died. Took the wagon to town, stopped on the way back to relieve himself, and passed out. He was on a hill, and the horses got frightened by something and backed the wagon down over him. Crushed the life right out of him."

"Where'd you come from — you and Joe?"

"Saskatchewan. My pa was a farmer. Joe's pa was a woodcutter. He came down here to cut wood along the Missouri, and I moved down here with my folks when I was twelve. We had a farm near Joe's camp, though a wildfire burned us out. Ma couldn't take this country anymore, so far from her own folks. She went back to Canada with my sisters and little brother. Pa and I stayed here, Pa working at Joe's camp till a heart stroke took him. Joe and I married and we staked our claim here. Ma's dead, I heard. My sisters all scattered. Ivy's somewhere in the Rocky Mountains — Colorado or Wyoming."

She looked up at Yakima, who stared down at her now, watching the reflected flames dance in her light brown eyes. "This here's all I got, and it's a good enough life, I reckon." She lowered her hand between his legs, gently squeezed, and pressed her lips against the underside of his arm. "I reckon it won't be near as good after you're gone, Yakima. But I'm having a good time tonight, and I think you'll agree with me" — she smiled, fondling him and getting the desired response — "when I say I think we oughta do it again."

They did it several more times. The last time, she'd crawled on top of him and was hammering down on his hips, her hair caressing his chest, when Yakima heard as though from a distant dreamworld Wolf raise a shrill whinny. Aubrey continued to sigh and moan as she rose and fell, bouncing on her knees and kneading the hard slabs of his chest with the heels of her hands.

There was a loud crash.

Yakima lifted his head suddenly as Aubrey screamed.

It took him nearly a full second, staring toward the kitchen, to realize that someone had kicked the front door open.

CHAPTER 12

Four men in heavy coats and scarves burst into the cabin, one after the other. The first man was tall and blue-eyed, with sandy brows and a thin, sandy beard. As he turned toward Yakima and Aubrey, his eyes blazed and his face turned as red as the fire dancing in the hearth to his right.

Aubrey's back was facing the door and the kitchen, as she straddled Yakima. As the man bounded toward her, a Spencer carbine in one hand, the woman screamed, "Cal, get outta here!"

Aubrey was twisting around, trying to stand, but before she could rise, the tall man grabbed her by the hair and jerked her straight backward. Yakima, coming out of the fog of lovemaking, looked around wildly for a weapon, spying nothing but the fireplace poker leaning against the hearth to his left. He got his hand around the iron shaft, but before he could lift it, one of the other three men slammed a cold boot into his ribs. Yakima dropped the poker and fell back with a grunt, his head grazing the side of the fireplace hearth.

Fury burned through him on the heels of the pain in his side. As he saw the other three men — big men in heavy fur coats and hats and all holding rifles in gloved hands, sneering and grinning — he swung his right leg from left to right in a fierce scissoring motion, putting all his strength behind the kick. He'd learned such a move along with a handful of other Eastern fighting techniques from a Shaolin monk friend he'd known only as Ralph and with whom he'd once laid rails for the Transcontinental.

The man on the left grimaced as his own right leg hammered out from beneath him. He triggered his trapdoor Springfield on his way to the floor, the slug screeching over Yakima's head to chew into the wall behind him.

The first man kicked the man beside him as he went down, and this man twisted to his left, triggering his own rifle, a single-shot Sharps, into the wall behind Yakima as well. Both shots resounded sharply and loudly in the close quarters, one after the other, both instantly filling the room with the pepper of powder smoke.

As the man in the middle of the trio stumbled into the man beside him, Yakima reached again for the fireplace poker. He rolled straight back and onto his shoulders, building force, then shot up onto his heels as though he'd been fired from a cannon. Bounding straight up from his heels and into a standing position, he swung the poker from left to right. The heavy iron rod connected soundly with the side of the third man's head. He screamed as he flew sideways into a handmade rocker and over the chair to the floor.

Yakima swung his gaze toward the kitchen, where the first man who'd stormed into the cabin had Aubrey bent forward over this end of the table and was shouting at her while ramming his pelvis against her rump.

"You won't even ask me in for a cup of *coffee,* but you'll fuck this murdering savage on your *floor?*" he bellowed.

The stench of forty-rod mixed with the rotten egg odor of powder smoke, betraying that the four attackers had well fortified themselves before making their move. Yakima had just started to lunge toward the man Aubrey had called Cal and who was unbuttoning his pants as he continued to wail at the naked woman, when the second man he'd laid out heaved himself up off the floor and bulled, wailing, into Yakima's belly.

The half-breed's diverted attention had made him vulnerable, and before he could brace himself, his attacker had lifted him up off his feet and pushed him back toward a rear corner of the cabin. The floor came up to smack Yakima hard about the head and shoulders.

"Get out!" he could hear Aubrey screaming as though from a distant room as rockets exploded behind his eyes. "Get out of here, damn you!"

Then she was sobbing and Yakima was realizing he'd raised his left arm. The man who'd bulled him over was driving a large, gloved fist toward Yakima's jaw, but the man's fist glanced off Yakima's forearm a half second before the half-breed, regaining his wits, drove his own right fist soundly into the man's stony, clean-shaven face.

The man grunted, blowing his sour whiskey breath, as his head jerked sideways and his face slackened, eyes slitting with pain. Bunching his own lips, Yakima hammered the man's jaw once, twice, three more times, each time making a gash beside his mouth a little wider and longer and rolling his eyes back up into his head.

Yakima heaved himself up into a sitting position.

At the same time, he saw both the other men who'd come after him move toward him with their rifles in their hands. The man he'd just sucker punched wheeled back toward Yakima, grimacing as he thrust his right fist up toward Yakima's head. One of the men behind him triggered his rifle. Yakima squeezed his eyes closed for a half second. When he opened them again, he saw the man who'd been about to punch him stare weirdly down at him. Blood was oozing out the back of the man's head, speckled with white brains and bone. It was oozing out the man's blown-away right temple, as well, and Yakima could feel the warm wetness on his upper left shoulder.

"Holy shit, Stamp," yelled the second man with a rifle, eyes wide in shock, "you shot Anderson, ya damn fool!"

As Anderson slumped down against Yakima, as though drifting off for a nap, both of the other two men in the parlor side of the cabin stared in shock and bewilderment, rifles sagging in their arms. Aubrey screamed and rolled off the side of the kitchen table, as Cal turned toward Yakima and the dead man, his pants halfway down, showing his red, threadbare long-handles, the fly of which was open. He sort of staggered forward, into the parlor, jaw hanging.

"You was s'posed to kill the breed," he drawled. His hat was off, and he raised a hand to the back of his head as though to smooth down a rooster tail. "Not s'posed to beef each other . . ."

Yakima rested back on his outstretched arms as the other two men bore down on him, rage returning to their drink-glassy gazes.

"Well, what're you waitin' for, Creed?" Cal said, throwing out an arm and wobbling drunkenly. "Take him out and kill him, and we'll haul him over to Coyote Ridge, and let Ma Las—"

The loud, metallic rasp of a cocking lever cut him off. He'd just started to turn his head, as the other two men were turning theirs also toward the kitchen, when a rifle barked. Yakima couldn't see who'd fired the rifle, because one of the other men stood directly between him and the kitchen, and he couldn't wrap his mind around the idea that Aubrey had fired it until the man in front of him stepped aside. The naked woman was ramming another round into the Spencer's breech even as Cal staggered sideways, sort of twisting around like a dog to see where he'd been shot.

Aubrey's face was as white as snow and implacable as granite as she raised the rifle to her shoulder once more and tilted her head to press her cheek against the stock.

"Hey!" shouted the man in front of Yakima, twisting around toward the woman.

"Hey, now — hey, now — hey, now!" screamed the other man, Creed, though that last was cut off by the Spencer's echoing report off the cabin's stout log walls.

The Spencer barked once more, and then both men were piled up around Yakima, shaking and flapping their limbs and gurgling as their brains slithered out of their skulls. One of the men, the man who'd shot Anderson and who'd been the other one of the survivors of Cottonwood Canyon, stared up from the floor at the half-breed as though in desperate pleading.

Then his eyelids fluttered. He sighed. His eyelids closed halfway, and he lay still.

In the kitchen, Aubrey slowly lowered Cal's smoking rifle from her shoulder and shuttled her gaze between the two dead men nearest Yakima and then to the man who'd been about to rape her and who now lay belly down on the floor in front of the fire and sizzling stew pot. His pants were nearly down to his ankles. Blood poured out the hole in his side to pool between his side and his left arm.

Yakima slowly gained his feet. The fire was

dying down and couldn't keep up against the cold flowing through the wide-open door. He moved forward, stepped over the two dead men before him and the fourth man in front of the fire, and closed the door. He turned to Aubrey, who held the rifle down low across her thighs and was staring down in shock at the third man she'd killed.

Yakima grabbed the bearskin they'd made love on, jerking it out from beneath the dead man Cal, and, more concerned with her own nakedness than his own for the moment, went into the kitchen and wrapped the robe across her shoulders. As she continued to stare, her mind seemingly elsewhere, Yakima took the rifle from her hands and leaned it against a cupboard behind the table. He pulled a chair from the table and gently pushed her into it.

"I'm cold," she said, holding the robe around her shoulders and sort of hunkering down into it.

"I'll get the fire stoked."

He went over to the hearth and tossed three heavy, halved logs on the flames, ignoring the smoking stew pot for now, despite the smell of scorched meat and gravy it was adding to the stench of gun smoke and blood and whiskey sweat in the cabin, and began dressing. When he'd stepped into his boots, he got his coat off one of the hooks by the door and pulled it on, as well. He got his Colt and cartridge belt out of the bedroom. Returning to the parlor, he slipped .44 shells from the loops on Anderson's shell belt and filled the Colt before adding six more shells to the loops on his own belt.

He spun the Colt's cylinder, slipped it into its holster but left the keeper thong hanging free. If there were more bushwhackers around, he'd likely have seen or heard from them by now, but he wasn't taking chances.

Donning his hat, he went over and crouched before Aubrey, who sat in the chair as before, holding her bare legs together, lifting her heels off the floor and leaning forward on the tips of her pink toes. Yakima placed his hands over her knees and looked into her eyes.

"You all right?"

"I'm all right. Just cold." She swallowed, blinked. "Are you all right?"

Yakima nodded. "I'm gonna have a look around and then drag these men out of here."

Aubrey looked around Yakima. "Did I kill all three of them?"

Yakima sandwiched her head in his hands, slid his thumbs across her pale cheeks. "I'm going to get them out of here. But I'm going to need you to stay alert, all right? Just in case there's more around. I doubt there are, but just in case." He ran his fingers over her ears and shoved his face up closer to hers. "You still with me?"

She nodded, and her mouth corners lifted slightly. "I'm with you, Yakima."

He kissed her. "I'm sorry."

"It's not your fault."

Yakima stood and went to the door. Hand on the latch, he listened through the wood. Hearing nothing, he went out and drew the door closed behind him, latching it softly. He unsheathed his Colt, ratcheted back the hammer, and walked out into the yard that was cloaked in chill darkness, stars showing through the thinner spots in the ragged clouds. Wolf was snorting anxiously inside the barn, while the geese barked and quarreled. The mule added its own brays, and the milk cow its lowing, to the sounds of discontent. In the distant hills in the direction of the river, wolves yipped and howled.

Slowly, cautiously, Yakima circled the cabin. When he was relatively certain there were no other gunmen around the place, he backtracked Cal and the other three into a crease in the buttes behind the cabin. Apprehension built inside him as, following the tracks, he realized that there were five sets, not four. And one set of the five led back into the buttes, where Yakima now found four horses tied to a nest of snow-laden chokecherry shrubs.

The horses nickered and coughed and skitter-stepped, wary of the strange-smelling stranger, as Yakima looked around and was not happy to find the tracks of a fifth horse. The horse's tracks intersected the tracks of the fifth man, who'd apparently remounted his horse and ridden away.

Ridden away at a gallop, heading back in the direction from which he and the other four attackers had come. In the direction of town. . . .

"Damn." Yakima's sudden oath in the quiet night startled even himself. Two of the horses skitter-stepped away from him.

With his confounded gaze, Yakima followed the purple tracks in the gray snow as they meandered off through the crease between the buttes. He cursed again as he worried a molar with his tongue.

The wolves continued to yip and yowl.

Heavy with dread, Yakima headed back to the cabin to dispose of the dead men.

CHAPTER 13

English Charlie Waters reined up at the fork in the trail. He was breathing hard, his eyes bright with drink and terror.

He stared in drunken confusion at the forking trails, one leading to a woodcutters' camp, one leading back toward Wild Rose, and the third rising and falling over the snowy, night-cloaked bluffs and into the country of Coyote Ridge Ranch. English took his old strawberry gelding's reins in his teeth and reached back with his lone, left arm to dig around in his saddlebags. When he found the whiskey bottle he'd been looking for, he popped the cork with his teeth and took a long pull.

The whiskey hit his stomach like a soothing, blazing tonic. The calm flowed through his limbs and into his head, rearranging his scattered thoughts until they each settled like billiard balls in separate pockets. He drew a deep breath and looked up the trail that led westward toward Wild Rose.

Why go there? he asked himself. What was waiting for him there?

Of course, he should go back and report what had just happened at the Coffin farm to Sheriff Hagan. But then he'd have to explain how he and Galvin Creed, Bill Anderson, and Stamp Halvorssen had been roped by Cal Driscoll into heading out to the Coffin place to take down the half-breed he'd seen there making time with Aubrey Coffin.

And the sundry events that followed. . . .

True, he'd had nothing to do with those. Having only one arm, he'd been allowed to observe and to keep an eye on the horses in case wolves would try to haze them away. Still, he'd been part of a bad thing. He'd seen part of it through the window.

A very bad thing.

English took another slug from the bottle, smacked his lips, ran his coat sleeve across his mouth, and shook his head. No, there was nothing for him in Wild Rose but trouble. Now, the Coyote Rim Ranch was a different story, he mused as he stared up the trail that rose and fell over the star-trimmed northeastern bluffs. If he could get on Ma Lassiter's good side, there just might be a job in it for him. And telling Ma where she could find the half-breed who'd killed her only son would definitely get him on the irascible old woman's good side.

If she had a good side, English thought with a wry chuff.

What the hell? It was worth a try. A long, cold winter was coming, and English Charlie Waters was out of a stake, with nowhere to go. Having only one arm severely limited his options. He wished he'd headed for Mexico when he still had some gambling winnings, but it was too late for that now. Now he had to worry about putting a shelter over his and his horse's heads, so he didn't starve or freeze to death. In town, he'd pretty much run through his credit at all the saloons and whorehouses, and no one there was bound to offer a job to a one-armed limey drunk.

Ma had a big place. Maybe she'd hire him to be her houseboy. One-armed he might be, but he could split wood and cook, fer Christ's bleedin' sake. . . .

English Charlie punched the cork back into the bottle, returned the bottle to his saddlebags, and booted the strawberry onto the right tine in the trail's fork. He paralleled the trail to the woodcutters' camp for a time; then, when that trail doglegged west toward a jog of low, wooded hills, English kept heading northeast.

The night got colder and colder, and by the time the rider could see Bottineau Landing in the river's canyon below him and to his right, he'd started to believe he might freeze to death before he arrived at the Coyote Ridge headquarters. English paused under a giant, naked cottonwood, fished the bottle back out of his saddlebags, and indulged in another deep pull.

An owl cooed. The call in the otherwise cold, silent night caused English to jerk with a start. He pulled the bottle down too quickly and sent a good bit of the prized forty-rod — who knew where or when he was going to acquire another bottle? — dribbling down his chin and spade beard and onto the front of his gray wolf coat, where it glistened in the snow-reflected starlight.

"Of all the bloody goddamn . . . !" English held the bottle up toward the stars, checking the level of whiskey remaining, then looking around for the culprit. "Fuggin' owl."

The bottle shattered. Glass and whiskey were blown off to his left while several shards and a good bit of the prized tanglefoot drenched English's lap.

"What the *bloody hell?*" English bellowed

as the echoing crack of a rifle reached his ears.

The strawberry lurched and curveted. English Charlie released what remained of the bottle in his hand and grabbed the saddle horn to keep from being thrown. A man's laugh sounded. English reached for his rifle jutting from its saddle scabbard on the horse's left side. The strawberry took advantage of the sudden slack in its reins to pitch back on its hind legs while loosing a shrill whinny.

English screamed as he was thrown off the horse's left hip and hit the ground with an impact that sent a splintering, tooth-gnashing pain throughout his chest and rib cage and fired red, white, and blue flares behind his eyes. The dark shape of the strawberry jerked away from him, and he could hear the thuds of its galloping hooves beneath the cracked bells tolling loudly in his ears.

He couldn't have been hurt too badly, however. The pain quickly abated behind the warm flush of the forty-rod, and he found himself rising to his hand and knees looking despondently at the wet spot in the snow from which shards of glistening glass poked up.

"Bloody bastards," English cried. "Bloody,

bloody *bastards!*"

He heard more hoof thuds, these growing louder. Looking up the trail, he saw two horseback riders moving toward him at slow trots, both men silhouetted against the starry sky above and behind them and holding Winchester carbines straight up from their thighs. Their breath frosted in the air around their heads as they rode straight-backed, shoulders broad and tense, faces dark as spectral visages beneath the broad brims of their hats.

Both men reined up in front of English Charlie. They were only ten yards away, but English still couldn't make out their faces behind the gray puffs of their own breaths and those of their horses. Apparently, they could see him, or could see the empty right sleeve pinned to the hem of his coat.

"Damn, English," the man on the right said. "What the hell are you doin' out here? Don't you know it's dark, and winter's comin'?"

"You bastards had no call to blast my bottle!"

"You're lucky that's all we blasted, you crazy English fool," said the man on the left.

English recognized both voices as belonging to Jack-Henry Vincent and Drew Beresford. Coyote Ridge riders. Riders whom Ma

Lassiter had been wintering over for the last five years or so, a long time in the life of a cowpuncher, though these men were far from mere "punchers." Like most of Ma's men, they were what some would "cold-steel savvy."

Jack-Henry added, "We been havin' rustlin' problems of late, and Ma's told us to shoot first and ask questions later. So I had every right to go ahead and blow your head off, and the only reason I didn't was that I was wondering what a rustler would be doin' out here *pie-eyed.* Could tell you was drunk from a half mile away in the dark!"

"It's Jack-Henry's ornate curiosity that saved your worthless limey ass." Beresford sniffed and set his rifle barrel on his shoulder.

"*In*-nate," English said. He'd had some schooling back in England before heading to the Territories to seek his fortune, which had so far eluded him to his everlasting frustration. He still liked to read a dime novel now and then, to ease him out of a long debauch. "It's *in*-nate, ya damn peckerwood. *Ornate* means a decoration."

Vincent turned toward Beresford. "Look who's ridden all the way out here to give you an English lesson."

Still on his knees, and feeling the burn of

anger welling up behind the alcohol gauze in which his entire body felt loosely wrapped, English snarled, "I came out here 'cause I got some information for Ma. Now, kindly run my strawberry down and take me to her."

Beresford stared grimly down. "What information?"

"Gotta tell her in person." English curled his upper lip. "It's complicated. You two'd get it wrong."

"Oh, yeah?" said Vincent, aiming his rifle at English with one hand, holding his reins in the other. He thumbed the hammer back with an ominous, ratcheting click. "I think I just caught you tryin' to long-loop one of Ma's yearlings."

"Hold on, now!" English raised his lone arm high above his head, realizing he'd made a mistake. His predilection for the tanglefoot often caused him to take such missteps, but while he realized his problem, he'd never considered doing anything about it.

"Hold on, Jack-Henry. Why waste a bullet on this crippled old dog?" Beresford reined his chestnut bronc around. "I'm gonna fetch his horse."

Jack-Henry stared down the barrel of his carbine at English, who felt a prickling under his collar. All he could see of the gunman's face was a dark oval with possibly the long line of a faintly star-limned nose. English's heart thudded, but it began to slow when he heard the click of Jack-Henry depressing the Winchester's hammer.

Jack-Henry spat to one side, then reined his horse around and spurred it slowly up trail, in the direction in which Beresford had disappeared.

Beresford returned a few minutes later, leading the snorting strawberry. English climbed aboard, and then he and Beresford booted their mounts up and over the next low ridge, catching up to the moodily quiet Jack-Henry Vincent about a hundred yards beyond.

Vincent and Beresford rode silently ahead of English, who kept to himself, as well, only hunkered down low in his coat, shivering and hoping to God that Ma Lassiter would at least reward him with a drink and a bunk by a hot fire. Food would be nice, but the main thing was a bottle. His hand still hurt from the several glass shards that had poked him when Beresford had shot the bottle out of his hand.

English snorted, angry again. Simple sons o' bitches had no respect for nothin' or no one. . . .

After what felt like another hour on the cold, miserable trail through the snowy, night-shrouded buttes, but what was probably only fifteen or twenty minutes, English found himself following the two quiet Coyote Ridge riders down a long slope between flat-topped bluffs and into the sprawling headquarters of the Coyote Ridge Ranch. There was the main lodge ahead, sitting back against another bluff, with a windmill fronting it, the long L-shaped bunkhouse, its windows lit against the cold night, to the right. Several stock and hay barns were arranged willy-nilly to the left, along with a springhouse and another windmill and stock tank.

English had been out here a few times before, as he'd once cooked for Ma Lassiter during a fall roundup a couple of years ago. And he'd ridden out here to supply the woman with firewood when her men had been too busy with rustlers, Sioux, and cattle to cut their own one summer, so nothing about the place was new or surprising to the one-armed man. It was a Dakota ranch — remote and rough-hewn and built to weather both the high-plains climate as well as marauding Indians.

The house was big and plain and solid, like a barrack-house — a two-story log, shake-shingled affair with dormer windows jutting from the roof. The lower-story windows were lit, and smoke issued from the big river-stone hearth jutting above the roof on the right side. There was a broad, roofed front gallery decorated with elk and deer antlers, and as English and the other two riders pulled up in front of it, a figure moved in front of one of the windows and stepped out to the edge of the porch.

"What you fellas got there?" the man said, holding a rifle in his crossed arms. He was smoking a quirley. English caught a whiff of the tobacco smoke and salivated. "Find you a lost lamb, didja?"

Jack-Henry Vincent had just opened his mouth to speak when the front door clicked and squawked as it opened. A bulky figure in a pleated skirt and white blouse stepped out onto the gallery, pulling the door closed behind her.

"What's goin' on, boys?"

Ma Lassiter had a bobcat stole draped over her shoulders. A long black cigarillo smoldered between the stubby fingers of her left hand. In her right, the barrel of a silver-chased revolver flashed in the light from the windows behind her.

"Found us a one-armed trespasser out on the range, Ma." Jack-Henry canted his head toward English Charlie, who'd put his strawberry up between the other men.

"English Charlie?" Ma said, moving out to stand atop the gallery's four log steps flanked with transplanted spruce trees whose needles were mostly brown. "What the hell are you doin' out here on such a night?"

English Charlie pinched the short brim of his fur hat. "Evenin', Ma. How're you?"

"Spit it out, English. It's cold out here."

"Might be warmer inside," English said.

Ma Lassiter didn't bite on the implied suggestion. "Yes, it would."

To English's right, Beresford gave a rueful snort. Charlie cleared his throat, enjoying the smell of tobacco smoke on the faint, chill breeze and vaguely imagining how a slug of good whiskey would complement it.

"Been some doin's," he said, shivering and hunkering low in his saddle. "Doin's you oughta know about. Regardin' Wesley . . . and the man who killed him."

Ma narrowed her eyes skeptically as she raised the cigarillo to her lips and took a long drag. Blowing the smoke out her broad nostrils, she growled, "You don't say."

"Just came from the Coffin farm."

"What on earth does the Coffin farm have to do with Wesley?"

English Charlie grinned like the cat that ate the canary. "That's where the man who killed him — that green-eyed half-breed — is holed up."

Ma stared for a time. The men on either side of English Charlie turned their heads toward him with hushed interest. The man who'd been standing guard on the gallery moved down a few feet, better able to hear the conversation.

"Why would you say such a thing, English?" Ma asked.

"Seen it myself, my good woman," Charlie said, shivering now from not only the cold but for desperate want of a drink. "Driscoll saw him earlier, then came to town and got liquored up. He was in the Union all day, drinkin' and playin' cards with me, Bill Anderson, and Galvin Creed. Around about three o'clock, he asked us if we wanted to help him run down the breed, as he knew where to find him."

English couldn't help chuckling in spite of his misery. "With Driscoll's woman, don't ya know? Seen 'em in the window, we did. Ruttin' like a couple of dogs in an alley."

English winked. "I stayed outside since I ain't much good with a gun, bein' left-handed an' all, though I was born to use the other." He whistled an' shook his head.

"Well, it sure didn't go the way Driscoll had planned it. No, sir! Somehow that breed an' Mrs. Coffin got the upper hand. I ain't sure, 'cause I sorta had too much to drink, don't ya know, and musta dozed off there for a few minutes. All the shootin' and screamin' brought me around, an' when I looked in the window, sure enough, Mrs. Coffin had a smokin' Spencer rifle — Driscoll's own carbine — in her hands! Driscoll himself an' Anderson, Creed, and the barman was all lyin' in pools of their own blood."

"What'd you do?" Jack-Henry asked.

"Me? Hell, I did the only thing I *could* do under the circumstances. I ran!" English frowned when Jack-Henry and Beresford chuckled their disdain. "What was I supposed to do — a one-armed man who was never good with a shootin' iron even *before* Leo Pepper laid into me with that hatchet!"

"Calm down, English," Ma Lassiter said, staring up at him from atop the gallery steps, a bulky, dark statue partly silhouetted against the lantern-lit windows flanking her. "You did good, comin' out here to tell me what happened. Why don't you go on in, get yourself a drink, and make yourself comfortable by the fire?"

She glanced at Beresford. "Drew, tend his horse for him. You come on in now, English.

I got just the thing to take the chill out of your bones."

Instantly relieved and gleeful, English Charlie swung down from his saddle and tossed his reins up to the scowling Drew Beresford. He scrambled up the steps, heavy-footed and awkward since his feet were half frozen, and lurched for the cabin's front door and tramped on inside, making a beeline to warmth and whiskey.

Ma said to the three men around her, "You boys go on to bed. Get plenty of sleep, and be ready to ride at first light."

"The Coffin farm?" John-Henry asked.

"That's right," Ma Lassiter said with a nod.

"Sure you don't want a guard?" asked the man who'd been sitting on the porch when English Charlie and the other two men had ridden into the yard. "What about them Fury boys?"

"It's too cold for the Furys to come gunning for us tonight, Bob. Go on to bed. For the time bein', we got bigger fish to fry."

The three men headed off toward the bunkhouse, Beresford leading English Charlie's strawberry. On the cabin's gallery, the stocky woman twirled the big, silver-chased pistol in one hand and lifted the cigarillo to her mouth with the other, drawing the smoke deep into her lungs and blowing it out at the stars with a wistful look in her deep-set eyes.

Chapter 14

Yakima opened the cabin door and stepped out into the blue shadows of early morning, with the rising sun laying a burned-orange sheen across the snow. Closing the door, he took his rifle in both hands and glanced down at the four dead men he'd dragged out to the porch and arranged side by side in a line. He hadn't seen any point in covering them. They lay on their backs now, hatless but still wearing their coats, open-eyed and staring with varying degrees of dumb misery at the gallery's low roof.

The cool morning kicked up ghostly veils of snow that had fallen fresh the night before. It ruffled the fur of the men's coats, all of which, and the dead men's hair and brows, were rimed with frost.

Yakima looked around the yard. Nothing moved except for the blowing snow and the faintly, intermittently squawking windmill blades. No fresh tracks, either. Yakima was relieved. He wanted no more trouble here for Aubrey Coffin.

Setting the Yellowboy on his shoulder — he'd found about twenty rounds of ammo for his rifle and pistol in the dead men's gear — he started down the gallery's three steps. He winced at the hitch in his lower right back. Last night's dustup had opened the stab wound again; though Aubrey had patched it the cold now pulled at it. The door clicked behind him. He stopped and turned to watch Aubrey step out of the shack, her hair down, two heavy striped blankets wrapped around her shoulders. Her hair blew in the breeze as she pulled the door closed, glanced from the dead men to Yakima.

"Are you going to bury them?"

"No." He shook his head. "I'm going to take them back to town."

She frowned. "You can't be serious."

Yakima gave her a direct look. "It's time to end this once and for all. I'm taking these men to town, and I'm going to have a little sit-down chat with the sheriff."

He swung around and strode off toward the barn, where he'd stabled the men's horses and gear. He heard Aubrey go into the cabin, but she came out again quickly, and as she ran up from behind him, regarding him urgently, she was wearing her quilted coat, battered hat, and gloves, a red scarf wrapped loosely around her neck. "Yakima, please. That's a crazy idea. If you go back to town, they'll hang you."

"Who?" He chuckled without mirth as he continued to the barn. "Hell, I've killed damn near every able-bodied man there."

"I killed the last three."

Yakima stopped in front of the small barn door to the left of the two larger ones. "No one will ever know about that. I'm not going to tell them, and there's no point in you tellin' 'em, either. You killed them because of me."

"No." Aubrey shook her head. "I killed them because of me. You know what was about to happen."

"I led them here, Aubrey. I as good as killed 'em." Yakima lifted his hand and slid a lock of hair back from her cheek. His eyes crinkled in a smile of sorts as he said gently, "I'm pullin' foot. I want you to go on with your life and forget about all this."

"I can't do that. I can't forget any of it, Yakima."

"You don't have a choice, Mrs. Coffin."

He turned quickly away from her and went into the barn. She grabbed the door before he could close it, and followed him into the shadows rife with the smell of feed, shit, and ammonia. Immediately, knowing it was feeding time, the two white geese dropped like demonic angels from the loft, barking and quarreling and flapping their wings, lifting a fetid wind. That set the milk cow to lowing, the mule to braying, and the five horses including Wolf to stomping around and snorting and kicking the stall partitions.

Yakima was glad for the din. It kept Aubrey from continuing their argument. When he'd fed and watered all the horses he intended to take to town, he saddled Wolf and the others, tying the four horses belonging to the dead men tail to tail. Opening the two big doors, he led Wolf and the string of four others back out of the barn and into the cold morning.

He stopped in front of the cabin, heard the mule bray behind him.

Turning, he saw Aubrey leading her saddled mule out of the barn, an obstinate expression on her face.

Yakima grunted and shook his head. "No way." He went over, grabbed the dead Driscoll by his coat front, and heaved the man up and over his shoulder before laying him belly down across one of the spare horses.

Aubrey tied the mule's reins to the rack fronting the cabin. "I'm going with you."

"Crazy talk." Yakima tossed a soogan blanket over the corpse and began strapping Driscoll to his saddle. "I won't hear any more about it."

When he had Driscoll secured to the horse, Aubrey helped him secure each of the other dead men to the three other mounts, covering them with blankets and lashing their hands to their ankles beneath the horses' bellies. Yakima was glad for the help, as all the heavy lifting would likely have grieved the stab wound again.

"Much obliged," he said crisply, and set his hands on her shoulders. "But that's all the help I'll need."

"I'm going to tell the sheriff what really happened."

"No. You'll just cause trouble for yourself when there's no point. I've got enough that a little more won't make any difference. With luck, the local law dog'll listen to reason and this will all be over for us both."

When Aubrey opened her mouth to retort, he kissed her, wrapping his arms around her tightly, holding her close against him. At length, he pulled his head away from her, gave her a reassuring wink. "You take care."

She drew her mouth corners down,

crossed her arms on her chest.

Yakima grabbed his own reins and the lead line from the hitch rack and mounted up. He did not look back until he'd reached the edge of the yard, and was glad to see her standing where he'd left her, at the foot of the gallery steps, staring after him. The wind plucked at the fringed ends of her scarf.

The mule brayed and switched its tail.

Yakima climbed a hill and headed on down the other side, and the Coffin farm was gone from his view.

In his room in the Brule Hotel in Wild Rose, Sheriff Rance Hagan groaned. He released a lungful of pent-up air.

June Trevelyan lifted her head from beneath the covers, her lips stretching a devilish smile. "Good?"

She smacked her lips.

Hagan groaned again, slowly blinked his eyes, and sank back against his pillow propped up against the double bed's wooden headboard.

"Are you sure?" the teacher asked. "I want you to be happy, Rance. I want to make you happy."

"You do make me happy, June."

She shook her hair back from her shoulders, exposing her naked breasts. She was naked under the bedcovers, and Hagan felt the warmth of her legs scissoring against his. "I mean, I want to make you happy forever. Just me and only me, Rance." She lay down beside him, wrapped her hands around his arm, and snuggled against him, making little grunting sounds of satisfaction and comfort.

"That means you wanna pull out of this humble little pueblo, don't it?"

She smiled and nodded girlishly, walking two fingers down his arm. "Mm-hmm."

Hagan yawned and glanced at the gray window over the washstand. He'd slept late again. Must have been eight or nine o'clock in the morning. "You know I can't do that, June."

"You got a stake, Rance. And it's a long, cold winter settin' in."

Hagan pulled away from the woman, threw the covers back, and dropped his feet to the floor. Yawning again loudly, he ran his knuckles through his hair brusquely, trying to wake up. June was right. A long, cold winter was setting in. Trouble was, whenever Hagan imagined being someplace else, he couldn't imagine himself being any happier than he was here.

That was the trouble with getting older,

he thought. Your imagination got dull. Or was it too sharp? He chuffed. Maybe he'd figure it out one of these days. But while he was bored to death of this town, this county, and had little but revulsion for the people in it, he just couldn't summon enough energy to leave it.

"He's dead, Rance," June said, her voice a soft purr as she rolled onto her side and propped her chin on the heel of her hand. "Dead and buried in the snow. You don't owe Ma nothin' more than what you done by ridin' out tryin' to find him."

Hagan chuckled without mirth and turned a scowl on the woman. "Jesus H. Christ, June. He killed my deputy. He killed nearly a dozen men out in Cottonwood Canyon. How can I just walk away from that? How can you *expect* me to just walk away from that?"

The teacher widened her eyes as she rose on an elbow. "For the love of God, Rance. He's dead. The winter's done already taken him. You don't owe this town anything. You been a good sheriff for five years now. That's twice as long as any of the lawmen they've had in the past fifteen, since the place was just a little trading camp and military post with a whorehouse for every hider and soldier!"

Hagan dropped his head and ran his hands through his hair once more, groaning.

"Wesley wasn't worth the tin you pinned to his chest, Rance."

Hagan nodded. "I know that."

"His ma's a droopy-titted old she-buff dug into those hills out there, with a string of cold-steel artists she uses mainly for runnin' anyone off who threatens her considerable domain though she already calls half the damn county her own. You know how many innocent men she's hanged, callin' 'em rustlers or horse thieves when they were only trying to build up a place of their own out there?"

"Yeah, I know."

"And those men in Cottonwood Canyon — they were all drunk and runnin' off their leashes. They had no call to be out there. Just a pack of coyotes crazed by the smell of blood and some half-baked idea they'd get on Ma Lassiter's good side. Though what good that ever did anybody, I'd like to know! I knew a man who worked for her, an ex-solder like you. He worked good and hard for her, for twenty dollars a month and a roof and her stringy beef, and you know what she did when he got throwed and hit his head on a rock and it turned him into a babbling idiot?"

Hagan kept his head down, to nearly between his knees, pulling at his short-cropped hair as though to stifle the woman's voice in his ears. He hadn't heard this story about Ma Lassiter, but he'd heard others. He knew how it was going to go.

"She cut him loose with ten dollars in his pocket and an old nag of a horse that gave out before he reached the river ford. Wolves got both him and the horse. They found him in little bitty bloody pieces all up and down the Big Muddy by Moccasin Point. When they told Ma, she just laughed and said them wolves was a tad more merciful than she'd been. Said if she'd been a kinder person, she'd have put a bullet through his head after that horse threw him."

"All right, goddamn it, June!" Hagan heaved himself to his feet and swung around angrily. "I know all about Ma Lassiter and Wesley and the bunch in Cottonwood Canyon. I also know this town and county ain't been half bad to me. I'm wearing its badge, and by God I'm gonna continue wearing it until my term is up or they bring in someone they think can do a better job. Shit, you're right — it's a big world out there. But you know what, June? Everywhere you go is just the same as here."

"Ha!" the woman laughed as Hagan walked over to the washstand. "You think Denver or Cheyenne or, hell, San Francisco would be anything like *this?*"

Hagan poured water into the enamel-covered washbasin from the rusty tin pincher and splashed water on his face. He talked big. He talked tough. But was he really capable of handling any of this? The trouble was he wasn't really capable of mustering the gumption to walk away from it, either.

"You know what your problem is, Rance?"

"What's that?" he said wearily, continuing to wash.

"You like bein' a big frog in a little pond. But the boredom of this hideous place has made you a drunk, and now you're just too stuck and drunk and afraid to take a good hard look at yourself and see what I'm sayin' and make a change."

Hagan looked over his shoulder at her. She stared back at him, her eyes hard beneath her furrowed brows. She was sitting up now, and she'd crossed her arms over her naked breasts. He wanted to feel anger at her for saying those things, but the only emotion he could drum up for her was pity.

Truth was, June Trevelyan was just as

stuck as he was. And just as much of a bored, lonely drunk as he was. She loved him, as he loved her. And that's why she'd never run off to Bismarck with the next lucky gambler to pass through Wild Rose on his way downriver.

Oh, she might leave eventually. But at considerable cost to herself. She knew that, as did he. And that's why he suddenly felt like bawling his eyes out for both her and himself, and crawling back into bed with her and another bottle. Spending the whole damn day there. Hell, the whole winter . . .

He felt a little smile twitching his mouth. "I'm sorry I can't be who you want me to be, June. Over the years, I reckon I went and sank a taproot without realizing it. I'm just a small-town sheriff. And right now I gotta run down that breed, if he's alive, and I think he is. I saw the knife that Luther One-Eye stabbed him with, and it wasn't very big. So, like it or not —"

Several sets of shod hooves thudded in the snowy street below Hagan's window. He swung around and peered out through the frosted pane. "Oh, shit."

"Who is it?"

"Him."

CHAPTER 15

The front door of the saddle shop on the street's left side opened slowly, menacingly, the hinges grumbling ever so faintly.

Yakima jerked Wolf to a halt and drew back the hammer of his Yellowboy repeater, keeping the rifle resting across his saddlebows but aiming the barrel in the direction of the opening door. When the black gap between the door and the frame was a foot wide, a weathered old face capped in shaggy gray hair peered out. Lower down was a fist belonging to the face, and it was wrapped around nothing more harmful than a yellow broom handle.

The old saddle maker scowled at the half-breed, furrowing his shaggy gray brows and working his toothless gums in disapproval of the four horses lined out behind Yakima, each with a blanket-wrapped corpse slung across its saddle. He shook his withered old head and closed the door.

Yakima looked around. It was nearly midmorning, and a fine snow was falling from a sky the color of soiled rags, keeping most people off the street. There were a few here and there — men on boardwalks and on the loading dock of the mercantile. To a man, their eyes were on Yakima. He could see dim visages of folks peering out shop windows at him, as well.

No one seemed of a mind to stop him.

He clucked Wolf on ahead, wincing as a gust pelted him with grain-sized snow and grit, and tipped his hat brim down over his forehead. The four carcass-hauling horses clomping along behind him, he pulled up at the gray frame cabin set on short stone piles across from a brothel, on the right side of the street. It was a run-down-looking place, with a snow-dusted shake-shingled roof and a front gallery that sat askew and appeared to be missing some floorboards.

Its windows were dark. No smoke curled from the tin chimney pipe.

Yakima pulled Wolf up to one of the two hitch racks fronting the gallery, looked the place over, and, deeming it vacant, hipped around in the saddle to rake his eyes along the broad, rutted street coated with fresh snow and frozen mud puddles. More townsfolk had stepped out of their shops to give him and his grisly cargo the scrutinizing eye. A couple of men in trail garb — punchers, most likely — stood on the gallery of a gun shop, staring at Yakima and moving their jaws, conversing, the ends of their scarves flapping in the breeze.

Movement out in front of the Brule Hotel caught Yakima's attention, and he hauled his gaze to the narrow, three-story brick building to see a mustached man in a wool coat and cream Stetson stride down the place's front steps and turn up the street in Yakima's direction. A tin star shone on the man's coat. As he walked, he stared ahead grimly, curling his mustached upper lip with incredulity, maybe a little fear. His eyes looked dreadful beneath the bending brim of his hat.

One of the two men out in front of the gun shop said something as the sheriff passed them — something Yakima couldn't make out above the wind and sifting snow. The lawman kept walking toward his office, ignoring them.

He angled across the street, and, shuttling his skeptical gaze between Yakima and the four dead men, Hagan stopped at the last of the four horses and jerked the blanket up over the head of the barman, Halvorssen. He jerked the blanket back down over the dead man's head, glanced at Yakima again darkly, then moved up to the next horse in the string. When he'd uncovered the heads of the farmer, Driscoll, and the other two men, Anderson and Creed, he was standing a few feet off Wolf's right hip.

He stared up at Yakima. "You keep diminishing the population of my little town by leaps and bounds." He paused. "Come for more blood?"

"I came to talk."

Hagan stared up at the half-breed for a few stretched moments, his eyes bleak, then slid his gaze along both sides of the street around him, where a few more people had gathered — mostly shop-owners and bleary-eyed saloon regulars, a few whores wrapped in blankets — talking amongst themselves, their expressions similar to that of the sheriff. Grim.

Yakima read the man's thoughts: how was Hagan going to handle this?

"Come on inside." The sheriff threw an arm halfway up, beckoning, and started up the steps of the gallery, digging a key out of a coat pocket.

Yakima stepped down from his saddle, looped his reins and the lead rope over the hitch rack. Hagan grunted and cursed under his breath as he twisted the key in the rusty lock, then pushed the door open and went inside. Yakima mounted the gallery and stopped in the building's doorway, instinctively cautious, looking around the cold, dark room before him.

Hagan turned between the doorway and the large, cluttered desk, poking his hat back off his forehead and narrowing an eye. "We really oughta be havin' this conversation with bars between us — you know that, don't you, breed?"

Yakima held his rifle down low in his right hand, aimed at the floor. "I reckon. But that's not how it's gonna be."

Hagan's eyes flicked to the Yellowboy. "Come on in and close the door. Christ, it's cold in here." Shivering, he walked over to the potbelly stove that sat in the middle of the room. He opened the stove door, then rummaged through a wooden box beside the stove for tinder and kindling.

"Another long damn winter on the way," he muttered, as Yakima pulled a ladder-back chair against the wall and sank into it, fronting the sheriff's desk.

As the sheriff dropped to a knee with a grunt, shoving wads of paper and feather sticks into the potbelly's maw, Yakima looked around. Yellowed and curled wanted dodgers were tacked to a bulletin board on the wall to his right. Four empty cells at the back of the room. One was being used for storage, it appeared. A wooden crate marked U.S. ARMY sat on its cot, and the door was closed. The place smelled like gun oil and tobacco. It was dark, gloomy, and cold. A dead mouse lay in a trap near the front door, slumped forward, spidery back legs spread wide, adding the sweet musk of death to the fetor.

"Coffee?" Hagan was standing before the stove, holding a black pot up. A fledgling fire knocked and fluttered behind the stove's closed door.

"I won't be here that long."

Hagan looked into the wooden bucket on the crude plank table right of the stove, rattled the tin dipper around inside. He sighed. "Water's froze up, anyways."

He set the pot down, then, giving another shiver, moved around behind the desk and sagged into a swivel chair, reclining deeply as he hunched his shoulders and crossed his gloved hands on his belly. He was in roughly the same position as Yakima, his back to the wall, his head turned to peer across the desk at his visitor.

"Talk."

"For starters, I killed your deputy in self-defense."

Hagan stared at him, unblinking.

"Those men who followed me into Cottonwood Canyon had me run to ground on a ridge wall. Like with your deputy, it was either me or them."

"Well, you cleaned up right well." Hagan canted his head toward the closed front door. "What about them?"

Yakima stared back at the man, unsure how to proceed. Since the snow made it possible for him to be backtracked to the Coffin farm, it was best to keep his lying to a minimum.

"Mrs. Coffin found me passed out in the snow during that storm last week. I'd been stabbed. She didn't know what I'd been involved in, and she saved my life. Gave me food and shelter, nursed me back to health. Would have done it for a dog."

Hagan was frowning now. "Aubrey Coffin? Hell, I was out there the day after that storm."

"I told her what I'd been involved in, but she lied to protect me. Believed my story. A good woman. It seems she's had encounters with your deputy, Mr. Lassiter, before."

"Go on, go on."

"Yesterday, Driscoll stopped by. Must have seen me. Came to town, found out a half-breed was running off his leash, and talked a few buddies into riding out to the Coffin farm to make me a good Injun." Yakima stared at Hagan, caressing the hammer of his Winchester with his right thumb. "They didn't succeed."

Hagan turned his head forward to stare out across the dingy jailhouse office. "What a goddamn mess."

Yakima glanced at the cell with the closed door. "That the Gatling in there?"

Hagan glanced at the cell. "Yep."

"Keep it there, will you, Sheriff? I'd hate to have to use it on your townsmen again."

"Damn few left to use it on," Hagan grunted.

Yakima started to rise. Hagan turned to him. "Will you sign an affidavit attesting to all this? I'll write it out for you, read it to you before you make your mark."

Yakima snorted and rose from his chair. His tone was mocking, sarcastic. "White man speak with forked tongue. This Injun no sign anything. You sign it, then shove it up your ass."

He swung around and headed for the door.

"Breed?"

Yakima stopped with his hand on the door, turned to look over his shoulder. Hagan stared at him hard, cheeks gaunt behind brown beard stubble, eyes rheumy and tired. "Don't hurry back to my humble little town, now, y'hear?"

Yakima went out and closed the door. He stopped on the dilapidated gallery, bringing his Winchester up slightly and frowning warily at the man standing near the bottom of the porch steps. A tall, bandy-legged man with ruby cheeks and a walrus mustache, round spectacles perched on his nose. He wore a heavy coat and mittens. He lifted his mittened hands to his shoulders, palms out.

"I ain't armed."

Yakima moved down the steps and, leaving the packhorses tied at the rack, grabbed Wolf's reins. Taking a cautious look around the street, noting a few men staring curiously toward him but no one drawing a bead on him, he returned his gaze to the tall man by the porch steps, who just stood looking glumly up at him.

Yakima swung into the saddle, reined Wolf away from the sheriff's office, and put the black into a fast trot westward out of town.

The mercantiler, Aaron Latham, stared after him for a time, then mounted the gallery, knocked once on the sheriff's door, and went in. Hagan sat as before, leaning back low behind his desk, hunkered down in his coat, the collars of which were pulled up to his jaw. He looked moody, pensive.

"You let him go," Latham said. It was not an accusation, just an observation.

"You got good eyes, Aaron."

"How do you suppose that song's gonna set with the townfolk who lost friends and loved ones in Cottonwood Canyon?" Latham jerked his head toward the door, indicating the pack string. "And a saloon owner, Stamp Halvorssen?"

"I don't reckon there's much they can do about it." Hagan stared across the room. "All the men good with guns have done expired. The rest can grunt and fume . . . maybe vote me out of office in the next election." He turned to Latham. "That's just fine with me. Think I'll head for Denver or San Francisco."

Latham grinned. "June would like that."

Hagan flushed a little. No one had ever mentioned June's name around him before. Of course, the entire county knew about Hagan and the Wild Rose schoolmistress, but unions like theirs weren't mentioned much except in private.

Hagan sniffed, swallowed. "Yes, she would."

"There ain't much the town can do," Latham said, his tone dark now. He'd picked up the dead mouse and the trap behind the door, and rose from his creaky knees with a grunt. "But what about Ma Lassiter?"

Hagan looked at Latham, who carried the mouse and the trap over to the tin trash bin beside the desk. The old cowboy turned mercantiler had removed his mittens, and he was prying the trap up over the mouse's crushed head with a thick, brown index finger with a dead, black nail.

"Hell, that Injun'll be long out of the county by nightfall. There ain't much she can do but snarl like the old she-cat she is."

"Yeah," Latham said, watching the frozen, twisted mouse tumble out of the trap and hit the bin with a soft thud and a rustle of wastepaper. "You're likely right." He set the empty trap on the edge of Hagan's desk. "Got any coffee?"

"Water's froze."

"Ah, shit, Rance," Latham said, sagging into the chair the breed had vacated. "It's gonna be another long, cold one — ain't it?"

Hagan leaned forward, opened a desk drawer, and pulled out a bottle and two grimy shot glasses. "Sure as hell looks that way."

Chapter 16

Aubrey Coffin, on her hands and knees and working with a brush and soapy water at one of the several bloodstains on the wood floor in her cabin's sitting area, loosed a shrill sob and felt the wetness of tears fill her eyes and dribble down her cheeks. She sat back on her heels and looked around, blinking, surprised by her own sudden outburst.

She brushed at the tears with the back of her wrist.

Where had that come from?

She felt her shoulders jerk as another sob rolled up from deep in her chest. Angrily, she wiped her face on her shoulder and sniffed, looking around the cabin that, she realized, seemed so much emptier than it had only a few days ago. For a few days, she'd had company. Male company. And while most of that time she'd spent wondering who the man under her roof actually was, he had filled the cabin for her. Given her work to do, someone else to think about beyond herself. He'd kept her company even while he'd slept.

And their brief time together on this very floor was something neither Aubrey's mind nor body would likely soon forget. Above the smell of the blood, she could still smell the horses and leather smell of him, and the wild smell of sage and wind and rock it was touched with.

She drew away from the bloody, soapy water bucket. She turned toward the bedroom in which he'd lain and took a deep breath, savoring his aroma and clinging to her memory of his darkly rugged countenance, the warm fire in his jade eyes, his coarse black hair, the rough caress of his thick hands on the insides of her thighs.

She sat back on her rump, feeling her blood rush warmly. Sliding a lock of hair away from her eye, she looked around the room.

Her blood slowed. She'd built up the fire after finishing her barn chores, but the cold seemed to penetrate the cabin's stout log walls. She looked at the window on the right side of the timber door. It was gray as parchment. Snow spat against the sashed panes lumped with frost.

The wind chuffed and groaned against the faintly creaking walls.

Those were the only sounds. She didn't remember it ever being that silent out here. Maybe after Joe had died. She hated to admit it, but she'd welcomed the silence that fell around her in the wake of his passing.

It bit at her now. Frightened her, as though ghosts were watching. Ghosts of loneliness and despair, smiling at her, blinking their wretched eyes.

She sat there for a time, mesmerized by the quiet until the skin above the bridge of her nose wrinkled slightly and she became aware of another sound rising slowly above the creaking timbers and the mewling wind. Turning to the west window, she felt her sudden dread of the coming winter lightening, her heart lifting.

Could the sounds be Yakima?

It made no sense that he'd return, but she didn't dwell on the practicality of her hope. Instead, she tossed the brush into the water bucket, climbed to her feet, and hurried over to the west-facing window that looked out over a low woodpile. She couldn't see much for the frost, so she drew her sleeve down over the palm of her hand and used it to clear a spot and pressed her face close to the glass.

A cold stone dropped in her belly. More than one rider was approaching the farm. A dozen or so riders were spilling down the flat-topped hill in that direction and fanning out in a ragged line as they came. They were all bundled against the cold. The galloping hooves of their horses kicked up doggets of fresh snow and tossed it out behind them.

There was a lead rider — a bulky figure in a long buffalo coat, a buffalo hat that came down over the man's ears, and a long black muffler.

Only two spreads in the area held that many riders over for the winter: Ma Lassiter's and the Furys'.

As the riders reached the bottom of the hill and started across the narrow, brushy cut of the unnamed creek that ran along the edge of the yard, recognition dawned on Aubrey, loosening her jaw hinges as she stared out. Her eyes grew wide, and her heart thudded.

Ma Lassiter was the bulky lead rider wearing a feather-trimmed opera hat. The men behind her were Coyote Ridge cutthroats. Most of the county feared the rough-hewn bunch of alleged killers, and Aubrey was no exception. Her farm lay just close enough to the edge of what Ma Lassiter considered her own rightful graze that Aubrey knew there was always a chance that Ma might try to push her out.

And of course there was the fact of Aubrey's having given sanctuary to the man who'd killed Ma's only son. . . .

As the riders thudded on into the yard, Aubrey pulled away from the window. Her heart was beating faster. Her shotgun was leaning against the wall by the door. Grabbing her coat off a hook, she shrugged into it, picked up the shotgun, and breached it to make sure both barrels were loaded.

"Hello the house!" came the land baroness's mannish baritone. "You in there, Mrs. Coffin? Ma Lassiter here, an' I wanna talk to you. Can you spare a minute, please?" She added that last in a sarcastic tone that made Aubrey's thudding heart skip a beat.

Aubrey turned to the door. She took a moment to steal herself. *Breathe,* she told herself. *Just keep breathing. Remain calm.* Ma Lassiter had no right here, even less right to cause trouble here.

Taking the shotgun in one hand, Aubrey slowly opened the door, stepped out. She moved out onto the shallow porch, her eyes shuttling from Ma Lassiter to the men on each side of her — all looking cold and grim, including Ma herself, who resembled some round, hairy critter, all tooth and claw, as she sat her stout-barreled bay. With the ratty opera hat on her head, ears covered by a brown scarf, the woman leaned forward in her saddle. She wore a sneering, arrogant look on a face broad as a man's, with a short, wide nose. Moles jutted around her thin-lipped mouth and forehead like the heads of worms clamoring to get out from the skeleton beneath.

Her eyes were small and mean, and their color seemed to hover between dull brown and duller gray.

"Good day to you, Mrs. Coffin," she said with phony affability. Her eyes flicked to the shotgun that Aubrey held straight across her thighs. "Goin' out bird huntin', are you?"

Aubrey ignored that, kept her voice low and even, letting the woman know without having to say it that Ma was trespassing and that Aubrey was ready to protect her place with buckshot if she needed to. "What can I help you with, Mrs. Lassiter?"

"I hear tell there's been a man through here. Could be he still is here. Maybe even found him a home here. With you." The old woman's thin lips spread a vague, self-satisfied grin.

"That'd be my business, wouldn't it, Mrs.

Lassiter?"

"Under most circumstances, it would be. But this is somethin' different. You see, the man you've been harboring is not only a lowly half-breed Indian, but he's the lowly half-breed Indian who killed my boy Wesley in town last week."

Aubrey's brain convulsed, though she tried not to show it. How had the woman learned . . . ? Then she remembered the fifth set of horse tracks that Yakima had mentioned, indicating that there had been five riders here the previous night. Not four.

"He's not here." The fury welling within Aubrey shoved aside the fear — imagine the woman coming here hunting a man who'd only been defending himself from her firebrand of a low-heeled son! — and she couldn't help adding, "And you're right lucky he's not." She stretched a thin though slightly brittle smile. "You heard what happened in Cottonwood Canyon, I take it?"

Ma glanced at the man sitting a claybank to her left. "Check inside, Jack-Henry." She turned her glance to a couple of men flanking her. "Blaze, Boone — the barn."

"No!" Aubrey raised the double-barreled barn blaster high across her heaving bosom. "You have no right here. No right to go poking around!"

As Blaze and Boone booted their horses off toward the barn, Ma called to their backs, "If you find him, don't kill him less'n you have to." She turned her shrewd, mocking smile on Aubrey. "I'll reserve that pleasure for myself."

As Jack-Henry swung down from his saddle, holding a Winchester carbine in one hand, Aubrey thumbed back both of the shotgun's broad hammers and began raising the heavy gun to her shoulder. She'd gotten it only halfway there before she saw a long black whip swing out over Ma Lassiter's right shoulder. There was a crack like a pistol shot. The blacksnake unfurled as it careened toward Aubrey before the forked tip bit into her right shoulder with the sudden, sharp pain of a diamondback's penetrating bite.

Aubrey screamed, shocked by the sudden blow, as the impact of the whip twisted her around and slammed her backward. Inadvertently, she tripped one of the shotgun's triggers.

Boom!

The buckshot punched into the underside of the gallery's roof. Bits of wood, dust, and frozen sod rained down as Aubrey fell back against the cabin's front wall, knees buckling, her shoulder aching as though with the impact of an axe handle.

Jack-Henry chuckled as he picked up the shotgun. Holding the barn blaster against his left hip, the Winchester against his right hip, he turned to the cabin's closed door. With the rifle's barrel he tripped the latch, then gave the door a savage kick.

"Breed?" he shouted as the door slammed back against the front wall.

Jack-Henry stood in the open doorway, nearly filling it, aiming both the shotgun and the rifle out in front of him and pivoting slightly on his hips, waving the guns around as he inspected the cabin's interior. Out the corner of her eye, Aubrey saw the man move on inside the cabin. She climbed to her hands and knees, rage pounding inside her head like a heavy hammer on an anvil. Hardening her jaw, she turned to Ma Lassiter, but before she could scream her defiance, something else flew out from around the woman's bulky form.

The fluttering hondo at the end of a lariat.

Aubrey ducked too late. The loop dropped over her head. Just as she tried to raise her arms, Ma Lassiter gave a grunt and drew the rope back taut against her chest, expertly dallying the rope around her saddle horn and pressing her boot heels to her buckskin's flanks. The horse snorted, dropped its head slightly, and backed straight up quickly as if it had been bred for just such maneuvers and loved doing nothing more.

Aubrey groaned and gritted her teeth as the rope drew so tight around her that she thought it would cut her in two.

She was pulled straight forward onto her belly. As she fought to rise to her knees, Ma jerked her down the porch steps and out into the yard, plowing through the fresh tracks that Ma's buckskin made in the snow. Aubrey tried to keep her head up as she struggled against the creaking rope, but it was nearly impossible in such a position. A good bit of snow washed icily across her face and down the front of her coat and shirtwaist.

Terror racked her as the cold snow engulfed her. She felt a thread of relief when the rope slackened just enough that she came to a stop in the middle of the yard.

Looking up, she saw Ma swinging down from the buckskin's back with surprising agility for a woman of her age and girth. The woman had another rope in her hand. Immobilized by the lariat still holding her arms down fast to her sides, Aubrey watched helplessly as the big woman stomped toward her, kicking snow up around her high-topped fur boots and long buffalo coat.

"Please!" Aubrey cried. "Don't — !"

Ma Lassiter dropped to a knee and went to work with the second rope, and before Aubrey could wrap her mind around what was happening, she lay with her wrists tied behind her back, feet in the air, wrists tied to her ankles.

Like a calf trussed for branding.

"You can't . . . you can't do this . . . !" she screamed at the tops of her lungs. "You have no right here!"

Ma whistled softly, and the buckskin took a couple of steps toward her, causing the first rope to sag into the snow, releasing its painful grip on Aubrey's arms and torso. Ma whipped the loop up and over Aubrey's head. Though there was less pressure on her arms, she found herself even more immobilized than before.

"You're just gonna stay right there," Ma bellowed, red-faced and sharp-eyed.

She climbed up off each knee in turn with a mannish grunt as she turned her attention to the cabin. "Any sign of him, Jack-Henry?"

Aubrey was facing away from the cabin as she sobbed and groaned and struggled futilely against the rope binding her wrists to her ankles, so she couldn't see Jack-Henry. She heard the man yell, his voice muffled and echoing inside the cabin,

"Nothin' here, Mrs. Lassiter. Plenty of blood on the floor."

There were the thuds of boots on floor puncheons, and then Jack-Henry must have been standing in the open doorway because his voice was louder as he said, "No gear, either. Looks like the breed pulled foot."

Ma turned toward the barn. "Blaze, anything over there?"

Nothing but silence and the clomping and crunching of the other men circling the cabin and the outbuildings as they searched for Yakima. The small barn door opened with a wooden scrape and a high whine of hinges, and one of the two men came out, an impossibly tall, long-haired man shaking his hatted head and resting his carbine on his shoulder. The other man followed close behind him, and they were both kicking through the snow toward Aubrey.

Ma Lassiter gave Aubrey a fierce look, gloved hands on her hips. "Where'd he go?" Breath jetted from her mouth and broad nostrils. The tops of her cheeks were apple red.

Aubrey stretched her lips back from her teeth as she fought the ropes and gave a frustrated wail. "Even if I knew I wouldn't tell you, you old *whore!*"

Ma buried one of her boots in Aubrey's

side. "Whore, is it?" She kicked her again, and Aubrey yelped at the stabbing pain in her ribs. "How dare you call *me* a whore! *You* were the one coupling on the *floor* with that *savage* who murdered my *boy!*"

She hauled her boot back again and buried it in Aubrey's hip socket.

Aubrey tried to twist away from the woman. Her shoulders felt as though they would pop from their sockets. She howled and sobbed.

"I'm gonna ask you one more time!" Ma shouted so shrilly that her voice cracked on the high notes. "And you remember — I treat women who double-cross me same as men!" Ma leaned forward, hands on her broad thighs. "Where's the breed that killed my Wesley?"

Aubrey steeled herself enough to lift her chin in desperate defiance, and shriek, "Go *fuck* yourself, you old *whore!*" Giddy with her own misery and rage, Aubrey found herself laughing, tears streaming down her snow-flecked cheeks. "Yakima killed your son because he *needed* killin'! He shoulda been killed *a long time ago!*"

Ma scowled down at Aubrey, who now sobbed uncontrollably.

"Oh, boy," Ma said. "Oh, boy."

She reached into a pocket of her buffalo

robe and pulled out a blacksnake coiled around a hide-wrapped wooden handle. She turned to the two men who'd searched the barn and were now standing around her and Aubrey looking grim and mean. "Boys, drag her to the corral over there. Take her coat off, and tie her wrists to the top pole."

"No!" Aubrey wailed.

As the two men picked up Aubrey and carried her, howling, over to the corral angling off the barn's north wall, Ma followed, kicking up snow, gritting her teeth, and shaking her head. "Oh, boy."

She whipped the snake out in front of her.

It cracked like a rifle shot, scaring up several crows from the barn roof.

CHAPTER 17

Sheriff Hagan reached back into his saddlebags for a fresh bottle. He popped the cork and took a pull.

He hadn't had a drink since the two he'd limited himself to early that morning with Aaron Latham, and this one, after the hour-long ride out to the Coffin farm in a chill wind spitting snow and sleet, blossomed in his belly like a beautiful spring flower. It spread behind his heart so that he didn't care so much about how wretched he'd become, and what a disappointment he was to the only woman who'd ever loved him besides his mother.

The sky pilots' and women's civic abstinence committees could take a running leap. Whiskey was a wonderful thing.

He hammered the cork back into the bottle, returned the bottle to his saddlebags, and looked down the hill he'd just crested at the Coffin farm. He blinked. His heart surged, thudded in his ears.

"H-yahh, boy!" he yelled against the sharp wind, driving his spurred heels into the copper's flanks and dropping at a racing gallop down the hill.

He rode past the burned-out barn laced with orange flames flickering against the cold wind and sleet-laced snow. He merely glanced at the cabin — it, too, was a burned-out hulk a couple of hundred feet away, the fire having consumed most of it before the sod roof dropped in on it, likely smothering it and being helped by the weather. The wind was quartering from the northwest, over Hagan's shoulder, and that's likely why he hadn't smelled the smoke.

He could smell it now, as well as the fetor of charred wood and burned animal flesh that was a sickly presence around the barn. Part of the corral had caught fire, but it hadn't burned long. And it hadn't reached the woman who'd been tied to the top pole, about halfway between the barn and the end of the corral and near a wooden hay crib. She hung flat against the corral, on her knees, her head up, brown hair hanging down and mingling with the open wounds that resembled red snakes crisscrossing her back.

Hagan leaped out of the saddle too quickly

for the whiskey he'd just consumed. His left boot came down on an icy patch, slipped out from under him. He fell hard on his right shoulder, breath punched from his lungs in a loud grunt. It dazed him. Slowly, clumsily, he regained his feet and stumbled over to the woman, dropped to a knee beside her, his face etched with revulsion at what had been done to her back and shoulders.

"Mrs. . . . Mrs. Coffin?" He wasn't sure if he should put a hand on her.

He slid her hair back away from the side of her face. Her eyes were closed, but her lips were stretched back from her lips in a pained grimace. Her chin rested lightly on an unpeeled pole. A muscle in her cheek twitched, and her left eyelid fluttered.

She was alive.

Hagan dug into his front pants pocket for his Barlow knife. Standing, he opened the knife and sawed through the rope tying her left wrist to the top corral pole. That hand flopped down to her side. He cut the other wrist free, and she fell to the ground with a sudden, agonized cry before he could catch her. She slumped forward, groaning, but he caught her before she could fall forward against the second corral pole from the bottom.

Her blouse had been almost entirely shredded from her back, both it and the camisole hanging free from her chest, as well. Looking around, he saw a quilted leather coat lying nearby — damp, snow-dusted, and cold. Too cold.

He glanced at his horse standing ground-tied behind him. Though Hagan hadn't expected to be out here long, he'd attached his soogan to the saddle, behind the cantle. After propping Mrs. Coffin against the hay crib, he ran over to his horse, avoiding the icy patch he'd slipped on before, and untied the hot roll. Returning to the woman, he draped the two sewn-together wool army blankets over the woman's shoulders.

Only half-conscious but obviously miserable, she shivered and drew the sides of the blanket closed over her breasts.

"Best get you to town," Hagan said. "You think you can ride?"

The woman didn't answer. In shock, Hagan suspected. It had been a rhetorical question, anyway. He had to get her to town, and all he had with which to get her there was his horse.

As he began to pull her to her feet, she gave another groan and dropped her head. Out. Hagan snaked one arm behind her back, the other beneath her legs. After some delicate back-and-bellying, he had her on his saddle and, holding her there with his outstretched arms, swung up behind her, sliding her forward so they could share as much of the saddle as possible.

He swung the horse around and, pulling the unconscious woman back against him, booted it back in the direction of Wild Rose, leaving the barn and cabin to smoke and sputter amidst licking flames behind him.

Yakima hunkered low against the driving snow and sleet, hearing it tick off his hat brim, as he put Wolf up and over another in a long series of hogbacks he'd traversed since leaving town.

At the bottom of the hogback and in the crease between it and the next one, Yakima drew the black to a halt and swung quickly down from his saddle. He shucked the Yellowboy from its boot, racked a shell into the chamber — a raspy grating sound that was nearly obliterated by the wind and snow — and jogged back up the hill he'd just descended. He ran at an angle, slipping and sliding in his high-topped fur moccasins, switchbacking until he was about five yards from the top.

In the tracks Wolf had made a minute ago, he dropped to his hands and knees, doffed his hat, and crabbed to the crest, keeping his head down, then lifting it slowly to edge a look over the top, back in the direction from which he'd come. The riders he'd spied angling toward him from the northeast were again on his back trail — two men obviously following his own recent tracks in the fresh snow.

Yakima lowered his head, staring at the oncoming riders through the tops of tough brown weeds poking up through the crusty gray snow cover.

Men from town? Possibly. But he'd swung directly south of Wild Rose soon after leaving it. These men had come from the northeast — the direction in which the Coffin farm lay.

Yakima didn't like the tight, hot feeling in the pit of his gut.

He stared at the riders. Slowly, they began dropping below his field of vision as they headed into a trough in the rolling hills. Lower and lower they went, horses' legs disappearing, then their heads, and then the hatted heads of their riders. Yakima stared out through the falling snow, across the tops of three or four more hills jutting between him and the men on his trail.

He watched the men rise to the top of another hill and continue to trot their horses toward him — gray-brown visages whom it was hard from this distance to separate from their horses. He could make out no distinguishing features of either the horses or their riders. He only knew they were men riding toward him.

Yakima watched intently as they dropped down into another valley, gone.

He waited, staring, caressing the trigger of his Yellowboy and occasionally blinking snow from his eyelashes, now and then brushing the moisture from his brows with a gloved hand. He waited a minute, and then he began scowling. The riders should have crested the next closest hill by now.

There was only the snow and the yellow-brown weed tops under a sky the color of cold iron.

Finally, his pulse quickening, wondering if the riders had left his trail only to ride up and around him, and knowing that most men out here knew this country much better than he did — every coulee and hillock, most likely — he stumbled back down the hill to his horse. He shoved his rifle down into its boot, swung up into the saddle, and booted Wolf up and over the crest of the next hill.

As he continued pushing south, he cast another glance behind him and felt the skin under his shirt collar bristle. Nothing back there but the white and gray hues of a fast-approaching high-plains winter.

He rode along a broad bench for a good fifteen minutes, looking cautiously around him in all directions, wary of an ambush, then dropped down into a broad canyon pocked with clumps of burr oak, sumac, hawthorn, chokecherry, and cottonwood. A game trail twisted through the brush at the bottom of the crease. The bloody scarlet remains of a wolf-killed white-tail buck lay in the brush amidst the myriad scuff marks that indicated the buck's fierce but futile battle.

Yakima followed the trail eastward along the gradually descending canyon floor.

He rode for ten minutes, hearing the whisper of the snow and the wind rustling the brush and making the brittle trunks of the burr oaks and willows creak. Occasionally, the muffled caw of an indignant crow lifted, drawing Yakima's cautious gaze.

The canyon opened like the broad end of a funnel. Beyond the funnel was the broad Missouri sliding like liquid iron between its broad, low banks. Its cold-looking currents were speckled with rock-sized ice chunks. Between Yakima and the river, in a clearing stippled with many stumps and clumps of piled tree limbs, lay a small gray cabin flanked by a privy.

Across from the cabin, to its left, were several sheds including what appeared to be a barn. On Yakima's side of the barn lay an unpeeled pole corral with no stock in it, and there didn't appear to have been any stock in it for a while, as there were no tracks in the snow and the grass had grown up around the cottonwood poles. The stumps and several piles of stacked logs along with a lumber dray parked in front of the barn bespoke a woodcutters' camp. Likely abandoned for the winter. The woodcutters would return when their customers, the boats plying the fickle waters of the Big Muddy, returned in the spring.

Yakima stopped Wolf a hundred yards from the cabin, swinging his gaze from right to left. No recent tracks in the snow. No movement around him. The horse did not look skittish or seem to be sensing anything unnatural about the environs.

Yakima looked behind him. Nothing.

He slipped out of the saddle and, holding the reins in one hand, his rifle in the other, led the horse on into the camp.

A half hour later, J. T. Fetterman walked up to a tree flanking the cabin that sat nestled in the woodcutters' camp. He gave the hovel a good looking-over, noting the smoke rising from the rusty tin chimney pipe poking out of the shack's snow-dusted sod roof. The smoke smelled like pine and fresh coffee.

Fetterman, a big, shaggy-headed outlaw from Missouri and a veteran of the War of Northern Aggression on the side of the South, tugged on his thick ginger beard and felt a smile lift his stinging, cold-rosy cheeks. That coffee was gonna taste good. He'd have a cup in his hand in just a minute or two.

He turned to where his partner, Louis Beaumont, known as "Pandhandle Louis," stood just inside a stony notch that a now-defunct spring had cut into the side of the steep hill behind the cabin. Beaumont showed only one eye, his long hooked nose in profile, and the Henry repeater he was holding cocked in his gloved right hand, barrel aimed skyward. The Texas gunslinger's cold gray eye stared unblinking, shrewd lines spoking from its corner. The spokes deepened and lengthened as Panhandle Louis frowned, incredulous at the grin on his partner's face.

Fetterman jerked his head up, beckoning. He'd realized as soon as he'd smelled the smoke what the grin on Fetterman's face was about.

Beaumont glanced at the cabin's rear, where only one frosty window shone, a flour sack curtain drawn across it. The Texas gunman stepped out of the notch and broke into a jog, holding the Henry barrel up in his right hand. When he reached the tree, sidling up to Fetterman, who stared around the tree's opposite side, Fetterman said softly, "You ready for a cup o' mud, Louis?"

Beaumont sniffed. Then he growled, "Yeah. I'd take a cup. Hot an' black."

"All right, then. You go around that side of the cabin. I'll go around this side. Meet you *in*-side for a cup o' mud!"

Beaumont sniffed again, then moved out from behind the tree and jogged up the cabin's left rear corner. At the same time, Fetterman jogged to the opposite corner and then along the cabin's west side.

At the front corner, he stopped, edged a look around to the front. Spying nothing in front of the place but the snow slanting against the weather-silvered logs, and tracks etching the snow around the firewood stacked against the front wall, he stepped around the corner and met Beaumont at the heavy, timbered door.

Fetterman looked down. Large moccasin

prints led from the woodpile to the front door. The Indian had obviously made a couple of trips for wood, was likely warming himself inside by a nice big fire.

Fetterman shared a shrewd glance with Beaumont, then stepped back, lunged forward, leading with his right foot, and kicked the door inward with a loud thudding, crunching sound. As the door slammed against the front wall, the metal latch clinked to the hard-packed earthen floor. Chips from the doorframe sprayed.

Fetterman bolted inside and stepped to one side, making room for Beaumont, who followed him in and stepped to the other side, both men careful not to let themselves be outlined by the gaping front doorway. The cabin's interior was dark and smoky and filled with the scorched fetor and hiss of boiling-over coffee. Neither man could see much but a few sticks of rough-hewn furniture, so they began triggering their rifles, kicking up a tooth-gnashing cacophony, causing furniture to shatter and dust to sift down from the rafters.

The shooters' shell casings bounced off the wall behind them and rolled around their boots.

Fetterman emptied his rifle a few seconds before Panhandle Louis did.

Silence then, except for the pop and spatter of burning coffee on a glowing stove lid.

The men stared, squinting against the eye-watering powder smoke, now able to see even less than they'd been able to see before.

The shooters moved around, coughing against the smoke. Finally, having found nothing inside the cabin except for bullet-torn furniture and airtight tins, they filed back out into the yard, looking skeptical, vaguely chagrined, worried.

Ten feet in front of the cabin, both men stopped and glanced at each other. "Where in the hell . . . ?" Texas Louis said.

"Right here," said a low voice behind and above them, barely audible above the snow and the steadily chuffing wind.

They wheeled, throwing aside their empty rifles and reaching for the handles of their six-shooters jutting above tucked-back coat flaps. From his perch atop the sod roof, Yakima bore down on both men, squinting down the barrel of his cocked Yellowboy repeater. He planted a bead on Fetterman's broad chest and squeezed the trigger.

The Winchester leaped and roared.

Yakima ejected the spent brass, seated a fresh round. He drew a bead on Texas Louis's chest as the man, knowing he'd never get his Schofield raised in time, screamed wildly. Yakima cut off the scream by punching a neat round hole through the center of the gunman's red-and-green-striped blanket coat.

The man stumbled backward, twisted around, tripped over his partner's quivering supine form, and fell forward in the freshly fallen snow. He lifted his head, grunting and groaning. Yakima drilled another round through the back of it, punching the man's face down hard in the snow.

Yakima crawled to the edge of the roof over the woodpile. He dropped the Yellowboy onto the pile below the overhanging eave. Grabbing the edge of the roof with his gloved hands, he dropped his legs over the side, then dropped easy as a bobcat down to the pile. From there, Yellowboy in hand, he leaped to the ground, wincing only slightly at the hitch in his lower right back.

Glancing at the two dead gunmen turning the snow around them red, he whistled. Hooves thudded as Wolf came running from behind the barn, his reins wrapped around his saddle horn. Yakima jogged over to the horse, swung up into the saddle, grabbed his reins from around the horn, and booted Wolf around the cabin, following the tracks of his two deceased shadowers.

He found the men's horses a minute later,

tied to the same cottonwood in a coulee running into the canyon in which the woodcutters' camp lay. Quickly, he checked the brands on the horses' withers — the letters *C* and *R* for "Coyote Ridge" separated by a squiggly line indicating a ridge.

Jaw set hard, Yakima turned the two horses loose and rode hell-for-leather back in the direction of the Coffin farm.

Chapter 18

Sheriff Hagan wasn't sure Mrs. Coffin was still alive as, his head down and wincing against the weather, he rode into Wild Rose set behind a gauze curtain of snow now falling faster and heavier than before. Only a few people were out, men in fur coats hustling here and there. As Hagan rode past the mercantile, Aaron Latham came out in shirtsleeves and walked out to the edge of his loading dock.

"Good Lord, Rance," the mercantiler intoned. "Who you got there?"

"Mrs. Coffin."

"Where you takin' her?"

"Over to the school," Hagan said as he passed, not sure if he was hauling a corpse over to June's quarters at the schoolhouse.

The town had lost its doctor in a buggy accident that summer and hadn't found a replacement yet. The barber, Terrence Dawson, had been a medico in the army, but he was so arthritic and forgetful that most folks made do however they could. June was Hagan's way of making do, as the teacher had had to serve as doctor to her students injured on the playground or occasionally kicked or thrown by their horses. She'd probably done as much doctoring as Dawson or anyone else in town. And she was a woman — so the school was where Hagan was headed.

"Hang on, Rance!" Latham called.

Hagan pulled back on his bay's reins and scowled impatiently over his right shoulder at the bandy-legged mercantiler.

"Ma Lassiter was here lookin' for the breed. She tracked him to the jailhouse. Then tracked him on out of town."

Latham dropped his gaze to the woman slumped against Hagan's chest. Hagan felt his brows form a straight, firm line over his eyes. Ma. That she'd been the one responsible for Aubrey Coffin's condition, there was no doubt. The tracks at the Coffin farm had told him it had been a large group that had pillaged the place, and he'd followed the tracks right into Wild Rose.

Hagan did doubt, however, that there would be anything he could do about it. Frustration and rage burned like a bullet graze at the base of his spine. "If she comes back, you let me know."

"Got me a feelin' you'll know before I do, Rance."

Hagan turned his head forward and clucked the tired bay on down the street and then down a side street and through a snowy alley, taking the shortest route to the school that sat on the town's southwest edge. It was flanked by Indian Wash in which June's students played during recess and before and after school. Buttes rose on the wash's far side. The school itself sat on a low hill, on a yard that was now covered in snow but that had long ago been hard-packed and scoured of grass and brush by the busy feet of frolicking children.

One lone swing creaked on a chain in the wind, about fifty feet from the front door. The bell in the bell tower over the door clanked faintly in the wind. Hagan put the bay up the hill, reined to a halt in front of the high wooden steps, and, holding the woman with one hand, swung down from the saddle. He eased her down into his arms, holding the blankets tight against her nearly naked torso, and headed up the steps to the front door.

He kicked the door twice, then fumbled with the knob until he heard the latch click. He stomped inside, his boot thuds and spur *chings* resounding in the cave-like room that smelled like chalk and ink and beeswax.

"Rance!" June said as she swung her head toward him from the front of the room, where she stood with an open book held against her chest. Two little boys in flannel shirts and patched coveralls were at the chalkboard, looking away from the figures they'd drawn there in large, boyish script, eyes wide in shock and fascination as the sheriff moved along the center aisle with the woman draped across his arms like a sack of potatoes.

"Snowin' outside, June," Hagan said, grunting at the stiffness in his cold limbs as well as at the weight in his arms. "You think you could let school out early?"

There were only three other students, three girls between the ages of six and ten, all standing now at their desks to get a look at what Hagan was carrying.

"Of course," June said, slamming her book closed and setting it on her desk. "You're excused, children. Bundle up well, now — you heard the sheriff. Weather's bad."

White-faced, June looked down at the even whiter face of the unconscious woman in Hagan's arms. "Mrs. . . . ?"

She looked at Hagan as though she couldn't remember the woman's name.

"Coffin. She'd had the" — Hagan paused to look around, seeing that the children were all scrambling noisily into the coatroom — "holy hell beaten out of her. *Whipped* out of her. Can you help her?"

"Hell, I don't know!"

June moved to the door flanking her desk on its foot-high dais — a wooden door with a curtained window in the upper panel. She opened the door and led Hagan into her three-room living quarters consisting of a kitchen, parlor, and bedroom. She had a fire going in the woodstove in the parlor, Hagan noticed as he carried Aubrey Coffin toward the bedroom off the parlor's left wall.

June hurried past him to slide the lace sheet curtain that hung over the doorway aside, and Hagan went on through and lay Mrs. Coffin, wrapped in his soogan, onto the bed in the cramped, drafty room.

Mrs. Coffin groaned when her back hit the bed, face crumpling. She curled her legs a little and twisted her body, trying to relieve some of the pressure on the wounds. As Hagan straightened, wincing at the kinks in his back, June hiked a leg onto the edge of the bed and gently rolled Mrs. Coffin onto her left side and peeled the blankets away from her back.

Mrs. Coffin cried out in agony.

"Oh, God," June said, looking over her shoulder at Hagan, eyes wide, lower jaw hanging. "Who did this?"

"Ma Lassiter."

"Why?"

"Long story, June. Can you help her?" Hagan pitched his voice with urgent pleading. "There's no one else."

June looked again at Mrs. Coffin's back, gently, slowly peeling the blankets away from the deep, snake-shaped abrasions. "I'll try." She whipped her head around to Hagan, and her eyes were hard with commanding. "Fetch me a boatload of wood, Rance. I'm gonna have to thaw the poor woman out. And then I'm gonna need a lot of hot water."

Hagan nodded.

"And when you're done with that, I'm gonna need more whiskey than what I have here. A hell of a lot more!"

"You got it, June," Hagan said, wheeling from the room.

His heart was hammering with both fear and fury.

Ma Lassiter . . .

Ma Lassiter's eyes narrowed in their doughy, warty sockets as she stared straight over her horse's twitching ears at the two men standing in front of the woodcutters' cabin, in Jackson Hollow. She was flanked by Jack-Henry Vincent and Drew Beresford, who'd accompanied her when she'd split her gang up to scour the countryside for the half-breed, whose trail they had lost in a creek bed about seven miles south of Wild Rose, several hours ago.

"Ah, shit," Beresford grunted to her right, as he, too, stared at the men fronting the cabin, both of whom were standing casually, holding their rifles in one hand, holding lit quirleys despite the falling snow with the other. Their horses stood ground-reined behind them, laying their ears back as their tails blew up against their hips.

"What?" Ma said. Her eyes weren't as good as they once were. "What is it?"

"Two men down," Jack-Henry said to her left. "Our men, looks like."

"How can you tell?"

" 'Cause Bill and Tony ain't smilin'."

Only as she put her horse up to within fifteen feet of Bill Boyer and Tony Rodelo did Ma Lassiter see that there were indeed two men lying dead in the snow at their feet. Snow blew across their humped bodies, obscuring their features, but she saw now the alpaca chaps favored by J. T. Fetterman and the blanket coat with the hide-patched sleeve worn by "Pandhandle" Louis Beaumont. Ma stared down in disgust at the two men, stiff and waxy now in death, who'd let themselves get beefed by the breed.

She spat to one side, ran a buffalo hide sleeve across her runny nose, and adjusted her dentures. "Any sign of our quarry?" she asked the two men cupping quirleys in their gloved palms against the wind.

"Seen tracks in a coulee behind the cabin," replied Rodelo in his slight Spanish accent. "Most are covered, but where the wind sheltered them they look to be heading back north."

"North?"

Tony Rodelo blinked. Bill Boyer just stood stony-faced, sucking the quirley, the wind blowing his rabbit-fur hat with earflaps. He had his Sharps carbine resting atop his right shoulder.

"North, huh?" Ma said but only to herself this time as she stared at the hills rising dimly behind the snow veil on the other side of the hollow.

Why would he be heading north? Wild Rose was north. She figured he'd keep riding south to get shed of this country and those who wanted him dead in it.

North just didn't make sense.

Or did it?

"Let's head on home, boys," Ma said after a while. "Storm's settin' in to be a good one. We'll continue lookin' for that smelly savage when it lets up."

She turned her horse around and booted the tired beast into a loose-kneed trot.

"What about Panhandle and Fetterman?" one of the men called behind her, his voice barely audible beneath the near-constant wind.

"Leave 'em," Ma called, not turning her head. "Wildcats gotta eat, too!"

Yakima stood beside Wolf, staring blankly at the burned-out hulk of the Coffin cabin. His chest rose and fell heavily as he held the black's reins in one hand, his Yellowboy in the other. He'd already looked around the cabin well enough to know that Aubrey wasn't in there. It hadn't burned well enough to leave no trace of her. Besides — and this wasn't a pleasing thought but a practical one — he would have smelled her.

As he could smell the mule and the milk cow and likely the geese that had been trapped in the barn. . . .

Of course, whoever had done this could have locked her in the barn. But he could distinguish the smell of charred human flesh from that of animals. The fact that he didn't smell that here, and the tracks near the corral and leading off toward town — the faint tracks of a single rider who'd come and left a good hour or longer after the half dozen riders from Coyote Ridge had come and gone — told him there was a chance she'd survived and been taken away.

But in what condition?

Yakima swung up into the saddle. Casting another raking gaze across the ruins of the Coffin farm, he put moccasined heels to the black's flanks and followed the tracks of the single rider up through the bluffs behind the barn. On the tableland it was snowing harder, and the tracks had long since been erased by the snow. Yakima hunkered low in the saddle, turned his collar up to his jaw, and urged Wolf forward though, judging by the snorts and occasional indignant whinnies, the black obviously thought the better course of action would be to head into a wooded hollow and hole up by a hot fire.

"Keep goin', boy," Yakima growled, his voice sounding small in the tearing wind. "Get you warm . . . get us both warm . . . soon."

Across the wind- and snow-basted prairie horse and rider traveled. The wind felt like fire against Yakima's unshaven cheeks, and he found himself hunkering low and keeping his eyes closed against the pelting snow.

After an interminable time he could smell the town on the northwest wind — the mixed stench of wood smoke, privy pits, and the sundry hybrid, ammoniac fetors of stock manure. Even in the winter a man could smell a frontier town. He gave an ironic snort, welcoming the odor. Wolf must have been pleased, as well; the black whinnied. Yakima had his eyes closed as the horse climbed a steep slope, but now as the stallion stopped suddenly, Yakima slitted his lids.

Instantly, his right hand dropped to the horn grips of his .44, but the pistol was covered by the hem of his coat. Ahead, six riders sat in the trail about fifty yards in front of him. Likely more Coyote Ridge men. An instantly thawing fury blazed through him. These were part of the group that had burned Aubrey's farm, attacked her . . . One in a long buffalo robe and fur hat threw a mittened hand toward Yakima.

"That's that black I saw by the Coffin farm!"

Awkwardly, the man in the buffalo robe reached inside a pocket of his coat, hauling out a revolver. At the same time, the other men shook or bit off their right-hand gloves and shucked rifles out of their saddle boots. One was fast. Too fast. Yakima's fury blazed through him like red-hot sabers, but his muscles were still cold and sluggish for quick, efficient movement. His right hand moved toward his own repeater, but it was slow and heavy as lead. No use. Yakima threw himself out of the saddle as a man in a bobcat coat cut loose with a carbine, the shot sounding little louder than a sneeze against the wind.

Yakima hit the ground and rolled back down the ravine. He piled up against a snag of snow-mantled brush, ripped his coat up and over the handle of his .44, and shucked the gun from its holster. He bit off his right-hand glove and poked his index finger through the trigger guard. The finger was so cold that he couldn't feel the trigger.

Staring toward the lip of the ridge, he saw no riders yet. He heaved to his feet and took off high-stepping through the brush toward the ravine's bottom. When he reached the bottom he heard hoof thuds in the snow behind him.

"There!" a man shouted.

He glanced behind to see all six riders galloping down the ridge on Yakima's path. The snow was too deep for the horses, and one fell, its rider giving a startled yell as he went down hard and rolled. The other horses floundered but continued coming.

Yakima turned forward and ran down the ravine that slanted lower and lower. Pistols and rifles popped behind him, bullets thumping into the snow around him. He stopped, twisted around, and fired two quick rounds. It did not hold the riders. Even the man who'd taken the tumble was scrambling back into the saddle of his snow-dusted horse.

Yakima dropped to a knee, took careful aim, and blew one of the riders out of his saddle. The others checked their mounts down, shouting, one with a rifle continuing to lever and fire. Taking advantage of the hunters' hesitation, Yakima turned and ran down the bending ravine, soon finding himself in a broader canyon running perpendicular to the lesser cut.

Here were large cottonwoods, box elders, and cedars. Rocks and boulders lined the narrow creek that twisted between shallow banks. The water was black against the gray of the snow, its edges scalloped with the beginnings of the long freeze.

Yakima ran toward the creek, glad to see fresh tracks scuffing and scoring the new-fallen snow. Woodcutters had been here recently; he saw several felled trees sectioned off into hearth-length logs, the fresh cuts and sawdust showing yellow against the mounded white. No sign of the cutters. When the storm had settled in, they must have headed back to town, probably only a few minutes ago, judging by the freshness of the tracks.

Yakima made for one of the fallen trees around which the snow shone with many horse and man tracks as well as the deep indentations of iron-shod wheels. He leaped through a Juneberry thicket and hunkered down behind a stump that smelled verdant with the recent cutting.

Cursing himself for not grabbing his Winchester, he flicked open his Colt's loading gate. With numb, awkward fingers, he extracted the spent shell casings and replaced them with fresh. He spun the wheel, pressed his back against the rough-barked stump, and lifted his right hand to blow some warmth on it. He could just barely feel the appendage. If these six were determined to run him down, he'd have a hell of a time holding them off with a frozen gun hand.

Hearing hooves crunching snow, he hunkered lower behind the cottonwood stump. Beneath the howling wind and scratching branches around him, he heard the riders talking in raised voices, yelling above the storm. He edged a look around the stump.

The five men sat their mounts at the mouth of the ravine that Yakima had left. They were looking around, turning their heads this way and that. Finally, one gestured to his left, then his right, and the riders split up, two heading up the larger canyon, two heading down. One rode straight into the brush to Yakima's left, on an intersection course with the creek.

Yakima pulled his head back behind the stump once more. Again, he blew warm air on his gun hand, though it did little good. He'd be lucky to get off one half-assed shot with that frozen trigger finger. He could just barely feel the corrugated steel of the hammer with his thumb.

The slow thump of plodding hooves sounded on the other side of the stump, making the brush crackle.

Chapter 19

The hoof thuds stopped only a few yards from Yakima.

The man called in a mocking singsong, "Come out, come out, wherever you are, CR man. . . ."

Pressing his back against the stump, Yakima furled his snow-mantled black brows. CR man? He turned his head sideways to the stump and slid his head out just far enough to one side of it that he could get a look at the man sitting a long-legged bay about thirty yards beyond him and on the other side of a felled and sectioned box elder.

Just above the rider's right leg clad in dark brown wool, a brand shone against the horse's wither. The blaze was an F and an R separated by a slightly slanted lightning bolt. Yakima blinked, squeezing the horn grips of his .44 in his numb right hand. He pulled his head back behind the stump and ran the pistol's front sight across his frost-burned cheekbone.

Fury? He'd thought these were Coyote Ridge riders. . . .

Befuddlement wrapped him in a cold blanket of confusion. Hoof thuds rose again from both up and down the stream.

"Richard, you see anything?" a distant voice called.

The man nearest Yakima said, "Nah, I think he's hunkered down in the brush closer to the stream. We could haze him outta there, if we wanted to. . . ." He didn't sound like he wanted to.

"Come on," said the more distant voice.

Yakima heard the nearest man's horse moving back through the snow and brush. Then there was only the wind through which the more distant voice called, "Hey, CR man. Mighty cold out here. We're headin' to town, get us a *drink!* You wanna finish this, that's where you'll find us!"

Vaguely beneath the howling wood and creaking tree trunks, Yakima heard the riders shuffling back up the feeder ravine down which they'd come. After a time, Yakima looked out from behind the stump, spying nothing but the shifting veil of white. The mouth of the feeder ravine shone like gaping white jaws, the marks of the recent riders showing gray in the snow at its floor.

Yakima straightened and walked out of the brush. He looked around for a time, cautious, then slid his Colt back into its holster and put his glove on, opening and closing his hand to work some blood back into it.

Fury riders. Why the hell were they chasing him?

Only one way to find out.

He pulled his hat brim low but kept a careful eye on the terrain around him as he trudged back the way he'd come. Where the one Fury rider he'd shot out of the saddle had been, there was only a scarlet wash of blood in the snow. The man himself was gone, retrieved by the others.

At the lip of the ravine he'd mounted a moment before he'd spied the Furys, he whistled and waited for the black to gallop toward him from out of the storm. Then he hauled himself stiffly into the saddle and batted his heels against the stallion's flanks. Fortunately, it was only a short time before the town rose like separate gray ghosts before him, slowly delineating itself in the gauzy weather until Yakima could see a corral and a stable and then the leaning sign by a twisted cottonwood announcing WILD

ROSE in letters all but obliterated by the snow.

The drifts were piling up fast on boardwalks. The snow blew in windy gusts against the sides of the buildings. It howled down alleys between shops and made shingle chains squawk raucously. The middle of the street was nearly swept clear by the wind, showing the hard, frozen ruts and chuckholes.

No one was out. But he followed the six sets of recent hoofprints to the Dakota Plains Saloon sitting about halfway down the town's main street, on the north side. Six horses stood tied at the hitch rack, heads down, tails blowing out behind them. A mouse brown dun had a dead man strapped belly down across its saddle. There was no blanket to cover the man, and his woolly chaps and his hair danced in the snow-laden wind.

Yakima looked at the front of the saloon, large windows on either side of the double doors. Several sets of boot tracks shone on the steps and front porch, disappearing at the doors. Sliding his Winchester from his saddle boot, he swung down from the saddle, looked behind him and all around, paying special attention to the saloon's windows, from where he was liable to get bushwhacked. He looked at the second and third stories, then levered a shell into the Yellowboy's breech and climbed the porch steps. Slowly, he crossed the porch, turned the knob of the right-side door, and pushed the door open.

He stepped back away from the door for a moment, expecting to be met with a storm of rifle fire. When it didn't come, he bolted inside, stepped to his left so the open door wouldn't backlight him, and tensely looked around, his right index finger curled taut against the rifle's trigger.

He blinked and squinted into the shadows, trying to adjust his eyes to the cavelike darkness inside the saloon.

"You born in a barn, amigo?" said a man to his right. "Kindly shut the door — you're lettin' the heat out."

Yakima slid his eyes to the speaker, saw a man in a wolf fur coat and woolly chaps standing sideways to the polished mahogany bar. His hat was off, and short blond hair sat close against his bullet-shaped head. His nose and cheeks were red, blue eyes rheumy. He was holding the handle of a beer schooner atop the bar. A half-empty shot glass flanked the beer. He had a rifle resting on the bar, as well.

Four more men sat a table directly in front

of Yakima, under a timber cross beam trimmed with a good dozen deer antlers of all sizes. He recognized these four from the canyon outside town, as well. Two appeared to be twins — small-boned men with sweeping mustaches and dark, expressionless eyes. One wore a bobcat hide coat, the other a ratty bear coat, both unbuttoned. Their hats were on the table before them, near beer schooners and shot glasses. They sat side by side like two brothers posing there for a picture, and they were just awaiting the photographer.

The other two sat at each end of the table, as if they'd be in the same picture but off to the sides, leaving the brothers the focal point. One was thickset and older, with a rope scar around his neck. The other was slender and very young — a rooster-tailed towhead who was not yet twenty. Freckles were splashed across his broad nose and pale, faintly pitted cheeks. He wore a loosely knit cream scarf around his neck, and he sat back in his chair, casually, a boot hiked on a knee. He had a bemused look on his young face. Melted snow dribbled from the soles of the boot to the rough wooden floor.

Someone else drew a deep breath, and Yakima slid his gaze to his left. He'd been wrong about there only being the five in the room. A stocky Indian in a soiled apron stood as if he'd been carved from dark maple against the far left wall, beside the cracking and ticking, bullet-shaped black woodstove. He had a log in each hand, and the door to the stove was open.

The dark gent in the bobcat hide coat said without expression, "Horace, why don't you finish stoking the stove and pour the breed a whiskey on me?"

"You might try closin' that goddamn door first," said the blond man at the bar.

Yakima kept his rifle aimed into the room as he reached back, grabbed the knob of the open door, and pulled it closed. Slowly, he moved forward, swinging his gaze from the blond man at the bar to the two dark-haired, dark-mustached twins at the table before him. All four men at the table had their hands where Yakima could see them. The man at the bar had one fist on his right hip, just above an ivory-gripped Peacemaker. But he appeared in no hurry to draw the gun.

As the stocky Indian closed the stove door and then limped across the room and behind the bar, Yakima said, "First you bushwhack me. Then you buy me a drink. Custom of the country?"

The blond gent chuckled, then picked up

his beer to take a drink. The two dark gents stared without expression at the half-breed. "You can off-cock that rifle," said the dark-haired man in the ratty bear coat.

"Can I?"

"We thought you was a Coyote Ridge rider," said the man in the bear coat. "We seen what they did to the Coffin farm and figured they was out to expand their territory just a little more. We don't like them, and they don't like us. They kill our riders, see?" He blinked once, slowly, but his dark, glassy eyes remained expressionless. "So we kill theirs."

"You're the Furys."

"I'm Emil," said the man in the bobcat coat. Canting his head toward his lookalike beside him, he said, "That's my brother, Emmett. That over there at the bar is our cousin, Pat Anderson. There's more kin back to the ranch, but we was headed to town for supplies when we saw the burned-out Coffin ranch and been on the lookout for CR riders since. Like my brother said, we thought you was one. We do apologize."

The blond gent glanced at the stocky Indian drawing a beer from a brass-handled spigot behind the bar. "Horace here told us you was the one who sent Wes Lassiter to his reward. You might be a breed, but, like our amigo Horace here, you can't be all bad. Shit, if it was springtime and we was hirin', we might even give you a job." He grinned and lifted his beer in salute, took another sip.

Yakima stood in the middle of the room, depressing the hammer of his Yellowboy and lowering the barrel toward the floor. "Do you know where Mrs. Coffin is?"

The men glanced around at each other.

"Nope," said cousin Pat. "Dead, most like."

That bit Yakima deep, but he didn't let it show. Now that he had things straight with the Furys, he needed to find the sheriff and see about Aubrey. If anyone in town knew anything about her, Hagan should.

"I'll take that beer some other time." Yakima turned toward the door, then stopped and turned back, glowering.

"Why do you and the Lassiters keep goin' at each other like bobcats locked in the same privy?" He hiked an incredulous shoulder. "Just the usual old greed?"

"There was a little misunderstandin', years back," said cousin Pat with a sigh. "Just a small thing, really, but since she never did like us for bein' as ambitious as she was, it sorta grew over the years. No end in sight, either." He pursed his lips and shook his head.

His cousins Emil and Emmett kept their hard eyes straight ahead.

Yakima turned and went out. He glanced at the dead man tied to the mouse brown gelding. Just another poor hombre caught in a misunderstanding. The half-breed grabbed his blowing reins, swung onto Wolf's back, and continued heading west. As he passed another saloon on his right, he could hear a piano and a woman's ribald laughter behind the closed front doors. The laugh resembled a weird, ghostlike echo of the moaning wind.

He continued on to the jailhouse, found the windows dark, the front door locked. Turning on the stoop, he squinted against the wind and snow and cast his gaze at the saloon from which the piano patter still emanated faintly. Someone there would likely know where the sheriff was. Yakima had heard grumblings earlier about Hagan's predilection for the bottle, and that's why the lawman had hired Wesley Lassiter, to lighten the sheriff's own load.

He might be holed up in one of the half dozen watering holes or brothels around the storm-locked town. But whoever had brought Aubrey to town would have reported to Hagan what he'd found at the

Coffin farm.

Yakima started down the snowy porch steps, and stopped. A man was standing on the boardwalk beneath the awning of Landry's Drugstore, next door to the jailhouse and across a fifty-foot gap between the two buildings. The same tall, bandy-legged man with the walrus mustache who'd been standing outside the jailhouse when Yakima had left earlier. He wore a thick wool coat and a Stetson tied down on his head with a wool muffler. His round glasses were spotted with snow.

"You'll find him at the schoolhouse," the man said, one hand raised to an awning post beside him. "Northwest edge of town."

Yakima stared at the man for a moment, then continued on down the steps of the jailhouse gallery and swung up into the saddle. He booted Wolf on up the street, then turned right at the first side street. He found the schoolhouse a few minutes later, sitting alone on a slight rise and fronted by a wooden swing hanging from a log frame by a chain. The swing was shunted back and forth by the wind, twisting and turning, the chain links rattling. The bell over the school's front door clanged.

As Yakima put Wolf up to the hitch rack fronting the school's front stoop, the door at the top of the white-painted steps opened. Sheriff Hagan stepped out — hatless but wearing an unbuttoned coat and a gun on his hip. He winced at the blast of cold air and drew the door closed behind him to keep the heat inside the building.

"What the hell'd you come back here for, you damn fool?" Hagan yelled above the wind. "You damn near got her killed!"

Yakima drew a deep breath. The man's words hit him like a runaway coal dray of guilt.

The sheriff hustled down the porch steps mantled in a good six inches of drifted snow. Grabbing Wolf's reins out of Yakima's hand, he canted his head toward the schoolhouse. "What're you waitin' for? She's inside. I'll stable your horse with mine, goddamn it!"

CHAPTER 20

Yakima still couldn't understand why Aubrey had been taken to a schoolhouse, but it was a vague concern. Heavy-footed, he climbed the steps to the front door and went on inside, frowning as he looked around the school and stomping snow from his boots onto the hemp mud mat under his feet. He scrubbed snow from his coat with his gloved hands, then doffed his hat and used it to pound snow from his buckskin trousers.

At the far end of the room, a door flanking the teacher's desk opened. A woman with chestnut hair piled in a bun atop her head and in a conservative shirtwaist and long, pleated wool skirt stepped into the main room. A cameo pin held her collar closed at her neck.

"Are you Henry?" she asked in an uninviting tone.

Yakima nodded as he gave his trousers one more hammering with his hat.

"She's in here." The woman stepped back through the door.

Wincing at the ache in his near-frozen toes but welcoming the heat pushing against him — the big potbelly stove was snapping and popping on the room's right side — Yakima tramped down the aisle between the student desks to the back of the room. He moved with customary caution through the half-open door and into the room beyond it, one hand automatically touching the horn grips of the .44 jutting above his coat flap.

"You won't need that here," the woman said, standing back against an eating table in the kitchen part of her living quarters. She had her hands on the edge of it, and she was studying Yakima critically.

He looked around. The kitchen was warm and humid, the single window steamed over. Two pots boiled water on the black range to his left. There was a whiskey bottle on the oilcloth-covered table. He hadn't thought teachers imbibed.

He turned to the woman. "Who're you?"

"June. Friend of the sheriff's. No doctor in town, and since I've had experience tending the young ones' scrapes and broken bones, he brought Mrs. Coffin here." She gave her head a toss to indicate the door opening off the kitchen. "In there, through the parlor. She's been in and out. I gave her some laudanum."

"What happened?"

"They took a blacksnake to her. Ten lashes. Good ones, but she'll live."

Yakima walked toward the doorway.

"She's been asking for you."

He stopped, looked at the woman, who turned her gaze away from him. He went on through the parlor that was only a little bigger than the kitchen, with two old chairs and a horsehide sofa and footstool, a single lamp on a table, and two tintypes hanging on the red-and-gold-papered walls. There were a dozen or so books on a plank shelf near the small, stone fireplace.

Yakima crossed the room and poked his head through the sheet hanging over the doorway, and saw Aubrey lying on the bed, covered in quilts, her head fanned out across her pillow. She lay on her stomach, her face turned away from the door and toward a small, sashed window that showed the falling snow through its blue, frosty panes. A small stove ticked.

Yakima doffed his hat and walked around to the other side of the bed. He dropped to a knee, removed his gloves, and reached up to slide a lock of hair back from Aubrey's cheek. Her eyes fluttered, opened. She stared at him for a moment as though not sure who he was.

Then her eyes seemed to clear, and she said in a thin voice, "It's not your fault."

"Shh."

Yakima pressed his lips to her cheek. He lifted the covers gently and peered under them at her back, which was wrapped with wide gauze strips. Blood shone through the gauze, which smelled of some kind of aromatic herbal ointment.

He eased the covers back down on the woman's back and let a deep-held breath out as he sagged down on his knees and lowered his head. His heart felt heavy and torn. Aubrey was looking at him with an angry cast to her gaze, moving her cracked, near-purple lips slightly.

She hardened her jaw a little. "Ma Lassiter."

"I know."

"Go, Yakima. Leave here."

"No."

"If you stay, you'll die."

"If I stay, she'll die. And all the men who were with her today."

Tears varnished Aubrey's eyes. "No."

Yakima kissed her again. "You get some sleep."

As he rose and carried his hat and his

gloves to the door, he heard Aubrey say very softly but beseechingly, "No . . ."

Ma Lassiter was actually feeling a little fear that she and her gang wouldn't make it back to the ranch but get stranded out on the snowy plains. With the storm growing stronger, they'd all freeze to death in a massive drift. Such a fate had come to even the toughest and strongest and most experienced out here on the Dakota prairie, where severe whiteouts could cause one to lose direction so that, chilled to the bone, the sense even that the ground was down and the sky was up began to seem dubious.

Ma was relieved when she saw the lights of her lodge winking in the gray-dark hollow before her. Her fear vanished, and she was relieved to send it on its way. She wasn't accustomed to the emotion, and it made her feel weak and out of control.

She didn't like it at all.

"You boys put my horse up," she yelled into the wind as she hauled her heavy bulk down from the saddle, tossing her reins at Drew Beresford.

The cowboy reached for the reins, but the wind caught them and blew them out away from him, so that he had to scramble around in a drift to find them again.

It was dark. The wind was howling. The snow blew sideways and was piling up drifts under the eaves of the bunkhouse and lodge in the form of frozen stormy sea waves.

"Shit!" Ma cried as she kicked through a drift and headed for the lodge, venting her disdain for the weather that had come between her and the man who'd murdered her son. Without Wes as deputy sheriff of Brule County — she'd intended to make sure he was elected sheriff at the next election, as she sensed Hagan no longer wanted the job, anyway — the Furys were likely to get the upper hand. They had more land, more cattle, and more money to pay for more and better gun-savvy riders.

Having Wesley in a position of lawful power would have been a great equalizer.

The lodge's lower-story windows were lit by flickering umber glows. She'd left English Charlie in the lodge that morning, with a long list of chores for the one-armed man to do before she got home. Ma hoped to Christ he'd done them and not merely depleted her whiskey stores. She hoped for his sake he'd done his work. In her current frame of mind, she couldn't be blamed for what she might do.

Even to a cripple.

Ma stomped up the porch steps buried

under a good foot of snow. The old iron triangle she'd once used to call her boys and their father to meals whipped and clattered from its old rope beneath the eves. Ma never used the triangle anymore. Even when Wes was alive and working out here, he'd eaten with the men in the bunkhouse. Ma cooked only for herself or, occasionally, she'd hire someone like English to cook and clean for her.

The triangle hadn't been used in years, but she left it there to remind her of happier times, when she had a husband and two boys to raise and, despite the hardships of raising beef on this barren steppe, the world looked up instead of down.

Now it just looked down, and Ma wondered why in the hell she continued to not only live in it but to bust her broad old ass trying to make a living raising cattle in it. On the other hand, what the hell else was she going to do? Put a gun to her head and drill a bullet through her brain? Pshaw! She had too much gravel to hang herself in her barn.

Now she threw the timbered door's latch, pushed the door open, kicked a couple of bushels of snow inside, and entered her high-ceilinged foyer. A figure appeared so suddenly before her that she stepped back with a start and reached for the .45 on her hip.

"Here ye are, mum," English Charlie said, wrapping a heavy star quilt over her shoulders with his lone left hand. "Here ye are — that's the girl. We'll get you warm. Seen ya comin', and I says to myself, 'Ma must be half froze! Charlie, get her a quilt!' " As he wrapped the blanket over the dumbfounded woman's heavy shoulders, over her coat, and kicked the door closed, English Charlie gave a near-violent shiver of his own. "Blast this weather. And I thought it was cold in me merry ole England. Never, ever seen anything like this over there!"

"Good Lord," Ma said, looking the one-armed limey over as though disbelieving her eyes. "Why . . . why, thank you, English. Is that a fire I hear popping in the parlor?"

"A fire, 'tis, ma'am. A big one!"

Charlie ushered the near-frozen woman into the parlor, where the heavy heat hammered Ma like a giant fist. A giant, soft fist, for a moment sucking the breath from her lungs and then, as sudden heat often did, making her feel even colder than before. As Charlie guided her to an overstuffed rawhide chair he'd angled close to the fire, Ma's teeth clattered. She drew her shoulders together and felt every muscle in her body spasming.

"Ohhhh," Ma said, drawn to the fire like a bat to the light. "Ohhhh . . . English, I've been dreaming about a fire for the past five hours. Ohhh . . ." She turned to warm her heavy ass shelving a good six inches out from her back. "Ohhh . . . that feels . . . so . . . *good . . . !*"

"Here, here, here," English Charlie said, taking the blanket off the woman's broad shoulders. "Let's get you out of the coat. Come, now, Ma — let Charlie have the quilt just for a minute, until we can get you out of this frozen coat. Why, it's all snow an' ice!" He managed to tear the blanket from her small, viselike fists. "Then I'll wrap the blanket around you once again, and I'll pour you a whiskey as large as all Dakota!"

"Good Lord," Ma said, trying to stamp some heat into her frozen feet inside their badger-fur boots and shivering as Charlie tossed her coat onto the floor, then replaced the quilt around her shoulders. She was staring in wide-eyed shock at the corrugated tin stock trough she used as a wood bin beside the hearth. It had been empty this morning, but it was now filled to overflowing with split oak and cottonwood logs. "You did some chores, English!"

"Only did what you asked me to do,

mum." English chuckled as he went over to a table on the opposite side of the room, where several whiskey bottles stood sentinel over a small pyramid of freshly scrubbed goblets. "You ask English to do a thing, he does it. Yessir, Ma — English Charlie ain't the same man he was last year or even last summer. He's turned over a new leaf, the one-armed Englishman has."

English Charlie brought a goblet half-filled with amber whiskey over to Ma, who took it in her pudgy, quivering fingers and threw back half the forty-rod in a single slug.

She shivered as the fire hit rock-bottom and the cold struggled against it like a bobcat in a cave with a rabid wolf. But then Ma took another slug, and the cold began crawling back into its corner while the warmth snarled and gained confidence.

"Oh, Jesus . . . God, that's good!" She finished the glass and handed it over to English Charlie, who looked down at it as though she were handing him a dead snake. "Well, go on, go on, English. Refill it for me."

"Righto!" English grabbed the glass, dropped it. Fortunately, it did not break on the cinder-scorched bobcat rug beneath his and Ma's feet. Smiling sheepishly, he picked it up.

"Oh, for cryin' in the shit, English!" Ma berated him as she turned to face the fire and sag back in the overstuffed chair. "How much of that have you had, Charlie? I told you, no drinkin' on the job."

Still shivering, she pulled the blanket tighter around her shoulders as she leaned forward to begin jerking at the rawhide laces of her fur boots.

"Only a nip or two, Ma. Only a nip or two. I been busy all day, cleanin' up around here — such a messy girl, Ma Lassiter! — and tendin' the woodpile. So blame cold out there if I didn't have just one or two teeny-weeny sips of the old who-hit-Angus, I'd be froze-up like the Big Muddy's gonna be at first light tomorrow."

Ma got one boot off, then looked down at the empty holster at her side. She frowned. "Where's my gun?"

"What's that?"

"Where's my gun, English?"

English Charlie was bringing another drink, a glassy smile on his long, hook-nosed face with its close-set, yellow-brown eyes that shone brightly in the firelight. "Sittin' on the table over yonder."

"Over yonder where?"

"Over there, Ma."

"You slipped it out of my holster?" Ma

asked, frowning indignantly as English Charlie handed over her second goblet of whiskey.

"Sure, when we were comin' into the room. You don't need that big gun on you, Ma. Why on earth do you need to go around armed in your house?" English Charlie blinked as he smiled.

"I go armed in my house, English Charlie, because I'm used to goin' around armed in my house. A habit carried over from the old days, I reckon." She leaned toward him, the whiskey hitting her now and stoking her inner fires. "When I was liable to find Injuns or bobcats in my kitchen . . . or hired help helpin' themselves to my booze and fuckin' some little Mex cleaning girl in my pantry, like I caught you doin' last summer with Rosalie. Remember that, English?"

"Yep," English Charlie said, nodding. "Still got the scar from the bullet crease." He brushed his hand across his forearm, grinning nervously. "But like I said, I turned over a new leaf, and there'll be no more of that."

"Better not be, English."

"Don't you want me to help you take off your boots, Ma?"

She'd just taken another liberal slug from her glass. Lowering the glass, Ma Lassiter furled her brows and worked her warty nose. “What’s that I smell?”

“Hmmm?”

“Smells like somethin’s burnin’, English!”

“Mercy!” English Charlie swung around and ran toward the doorway, stumbling on the rug and nearly falling before bouncing off the wall in the foyer and righting himself. He continued on into the kitchen, and Ma sat back, hearing pots and pans clattering as Charlie cursed just loudly enough for Ma to hear.

The forty-rod was warming her so well, making her feel so good, that she disregarded the din from the kitchen and snuggled down deeper into her chair. Her cold, old, tired bones felt as though they were filling with warm molasses, making her feel sweet. Her eyelids drooped, and she dozed, dreaming . . .

. . . It was nigh on ten years ago, after her man had left her, and she was riding in her buckboard wagon on the trail back from town, the back of the wagon filled with supplies. It was a hot July afternoon and she held her two pulling horses to easy trots as she curved around the big box elder at the mouth of Mooney’s Coulee. One of the pullers whinnied and shook its head. It was answered by a distant whinny behind.

Ma turned to peer over her shoulder, saw two riders on a low hill on her back trail. They were walking their horses abreast, riding with a casual, slope-shouldered air, holding their reins one-handed.

Ma glowered. She was near the place along the trail where a pie wedge of Fury graze angled into Coyote Ridge holdings, and by the raggedy-heeled look of the two riders behind her, they were Fury men, all right. Complete with holstered pistols flashing in the sunlight.

Just then, as she watched the two, they turned their heads to each other conspiratorially. A half second later, they each gave a raucous, jubilant whoop and put spurs to their horses' flanks.

Ma's scowl deepened on her fleshy features as she watched from beneath the brim of her man's felt hat as both riders galloped toward her, heads down and loosing loud Rebel yells. That they were up to no good was obvious. Ma reached for the Winchester she always carried beneath her seat, but just then the wagon struck a chuckhole, and the rifle's rear stock bounced beyond her reach.

Hooves sounded like the frenetic beating of war drums behind her. And then the riders were on both sides of her, waving their arms and yelling and triggering pistols into the air over the heads of Ma's pullers. A quick glance at the brands on both horses' hindquarters told her these hellions were most certainly Fury men.

"Get outta here, you rattlesnakes!" Ma screamed, hauling back on her horses' reins.

Too late. The Fury men had accomplished what they'd set out to do, and both pullers answered the malicious hoorawing by heaving forward against their collars and hames and breaking into wild, frenzied gallops. Ma had to give up on the rifle and hold on lest she be thrown overboard.

"Lousy sons o' no-good dirty bitches!" the woman screamed as the wagon pitched and bucked wildly beneath her broad bottom, every second threatening to throw her from the wagon. All she could do was hold on to the taut reins, sawing back on them in hopes of finally getting the team stopped.

At the moment, however, it was as if a cloud of angry hornets were hanging over their heads. They were both galloping full tilt and ignoring Ma's demanding reins pulls and helpless screams. Fury bit Ma deep as she watched the two riders gallop away on a single-track horse trail that swerved left of the main trail, heading toward chalky, cone-shaped buttes in the northwest.

"Bastards!" Ma cried, so enraged that she

was beyond thinking about getting her horses stopped and had gone on to thoughts of bloody revenge.

A horse and rider appeared out of nowhere from the trail's right side. Ma blinked. Her lower jaw hung slack. Her son, Wesley — all of seventeen years old but as good a rider already as this country had seen in many a year — heeled his pinto steed up beside the right puller. The young man, blond hair blowing out from under his black hat in the wind, leaned forward and reached out with his left hand. He grabbed the head stall of the right puller, held on to it for about fifty yards, and Ma could see that the boy was gradually slowing his pinto with a deft right hand on his reins.

She felt the wagon slowing until finally Wesley had the pullers stopped and standing amidst their own thick, sifting dust, sweat-silvered in the sunshine. They blew and hung their heads. Before Ma could say anything to her boy, Wesley hammered steel to the steed's flanks, and he flew off in a flurry of thrashing hooves, heading up the trail that the two rawhiders had taken as they'd laughed like Fourth of July rodeo revelers.

"Wesley!" Ma called, certain she'd seen the last of her firebrand boy. She hadn't seen him in two weeks, since he'd ridden off in a summer-restless tantrum, having had his fill of cleaning out stock ponds and irrigation ditches.

As she stood screaming his name, he disappeared over the top of a hill.

Ma turned her team into the shade of two cottonwoods along a dry creek bed and clambered down off the wagon. Her heart thudded angrily. She was grateful the boy had saved her from a possible pileup, but he should have listened when she called him back. That was the trouble with Wesley; it had been since he was old enough to start whipping. He never listened worth a damn. Pretty much did whatever he wanted.

Ma watered her team from her hat while keeping an eye on the hill over which her no-account son had disappeared. If he never showed again, which was likely in spite of how good he bragged he was with his .45, it wouldn't trouble her any. Losing trouble is no trouble at all. . . .

The thought had just slipped across her brain when a pistol cracked. The sound came again, again, and again, then twice more. Silence. Was that a scream Ma heard on the hot, dry breeze?

She waited, staring toward the chalky buttes.

Presently, a lone rider appeared on the horizon, galloping toward her.

Wesley.

"Here, Ma," the boy grunted as he drew rein up before the woman staring at him with a skeptical expression.

He tossed a small burlap tobacco pouch to her. She caught it against her bosom. Still eyeing her recalcitrant child dubiously, she opened the pouch and sucked a sharp breath when she saw the four bloody ears nestled at the sack's bottom.

She looked up at Wes. He was grinning.

She closed the sack by its leather drawstring and berated the boy for not minding her. But she kept the little trophy sack he'd given her, tossing it onto the wagon seat. She was mildly surprised when he followed her instructions to trail her back to the ranch and get to work, as the main windmill needed oiling and then there were corral gates that needed fixing, etc.

She made sure he didn't feel too proud of himself.

But that night, after supper when she was sitting down with a glass of whiskey in her favorite chair before a popping fire, she opened the sack and peered inside. She couldn't help smiling.

"That boy," she said, hearing the uncharacteristic fondness in her voice. "Maybe he'll make a man, after all."

Much later she learned that the two hard

cases who'd hazed her team were not Fury men at all but merely drifters who'd stolen a couple of ponies from the Fury remuda. But who they were didn't really matter. What mattered was her son's act of devotion, and the adeptness with which he handled a .45. A boy — no, a man — like that would come in damn handy out here. . . .

Ma looked at the ears once more, then closed the sack and tossed it into the fire. Flames bit at the bag, and a charcoal smoke rose from it.

"Pew!" the woman exclaimed. "Oh, what an awful *stink!*"

"Sorry, Ma — just a little trouble in here, but not more than I can manage!"

English Charlie's voice woke her. She snapped her head up, brain still swirling with the dream.

Wesley. Oh, the plans she'd had for that boy and the long-coveted demise of the Furys . . .

Hearing English Charlie nervously knocking pans around in the kitchen, and gradually reviving, Ma heaved herself up out of her chair with a grunt. She walked over to the table where she kept her liquor supply.

Lifting the lone bottle there, she frowned. She held the bottle up in front of her face, shook it. About two drops slid across the bottom, from side to side.

Ma Lassiter's face turned crimson as she bunched her lips and slammed the bottle back down on the table.

"English Charlie!"

She swung around and stomped across the room and into the foyer. She could hear him cursing under his breath in the kitchen as she entered it, saw him tossing two steaks so charred that they resembled old black shoes into a corrugated tin tub beside the range.

"English Charlie, you drunken fool!"

He swung around so quickly that he sent the second steak tumbling and crunching across the floor before it nestled up against a table leg. He looked at Ma glaring at him from the doorway, stretched his lips back from his face in a dreadful grin.

"You're drunk," Ma accused, her voice pitched low with menace. "That bottle in the parlor was half-full last night."

Charlie just stood grinning that dire grin as Ma stomped over to a cabinet, opened a door, and stared up at a shelf containing only vinegar bottles and molasses jars.

Ma gasped. She turned her puffy red face toward English Charlie. Charlie lowered his glassy eyes to the floor.

"There was a whole bottle of brandy in

this cabinet. A whole bottle!"

English Charlie lifted his lone hand, ran it through his hair, tugging at it in frustration. Slowly, he lifted his timid gaze. "I do apologize, Mrs. Lassiter. I am indeed sorry. I was workin' outside, you see, splittin' wood an' such, and it was so cold that I needed a few sips of the forty-rod to keep me warm, keep me goin'."

"You goddamn fool."

English Charlie winced. "I do apologize, ma'am." He sucked a shallow breath, swallowed. "Why don't I just go out and hack another couple steaks off that beef quarter hangin' in . . ."

He let his voice trail off when he saw the .36 Colt in Ma's small, fat fist. She narrowed her deep-set eyes in their doughy sockets as she glared at him over the gun that she now cocked with a ratcheting click. English Charlie should have known she'd be armed with a hideout somewhere in the folds of all that flesh. . . .

"Why don't you just get the hell out of my sight before I gut-shoot you, you worthless, one-armed drunk?"

The skin above the bridge of English Charlie's nose wrinkled. "Now? Tonight? Ma, it's cold outside!"

Ma raised her voice several octaves. "I said

get out!"

"All right, all right!" he said, reaching for the coat hanging on a hook by the kitchen's outside door. "I'll just mosey out to the bunkhouse tonight . . . sleep out there till you cool off. Tomorrow, I'll —"

"No."

Charlie shrugged into his coat, frowning with anxious befuddlement.

"I want you off my place now. Tonight."

"Oh, Ma, it's . . . why, it's *snowin'* outside. And *cold!* I wouldn't make it half a mi—"

Ma bellowed so loudly that the lantern mantles chimed, "I want you off my goddamn place tonight, and don't let me find you huddled up nowhere on my land. You understand me, English Charlie? Nowhere. You're a worthless, one-armed drunk, and all you're good for is feedin' the goddamn wolves!"

With that, she narrowed an eye and triggered a shot.

Bam!

The slug tore into the door just as English Charlie heaved it open and bolted out into the blowing, snowy night.

Chapter 21

The next morning, Yakima swallowed the last of his coffee and slid his chair back from June Trevelyan's table in her quarters at the back of the schoolhouse. "Much obliged for breakfast. For the shelter, too, and especially for tending Mrs. Coffin."

The teacher looked up at him from her steaming coffee mug, which she held in front of her chin with both hands. "Where are you going, Mr. Henry?"

"Headin' out." Yakima pulled his coat off the back of the chair.

June looked out a near window. The storm had stopped, but it was gray and so cold that the water had frozen that morning in the bucket she kept atop the dry sink. "Not exactly traveling weather."

"I travel in all kinds of weather."

Yakima buttoned his capote, donned his hat, and grabbed his soogan, which he'd rolled and set by the door earlier. He'd spread it out on the living room floor the night before, wanting to stay close to keep an eye on Aubrey, who'd slept all night, a good sign that she was on the mend despite the severity of the whipping she'd endured.

He turned to June, who sat as before, her coffee steaming before her, and canted his head at the door behind him. "School to-day?"

She hiked a shoulder. "Oh, one or two might brave the snow and the cold. It'll be a quiet day." She sipped her coffee. "I hope it's a quiet day for you, too, Mr. Henry."

"Tell Mrs. Coffin good-bye for me, will you?"

Yakima pinched his hat brim to the woman and, shouldering his rifle and his soogan, left the living quarters, and tramped on through the main part of the school, which was warming now with a fire that the teacher had built in the stove in anticipation of her students. Out on the stoop that he'd cleared of snow earlier, his own modest way of repaying the woman for the trouble of boarding him, he stopped and raised his collar against the cold.

Damn cold. A cold that bit bone-deep, chewed into a man's fiber, rubbed his skin like coarse sandpaper. His breath puffed in front of his face. Oh, well, he could handle the cold. He'd need to. Because he wasn't going to waste today hunkered down by a fire. Cold or no cold, he was going to give Ma Lassiter what she wanted — a visit from the half-breed who'd killed her son.

He went out to the stable in which Sheriff Hagan had bedded Wolf down, and was glad to find the horse looking bright-eyed and bushy-tailed despite the cold. He had a blanket over him, a bucket with only a few remaining kernels of cracked corn before him.

"You ready to ride, boy?" he asked, holding the horse's chin with one hand, running the other one affectionately down its snout while Wolf swished his tail eagerly. "A little cold never hurt, did it?" He released the horse and grabbed the saddle and blanket from a stall partition.

He remembered the long, serpentine wounds on Aubrey's back, and he hardened his jaw. "Nah. A little cold don't hurt . . . when you got a job to do."

Wolf snorted and pawed at the straw-strewn earthen floor of his stall.

When Yakima had the stallion bridled and saddled, he led it outside, mounted up, and headed on back toward the center of town, noting the sugary snowdrifts rising and falling around him. For the size of the drifts, there were still patches of barren ground where the wind had swept it clear, and Yakima guessed the storm had been more wind and cold than snow — only a foot or so had likely fallen. Not too much to prevent travel.

He headed up the main street that was a rumpled white quilt, with shopkeepers on both sides of the street shoveling and sweeping their porches and boardwalks clear. It was cold, but horses were tied to hitch racks fronting the two eateries in town, and at the Dakota Plains Saloon, where Yakima's trouble had begun a few days ago.

He stopped in front of the jailhouse. Someone had shoveled snow from the porch, but the place looked vacant, no smoke curling from the chimney pipe. Yakima stared at the door. He imagined the Gatling gun locked in a cell inside. . . .

He rode on up the street and pulled up to the hitch rack at the base of the broad loading dock of Latham's Mercantile. Smoke gushed from the stout chimney pipe rising from the building's steeply pitched roof.

Yakima looped his reins over the hitch rack, mounted the shoveled loading dock to which stubborn crusts of snow clung in the form of men's boot tracks. He opened the door, and as the bell rattled, he walked inside and closed the door.

Heat pressed against him. Ahead and right, a bullet-shaped black stove knocked and wheezed as Latham, the bandy-legged, walrus-mustached man whom Yakima had seen twice before at the sheriff's office, shoved a chunk of wood through the stove's open door. Stooped over, the apron-clad mercantiler glanced at Yakima, his eyes behind round spectacles acquiring a skeptical cast.

The man glanced toward the front of the store, where Sheriff Hagan was standing at the long counter over a steaming cup of coffee. Hagan stood with his back to the counter, hat tipped off his forehead. He looked from the mercantiler to Yakima now, not saying anything but only watching the half-breed with mute, fateful interest.

"I'll be needing some forty-four shells," Yakima told the mercantiler. "Two boxes. Two more in the forty-five caliber."

Latham grunted as he chunked another log into the stove's open door, then turned to speak to someone whom Yakima couldn't see. "I tell you, English," the mercantiler said, "I never seen a man so froze-up and still breathin'. What in the hell were you doin' out in this weather, anyway? When you lost your arm, did you lose all sense, too?"

Yakima walked toward the counter, now able to see the man sitting in a chair on the counter side of the stove. He was a small-boned, brown-haired, spade-bearded man wrapped in several blankets, leaning forward in his chair and shivering almost violently as he rubbed his hands together. His pale, bare feet were in a bucket of steaming water. The steam owned a salty tang.

"Ah, hell," said the man called English. "I was out to Ma Lassiter's, workin' for the old hag. Didn't last long. That woman's meaner'n . . ."

The man glanced at Yakima out the corner of his eye. He turned back to the stove, then turned sharply back to Yakima, lifting his head, eyes widening as though in recognition, lower jaw loosening.

Yakima held his gaze as he continued strolling toward the counter. The man followed him, turning his head while he continued to shiver.

Yakima turned to Hagan as he leaned an elbow on the counter, near a barrel of rock candy. "Cold mornin'," Yakima said.

"Too cold to be out in it."

As Latham came around the end of his counter, glowering at the half-breed, Yakima slipped a knife from the belt sheath beneath his coat, reached up, and cut a tube of sausage free of the cord from which it hung over the counter. "I'll take that, too." He glanced at a wheel of white cheese sitting atop a bin to his right. It had only a few green spots of mold on it. "And a pound of that."

"You can't be goin' where I think you're goin'," Hagan said as Latham lifted the glass lid from the cheese and began cutting into the wheel with a knife.

"I got nowhere else to go."

"Plumb crazy. She's got close to twenty men out there. Keeps 'em all winter long though the only work she'll have till spring is gun work — runnin' the settlers off who don't get driven out by the cold, or starve or try to steal her beef to stay alive. Might have a couple o' minor tussles with the Fury boys."

"Sounds like a right nice lady. It's a wonder you hired her son." Yakima glanced at Latham, who was wrapping the cheese in butcher paper, then looked at the cartridge boxes stacked on a shelf behind the man. "Don't forget the brass."

"Around here," Hagan said, slipping a flask from inside his coat and popping the cork from the lip, "you do what you have to do to survive."

"It's that way everywhere, Sheriff," Yakima said, watching as Hagan splashed a good portion of whiskey into his coffee.

Latham set the .44 and .45 shells on the counter, then figured the bill on a small pad with a pencil. "That'll be four dollars and two bits."

Yakima reached into a pocket, carefully counted out some coins, spilled them onto the counter, then picked up the cheese, sausage, and four boxes of shells and turned toward the door. He stopped when he saw that the eyes of the man sitting by the stove were on him. They had a drawn but owly cast.

Yakima took his possibles in the crook of his left arm, dug into his pocket again, and fished out a quarter. He flipped it toward the man in the chair, who gave a startled grunt as he flung up his left hand — it appeared the only hand he had — and grabbed the coin out of the air.

He looked at it, narrowed his wary, suspicious gaze at Yakima once more. "Been out to Lassiter's, have ya? Well, you look like you could use a drink. On me."

Yakima continued on to the door and went outside, where a morning wind was blowing the freshly fallen snow along the street and brushing Wolf's tail up beneath the horse's belly. Yakima moved down off the loading dock and tucked the possibles into the war sack hanging from his saddle horn.

Mounting up, he swung the black away from the mercantile, noting the southern wind sanding his right cheek, and headed out.

Aubrey lifted her chin from the pillow with a groan.

Her back felt as though someone had basted her with hot tar. It was by turns hot, then cold, then hot again. She set her jaw, squeezed her eyes closed as an especially sharp spasm passed, then opened her eyes and looked around the small room. The window to her right told her it was morning. Snow covered the ground, whipped into white frostinglike ridges and swirls. There was a gray shed about fifty yards beyond, and the lumber stacked against its rear wall was capped in snow. A pewter-colored cat sat atop the lumber, cleaning its right front paw.

Aubrey wondered for a moment where she was, and then she could smell — above the smell of the devil's claw, willow bark, and licorice root that Miss Trevelyan had used to treat her wounds — the smell of beeswax, chalk, and ink. School smells.

She was still in the school.

A door clicked in another room, hinges squawked, and footsteps sounded. They grew louder until the sheet over the door rustled. Lifting her head from the pillow, Aubrey glanced over her shoulder to see Miss Trevelyan poking her head into the room. She was dressed in a ruffled shirtwaist and a long pleated skirt, and her hair was up. Dressed for school. A pretty woman who was oddly refined for these parts, who had an air of learning about her but also a hard practicality. Aubrey could just as easily imagine her dealing cards as teaching school.

"You're awake."

Aubrey nodded and laid her cheek down on the pillow, her face turned toward the window. "Sorry. I guess I disturbed your class. I don't normally carry on so."

"It's all right. There's only one student. Lloyd Harmon comes rain or shine. I guess he enjoys getting away from the whorehouse his mother works in."

Aubrey sighed at both the little boy's plight and her own. She'd been in too much pain to think about her problems much, but she was beginning to realize that she no longer had a home. Her house, barn, stock — all were gone. She had only the clothes she'd been wearing when Yakima had brought her to town, and most of those were bloody and torn.

Miss Trevelyan came around to the side of the bed. "More laudanum? Or should I get you some breakfast?"

Aubrey felt a sob ripple up from deep in her chest. Tears squeezed out from beneath her tightly closed eyelids. "No. I'd like to feel the pain for a while. I reckon it's all I have." She thought of something, opened her eyes, looking around behind the teacher and listening. "Where's Yakima?"

Miss Trevelyan sat down on the edge of the bed. "Gone. Headed out this morning. He said to tell you good-bye."

"Where did he go?"

"He didn't say. But I have a feeling . . ." Miss Trevelyan let her voice trail off.

Aubrey rolled onto her side, scuttling up a little to rest her shoulders against the bed's headboard. "The Lassiters'."

The teacher turned sideways and raised her knee to the edge of the bed, entwining her hands in her lap. "That's where I'd put my money, if I was a betting woman. He seems right attached to you, Mrs. Coffin. He's been awfully worried about you, filled with regret for what happened out at your place. Hasn't said so, but I could see it in his eyes. Odd thing to see in a killer's face."

"Yakima's no killer."

Miss Trevelyan arched a brow. "Oh, what is he, then?"

"A man trying to get along. A man who happens to be of a little darker color than the rest of us, and who attracts more trouble than the rest of us because of it."

"He killed Deputy Lassiter. Now, I realize that killing wasn't much of a loss, but —"

"Lassiter drew on Yakima first."

"Some say so. Others aren't so sure." The teacher crossed her arms on her chest. "Well, if you ask me, any man who kills a half dozen or more men and leaves the town shorthanded in case of another Indian attack is not one to be given the benefit of the doubt."

Aubrey stared hard at the teacher, trying to calm her emotions. "I do appreciate your help, Miss Trevelyan. I'll be going soon."

June Trevelyan's own expression softened. "You best relax, Mrs. Coffin. Are you sure you wouldn't like some laudanum? It'll help with the sting."

"No, thank you, ma'am."

"Whiskey?"

Aubrey shook her head.

The two women sat there together for a time. In spite of the teacher's harsh judgment of Yakima, Aubrey found her presence a comfort. It was rare that she ever found herself in another woman's company, and she found deep comfort in the silent council, the female camaraderie despite their differences in opinion.

The silence descended heavily, however, as Aubrey's thoughts swirled. Her chest grew tight, her stomach cold. She had no one, nothing. She looked out the window. Cold and snowy out there.

As if reading her mind, Miss Trevelyan said softly, gently, "Where will you go?"

Aubrey drew a deep breath and shook her head. "I don't know."

"You're welcome to stay here as long as you like. I could do with the company."

Aubrey looked at her and found herself asking something that was none of her business. "You and the sheriff . . . you're . . . ?"

Miss Trevelyan dropped her hands to her lap again and looked down at them. "That's a good question."

"I'm sorry. I —"

"No, that's fine." The teacher returned Aubrey's gaze, the hardness she'd shown before suddenly gone, replaced with a gentleness bordering on sadness. "Maybe, given enough time, I'll be able to give you an answer." She paused. Lines cut into the bridge of her nose. "Your husband — he's been dead over a year now."

Aubrey nodded.

"Must get lonely, out there — what is it, five miles from town?"

"Six." Aubrey eased onto her back, resting her head against the pillow propped against the headboard. "And to tell you the truth, Miss Trevelyan, I've found Joe's absence a comfort."

She looked at June Trevelyan, expecting to find censure in the woman's gaze. It wasn't there, however. It was almost as if the woman understood without Aubrey even having to explain further.

"I reckon that's why I never married." She chuckled as she rose and crouched beside the brazier, opening the door. "Of course, a teacher living the way I do isn't exactly right, either — taking up with different men over the years, never marrying one because I just never seemed satisfied with *any one* — but I reckon a town the size of Wild Rose has to take what it can get in teachers." A thoughtful cast streaked across her eyes as she turned to regard Aubrey from over her shoulder. "There's something cowardly in men — don't you think? It's like a little boy's fear they never outgrow. . . ."

June scooped coal into the brazier, then closed the door with a bang and a screech as she turned the rusty latching lever into its rusty slot.

A man cleared his throat. Both women turned to the bedroom door. Sheriff Hagan was poking his head through the sheet curtain. He looked a tad chagrined.

"Sorry," he said haltingly, looking at Miss Trevelyan. "I tried to keep the noise down so I wouldn't wake Mrs. Coffin. Just checking on things here."

He and the teacher stared at each other for a long, awkward moment. Aubrey felt her breath grow short, and felt a guilt pang, as though she'd been somehow to blame for drawing out the teacher's confession about her feelings about the men in her life. She decided to change the subject with "Sheriff, did you see Yakima?"

"Yes, ma'am, I did."

"Is he going out to the Lassiter ranch?"

Hagan blinked. "I believe so."

"Alone?"

"I doubt anyone around here would ride with him."

"What about you?"

"No." Miss Trevelyan rose from her crouch in front of the stove and turned to

Aubrey. "Rance has no dog in that fight."

Hagan gave the teacher an annoyed look, then softened his expression as he turned to Aubrey. "Mrs. Coffin, I tried to talk him out of it. Even if I rode out there with him, we'd only be two against nearly twenty. Now, why don't you get some sleep? You'll feel better again real soon."

Hagan pulled his head back from the doorway, letting the sheet drop back into place. He walked into the kitchen part of June's quarters, opening and closing his fists in frustration.

CHAPTER 22

Hagan poured a cup of coffee, splashed some whiskey into it, gave it a stir, then sat down at June's kitchen table.

He'd lifted the cup to blow on the hot liquid when June came out of the parlor. She opened the door to the main schoolroom, muttered a few words to someone in there, likely the boy, Lloyd Harmon, whom Hagan had seen when he'd entered the school from the front. The boy had been preoccupied with the reader he had his bespectacled head buried in. Better to weather the storm for books and schooling, Hagan supposed, than be run ragged for firewood at the brothel in which your mother worked.

June closed the door to the main schoolroom and turned to the sheriff.

"Don't listen to her, Rance," she said, canting her head toward the parlor. "She's got it bad for the half-breed. Too much time alone out on that farm of hers, I reckon. It's not your fight."

Hagan sipped his coffee and set the mug down on the oilcloth-covered table. He cleared his throat and stared across the table at the range and the shelves above it, all lined with oilcloth on which June's bag of Arbuckles' and coffee grinder sat with Holden's cornmeal and several tins of baking powder and sugar and salt. But he saw none of that. His mind was elsewhere.

He was thinking of how complicated his life had gotten since that damn breed had ridden into this town. He was supposed to keep the peace here, but he'd been gone for no more than a day, chasing whiskey runners, and all hell had popped in his absence. Ma's son killed, a half dozen citizens cut down in their zeal to bring Wesley's killer to justice if for no other reason than they were bored and had some dim wish to get on Ma Lassiter's good side.

As if that had ever gotten anyone anywhere.

Hagan chuckled at the idea of justice. . . .

June came around the table, her eyes on Hagan, then grabbed a cup from a shelf, poured coffee from the pot on the range, and sat down across from the sheriff. "What are you thinking about, Rance?"

Hagan sipped his coffee, set his cup back down, then stretched his arms out across the table to set his hands on June's wrists. "June, what I'm thinking about is this — if we can hold out till spring, I aim to take you to San Francisco and show you the time of your life if I have to rob a bank to do it."

The teacher frowned, vaguely befuddled, skeptical.

"You deserve it," Hagan said.

He rose slightly from his chair, leaned across the table, took the woman's head in his hands, splaying his fingers across her ears, and planted a warm kiss on her lips. He smiled. He sat back down in his chair, and holding her still-perplexed gaze with his own, took two more swallows of the nourishing belly wash, then rose from his chair and grabbed his hat from a wall hook.

As he hiked his shell belt higher on his hips and began buttoning his coat, June said warily, "What do you have on your mind, Rance Hagan?"

"My job."

Hagan headed out into the main part of the school. June sat staring down at her steaming coffee, hearing Hagan speaking friendly words to Lloyd Harmon as his boots clomped and his spurs rang across the floorboards, echoing in the cavernous room in which the little boy from the brothel studied.

"Study hard, Lloyd," Hagan told the boy. "It's the only way to get ahead in this world!"

The front door opened and closed, and Hagan was gone.

June raked a deep breath and released it slowly as with her right index finger she traced a small circle on her lower lip.

Hagan went out to June's stable and saddled his copper-bottom gelding. He tied his soogan and rifle scabbard, then mounted up and headed on out toward the main part of town. Looking around as the horse tramped through the snow, Hagan hunkered low in his saddle and shivered.

He and June should be nestled down in the Brule House. If the mercury wasn't down around zero degrees, it was damn close. It might climb to five or ten above, but no higher, and it would drop to ten below after dark. He hoped he wouldn't have to use that soogan, because he'd need more than those two blankets in such cold as this.

He pulled up in front of the jailhouse, wincing as a gust from an icy breeze blew up a bridal veil of powdery snow and shrouded him in it. When he came out of it, he cursed and swung down from his saddle, tossed his reins over the hitch rack, and mounted the porch steps. He stopped at the top, scowling down at the door handle. Slivers had been scraped away from the frame around the lock.

Hagan reached forward with one hand while reaching under his coat for his Remington .45. Shoving the unlatched door open — the lock had obviously been jimmied, probably by a short-bladed knife such as an Arkansas toothpick — he rocked back the Remy's hammer and stepped into the cold office.

He looked around at the dark room in which his L-shaped desk sat directly in front of him, against the back wall. He looked at the four jail cells to the left of the desk. All the doors were open, including the door of the cell in which Hagan had locked the Gatling gun that the army had left here and had apparently forgotten about. Hagan walked over to the door, swung it wide, and stood in the opening.

The gun and the crate he'd stored it in were gone.

"That bastard," Hagan said.

He laughed.

■ ■ ■ ■

Crows cawed loudly, shredding the silence of the snowy, gray morning.

Yakima jerked back on Wolf's reins with a start and automatically reached for the Yellowboy snugged down in the scabbard beneath his right thigh. He stayed the move, letting his right hand come to rest on the rifle's stock, and watched five or six of the birds light from a pine standing on the trail's left side. Continuing to bark like hoarse dogs, they lit off over a giant, dead cottonwood spreading its naked, barkless branches up high against the gunmetal sky and winged off to the northeast — the same direction in which Yakima was headed.

Wolf gave a blow. The packhorse Yakima had rented in Wild Rose, after he'd swung back around for the Gatling gun, followed suit, loudly swishing its tail as though indignant about being pulled out of its warm barn and into this wretched weather.

Yakima glanced back at the zebra dun — a broad-barreled, stout-legged horse that he'd chosen because it looked like a good packer and snower. The crated Gatling gun, the crate's cover secured by ropes, was stretched out over the wooden pack frame attached to the dun's back. Properly weighted and balanced so that, if it needed to, the horse would have no trouble running with the load.

"Sorry, feller," Yakima said. "Damn cold, I know."

Knowing it wasn't good to have horses out in such weather — their large lungs were vulnerable to crystallization, especially if they were run hard — he pressed his heels against Wolf's flanks, and as the lead rope drew taut, straining against the half-breed's saddle horn it was tied to, he headed on up the trail.

The horses' hooves made muffled clomps in the sugary drifts, the snow swishing up around the animals' hocks. The trace was delineated by the faint, nearly filled-in tracks that Yakima assumed to be those of the one-armed man called English Charlie, who'd traveled from the Coyote Ridge Ranch to town late last night or early this morning. By the look the man had given Yakima at the mercantile, there was little doubt he'd ridden first from the Coffin farm, as well. He'd been that fifth rider.

Yakima drew a muffler across his mouth as he headed on over a jog of low hills and into the Antelope Buttes — steep hills nestled in rocks and gnarled oak, sumac, and cedar and scored by deep ravines that all snaked around the base of the dozen or so bluffs as they drained off toward the Missouri a few miles east. Here, according to a map he'd seen in the sheriff's office, a branch of Hatchet Creek cut through.

He remembered this rugged country from his ill-fated trip to Wild Rose from Winnipeg, Manitoba, the little prairie town on the Red River of the North to which he'd hauled freight as part of a crew out of southern Dakota — a relatively easy job, and one for which he'd been well paid. He only wished he'd had the good sense to head back south directly instead of dilly-dallying in Wild Rose.

Oh, well. What's done was done.

He put the horses up a steep grade into tangled brush and boulders, until he found the spot he was looking for — a small cave at the top of a steep incline. He unloaded the Gatling gun and its ammo and set the gun up in the cave, obscuring the entrance to the cave with rocks and snowy branches but taking a good look around so he could find the spot again when he had to.

He took the pack rig off the zebra dun, then hobbled the horse and left it to forage on its own. If all went as planned, he wouldn't be long in returning.

Mounting up, he put Wolf down out of the buttes, following the shallowest watercourses until he'd crossed the dry north fork of Hatchet Creek and was again on the tableland where the snow lay in hard crusts, with wind-swept open areas between. Brome and needle grass poked their spiky, blond heads above the snow that danced and scuttled across the ground like vapor snakes in the occasional breeze.

Yakima cut English Charlie's trail again soon. It wasn't long after that that he saw what had to be the Coyote Ridge headquarters rise before him along a bench on the other side of a twisting river course. It was a ragged collection of gray shacks and corrals from this distance, and flanked by a camelback ridge spiked with cedars and aspens. Frowning, he drew Wolf to a halt.

Two riders were headed toward him from a cottonwood copse ahead and right. As Yakima watched, they booted their mounts into lopes. One already had his rifle out and was carrying it barrel up from his right thigh. The other man, who wore a bulky sheepskin coat and sheepskin hat with earflaps, reached down to jerk a carbine from his own scabbard. He cocked the gun one-handed as he rode, and set the rifle across his saddlebow.

Yakima held Wolf's reins taut in his left hand. With his right hand, he reached down and slid the Yellowboy from its sheath. He cocked it one-handed and held it barrel up, the brass plate feeling cold against his thigh through his buckskin breeches and long-handles.

Yakima waited, hearing the loudening thuds and crunches of the oncoming horses on the frozen ground and crusty snow. The men's cold tack squawked crisply. The man on the right, wearing the sheepskin coat, was big through the chest and shoulders, with a thick red-blond mustache and a light-complected face rosy from the cold. The other man was slender, dark, and square-faced. He wore a black, felt hat snugged down over a black scarf concealing his ears and knotted snug beneath his chin.

The men slowed as they approached, stopped their horses about twenty yards from Yakima. Neither one said anything for a time, until the blond man with the sheep-skin coat and sheepskin hat with earflaps that made his face look like marbled pork pushing out of a sausage gut narrowed one eye with menace.

"This here's Coyote Ridge range, in case you're wonderin', friend."

"No, I wasn't wondering."

The two men looked at each other. Then the blond man, who appeared to be the chatty one while the other man stared dull-eyed and mute at Yakima, said, "Now, I know you can't be that crazy half-breed that done killed Ma's beloved Wesley. 'Cause it's said you're crazy, but no man is so crazy that he'd ride in here like a rabbit into a den of wolves."

The man grinned, showing yellow teeth beneath his brushy mustache, obviously hoping that what he'd said was so.

Yakima aped the man's expression. "Now, you boys wouldn't have been part of that wolf pack that paid a visit to the Coffin farm yesterday, would you?"

The man with the blond mustache slowly let his lips close over his teeth. The other man's eyes grew harder and darker.

Yakima lowered the Yellowboy's barrel, dropping the forestock into his left palm and blowing a hole through the blond-mustached man's left cheek. The man jerked back in his saddle as though his horse had only shifted its feet. As the other man stared wide-eyed and was just beginning to dumbly raise his own carbine, Yakima plunked a second round through that man's forehead, where two deep lines formed a tributary-like Y.

It was as good a target as any.

The man jerked back, dropping his rifle and bringing one hand up to the wound as though to make sure it was really there. The other arm hung slack at his side. His horse whinnied and pitched, and he tumbled back against his hot roll, then, as the horse jerked sideways, tumbled down off the mount's left hip, getting his left boot caught in its stirrup and hanging there and jerking as he died.

The horse continued to prance and side-step, whinnying its disapproval at the twin gun blasts. The square-faced man hung with his head and shoulders raking the ground, eyes staring dully at the sky.

The blond-mustached man sat his own saddle stiffly, back ramrod straight as he stared straight ahead at Yakima. As blood dribbled from the quarter-sized hole in his cheek, his eyes blinked. He seemed to want to say something, to maybe reprimand the man who'd just killed him, but he was too dead for words.

So as his horse stepped straight back and sort of lowered its head in chagrin, the blond-mustached man fell sideways from his saddle and piled up on the frosty ground like a ragged sack of grain dropped from a wagon.

Chapter 23

Ma's own violent snore woke her up.

Gasping and choking and then coughing on the phlegm she'd sucked down the wrong pipe, she jerked her head up from her pillow and spat over the side of the bed into her thunder mug. Sitting up in bed, she looked around, squinting at the gray light pushing at her second-floor bedroom's two windows.

She'd drunk so much tanglefoot the night before — she found a bottle of blackberry brandy where English Charlie hadn't been able to find it, in a sideboard drawer under tablecloths she hadn't used in nearly twenty years — that she hadn't bothered to draw the curtains when she'd finally staggered up to bed around midnight. She winced at the sting of the light against her drink-tender eyes and reflected on the fact that it was morning. Not dawn but morning, likely pushing on toward ten.

A muffled pistol shot sounded. Then another.

Continuing to hack phlegm from her throat, Ma dropped her bunion-gnarled feet to the floor, spat again into the thunder mug before heaving herself up and walking, limping on both tender ankles and feet, to the window.

"What's all the shootin' about?" she muttered, working her jaw like a cow chewing cud and directing her gaze to the long, L-shaped bunkhouse sitting about fifty yards down a slight slope from the main lodge.

A half dozen men, dressed for the cold weather, were standing around on the bunkhouse's front gallery. They were milling busily while four or five saddled horses stood tied to the hitch rack before them. The men themselves were staring up the hill rising in the northeast, down which three more riders were heading toward the ranch headquarters, one of the three trailing a horse by a lead line. Over this led horse lay what appeared a dead man.

Ma's heart leaped into her throat. Her fingers tingled, and her eyes widened as she stared across the yard.

The breed? Had these men killed the half-breed son of a bitch who'd shot her boy?

Ma swung away from the window, and moving much more fleetly than she had only a moment ago, she began stripping off her flannel nightgown and night sock and pulling on her man's long-handles and baggy corduroy trousers, then her oversized undershirt and gray wool work shirt. Five minutes later, she stomped into her boots and was jolting on down the stairs toward the front door, where she grabbed her feather-trimmed opera hat and coat and, shrugging into the coat, headed outside in a hurry.

Kicking snow around her ankles, she crossed the yard toward the bunkhouse and reached it just as the three riders and the dead man drew to a stop near the bunkhouse's front corner.

"Who is it?" Ma said as her foreman, Blaze Westin, moved off the gallery, a mug of coffee smoking in his gloved left hand, and tramped on over toward the paint horse that was hauling the dead man belly down across its blanket saddle.

Ma was breathless as she skirted one of her own riders' horses on her way to the paint. "Is it him? Did you boys get that rancid son of an Injun whore?"

Before any of the men could respond, Ma grabbed a fistful of the dead man's long coal black hair and lifted his head to look at his face. Scowling, Ma released the head, let it drop down against the horse's side, and turned to Blaze Westin, tipping her own head back to peer up at the extraordinarily tall man's face beneath the brim of his chocolate-brown Stetson. "That's Harvey Chief Stick, that Cree from Canada. He ain't the one that killed my Wes!"

"No, ma'am, he ain't," Westin said in his slow Texas drawl, shaking his head just as slowly. He had the thinnest lips Ma had ever seen, and long stringy hair he never washed. "But we found him and about five other Crees tryin' to run off some of your beef early this mornin'. McCall seen 'em an' rode back to the headquarters for help. We all rode out, split up when them Injuns did, but this one here — ole Harvey — is the only one we managed to run down. 'Pears they was tryin' to take advantage of that snow squall to do a little long-loopin' out here at Coyote Ridge."

"Ah, hell!" Ma continued to scowl up at Blaze Westin. "Blaze, I ain't interested in ole Harvey Chief Stick or any o' his band. I want that half-breed that killed Wes. You boys was supposed to git out after him at first light!"

"Now, Mrs. Lassiter," Westin said, frowning in that dumb, stubborn way the Texan had, "you wouldn't want Harvey's boys runnin' off their leash out here. Hell, they could be workin' for the Furys, an' . . ."

He let his voice trail off as Ma gave him a look that would have put a curl in the devil's tail. Finally, Westin drew a deep breath. "Well, I sent Donny Laroque and Red Berger out to see if they could cut the breed's trail for us. Figured to join 'em out there later, after we had Harvey run to ground." The tall Texan hiked a shoulder. "I reckon we can head out after 'em now."

"That would be a good idea, Blaze." Ma gave a caustic chuff as she wheeled and headed back toward the lodge standing tall, its roof mantled with snow, beneath the snow-covered ridge.

Behind her, Westin called, "You won't be joinin' us today, Mrs. Lassiter?" His tone sounded hopeful.

"No," Ma said. "I got the chilblains, I do. I ain't as young as I used to be." Truth was, having lost Wes had left her feeling dark and lacking in vim and vinegar. Yesterday's ride had about killed her. She was tired. She would let her crew run the half-breed down.

She turned and glared at the men gathered around the foreman and staring after her warily. "I want you boys to bring him back to me. He's got a reckonin' comin'! But if you can't bring him back to me kickin' an' squirmin', I want his *head.*" She glanced at her cottonwood-timbered gallery. "Just bring it on up to the house and nail it to the porch rail for me. Big ole death-grin on his face. Keep in mind, you bring him in alive you'll all get a bonus."

Growling like a she-griz who'd lost the Missouri pike she'd been fishing for, Ma turned, stomped up the lodge's porch steps, went on into the house, and slammed the door loudly behind her. She stomped snow from her boots and headed into the big living room to start a fire; the lodge was as cold as a cave. She'd only made it halfway to the large, dark hearth when she stopped suddenly, lifting her head in the air, sniffing.

Tobacco smoke.

"What the hell?"

She turned her head, following the scent with her nose. Seemed to be coming from her office, the door of which was open. She headed for it, stepped inside, wondering if in her inebriated state the night before she had left a cigarette stub smoldering in a wastebasket. Like to have burned the damn house down. . . .

Just inside her office door, she stopped. The office was a small room with a map of the county above the small fireplace in the back wall. To the right of the fireplace was a rolltop desk. The desk sat sideways to the office door, with a window flanking it. The gray light of the window revealed the bulky silhouette of a man sitting back in Ma's swivel, leather-upholstered Windsor chair, a flat-brimmed hat tipped back off his forehead.

He wore a three-point capote and high-topped, rabbit fur moccasins. One moccasin was hiked on a knee. A Winchester Yellowboy rifle with an octagonal barrel leaned against the desk to his left. A horn-gripped gun handle jutted above the flap of his capote, from a holster thonged on his right thigh.

Ma's eyes went back to the rifle. Half-consciously, she knew who her visitor was, and she was just as half-consciously surprised to see such a fancy-looking rifle, with an engraved, gold-chased receiver, in his possession. Such savages usually carried old-model carbines held together with wire or shrunken rawhide.

Ma reached for the pistol on her hip, and blinked hard. Her hand brushed only the wide leather belt holding her pants up. She'd been in such a hurry to see the dead man outside that she hadn't strapped on her .45 and shell belt.

She stared at the casually reclining figure before her, unable to see his face against the glowing gray window. A nuthatch flitted in the long-needled branches of the pine behind him. A fine black stallion was tied to a branch of the pine, looking in the window and twitching one ear. The man had a tightly rolled cigarette in the hand propped on Ma's desk, and now he slowly raised the quirley to his lips.

It glowed.

He blew the smoke out into the office before him, and said softly, casually, "I know what you're thinking. But if you open your mouth to scream, I'll gun you before you get the first note out."

"I don't scream."

"If you try to make a run for the front door, I'll drill you through your head before you put your second boot down."

"That about covers it, don't it?"

"Not quite."

Yakima slid his Colt from its holster, heard the satisfying clicks as the hammer rocked back, turning the cylinder, and held it at full cock. He aimed the gun at the bulky figure of the woman in the doorway before him, feeling an intense heat behind his ears and an urgency in his trigger finger. In his mind, he could hear Aubrey's screams as this woman had taken a bullwhip to her while her men burned her cabin and barn and killed her stock and left her to freeze in the storm.

Yakima tightened his jaw as he rocked forward in the chair and gained his feet. He stepped to one side, in front of the cold fireplace. "Over here."

"Why? What are you gonna do?"

Yakima detected a satisfying note of fear in the woman's voice. "You're gonna practice your penmanship. Now get over here and sit down behind your desk. Come on — I don't have all morning. If you do what I tell you, I might even let you live . . . though the bitch who shit out the likes of Wesley Lassiter sure as hell don't deserve it."

"You son of a bitch," the woman sobbed angrily. "You killed my boy!"

"And I'm gonna gut-shoot you and leave you howling if you don't get over here."

The woman gave a groan of fury and frustration and walked toward Yakima. She stopped before him, and he could see the fleshy, ugly mess of her wart-stippled face, the pinched witch's eyes in pouched sockets. He waved the gun at the desk, and she sat down, making the chair creak beneath her weight.

"Get out pen, ink, and paper."

Ma Lassiter frowned up at him, jutting her lower jaw. "What is this bullshit, breed?"

Yakima just stared down at her. His finger drew a little tighter across the trigger. She must have seen the resolve in his eye, the eagerness to drill a bullet through her, so, with a shaking right hand, she opened a drawer and pulled out a tablet of lined note-paper. She pulled a tray containing a pen and ink bottle out from under the nest of pigeonholes stuffed with rolled-up papers. She slid a cloth-bound brand book aside and set the pad in its place.

"If you want to learn how to read and write, breed," the woman said, gritting her teeth, "I hear there's a good teacher in town."

"Dip your pen."

When she'd done what he'd told her to do, he pressed his cocked Colt to the back of her head. After fuming and fussing and then grunting against the pain of the Colt pressed to her head, she wrote in a script improbably ornate for such a crude, evil woman:

To Whom It May Concern:

I, being of sound mind, and having come

to deeply regret burning the Coffin farm and whipping Aubrey Coffin to within an inch of her life and leaving her to die, have decided that the only way to repay the woman and to do what is right is to sign over my own ranch to Mrs. Coffin. With this pen, I hereby sign over the headquarters of the Coyote Ridge Ranch and all my surrounding land and its stock holdings and water and mineral rights to Mrs. Aubrey Coffin. All I own except for the clothes on my back are as of this date now hers.

Abigail Lassiter

"No one'll believe this," Ma said, her voice quavering with exasperation as she threw her pen down.

"I wouldn't be so —"

Someone rapped on the front door.

"Help!" Ma screamed. "He's here! He's — !"

Yakima slammed his pistol against the back of the woman's head.

CHAPTER 24

As he heard the front door open and a couple of sets of boots pounding the floorboards, Yakima reached over Ma Lassiter slumped over her desk. He tore the sheet from the tablet, folded it quickly, and stuck it into his shirt pocket. He turned toward the room's open door just beyond which two men appeared, widening their eyes and raising carbines.

Yakima swung his Colt around and fired.

One of the men yowled and grabbed his shoulder as he fired his carbine into the rug on the office's floor. As the other man raised his rifle to his shoulder, Yakima grabbed his Yellowboy and threw himself against the window flanking the desk. Glass shattered around him, a few shards cutting into his coat and buckskins, as he dove on through and hit the snowy ground on his left shoulder.

He rolled, getting his feet beneath him and

coming up quickly, holding the rifle in his left hand and triggering his pistol through the broken window with the other. Inside, a rifle flashed. The bullet screeched over Yakima's head and chewed a dogget out of the pine to which Wolf was tied. Firing one more shot into the Lassiter lodge, Yakima leaped into the saddle and ground his heels against Wolf's flanks.

As the horse leaped forward and began racing across the weed-bristling, snow-blanketed backyard, angling north toward hogback hills, Yakima heard shouts and hoof thuds — men storming around the lodge from the front. A man's shrill shout rose from inside Ma Lassiter's office.

"Back here!" Ma's hoarse voice shouted out the window.

Pop! Pop!

Two bullets curled the air around Yakima's ears, one slug chewing shards from a snow-glazed rock ahead of him, another slicing a dead twig from a box elder towering over a gully on the half-breed's left. Ma must have had a gun in her desk, and was using it now.

"That Injun bastard invaded *my* house, and now's he's gettin' *away!*" Ma squealed. "Bring me a *horse!*"

Yakima barely heard that last. Wolf was leaping the gully where it curled along the base of the buttes, hooves thudding the frozen ground, tack squawking loudly, and then he lunged at an angle up the ridge. Halfway up, Yakima turned to peer at the ranch yard behind him. A half dozen riders were galloping across the ground he'd just covered, horses lunging through crusty drifts and plowing through the scraggly remains of last summer's garden.

One man raised a carbine to his shoulder as he rode, his reins in one gloved hand. The carbine stabbed umber flames, puffed smoke. As several other riders rode around him and on ahead, he hung back slightly as he racked a fresh round and tried again.

Yakima turned forward, hunkering low as Wolf took the incline in long, lunging strides. As he and the black crested the ridgeline, he heard the men shouting and the screech of tack as they leaped the gully and started up the slope.

Yakima turned Wolf east, following the same tracks he'd made when he'd circled the ranch yard from the south, angling around to its rear from the east. He rode hard. The black could handle the snow that the wind had swept into two- and three-foot drifts. It could also handle the gulleys that scored this country slanting gently eastward toward the broad canyon through which the Missouri slid. The cold was another matter. . . .

Those canyons cut by Hatchet Creek were what he was heading for. The men behind him would have a tough time keeping up to him through such rugged country, and he could lead them like lambs to the slaughter as he made his steady, purposeful way back to the Gatling gun nestled in its cave — loaded and waiting.

As he and Wolf ascended the slope of another deep gully and crested the ridge, guns barked loudly behind. Keeping Wolf moving, Yakima turned to see a good eight men behind him now — closer than he'd wanted. He'd expected to have a cleaner leave-taking of the Lassiter ranch, hadn't counted on men interrupting him during his business with Ma.

He'd hoped for a solid ten- or fifteen-minute head start.

Shit, they were hard on his heels. All seemed to be triggering lead, and a few of those hot bees were screeching too close for comfort and thumping into the ground around Wolf's hammering hooves. Yakima reined up suddenly, swung Wolf around, racked a shell into the Yellowboy's breech, and sent four of his own lead hornets whistling toward the riders hammering toward him in a ragged line.

They all ducked, but one drew his head down especially hard as his hat was ripped off his head and went sailing off in the breeze. One horse bucked, nearly throwing its rider. The shaggy line of pursuers split into two groups as they returned Yakima's fire, but by then the half-breed had kicked his black into another ground-chewing gallop, outdistancing the Coyote Ridge riders' bullets.

That bought him some time. The gap between him and them opened to a hundred yards, then two hundred, and then he dropped into a little crease in the prairie that angled into a bowl-shaped valley. He only went a few yards down, and then he slid out of the saddle, hitting the slope with legs splayed, one up, one down, as Wolf continued down away from him.

Yakima ran back up to the lip of the ridge and hunkered beneath the cutbank crowned with a large, square boulder with a crack through its middle. He shoved his left shoulder against a corner of the rock and gripped the Yellowboy in both his gloved hands, waiting.

He could hear the thuds of oncoming horses. They grew louder until he heard the raspy breaths of the horses and the muttered conversation of two or three men until they seemed to be twenty, maybe thirty yards away. He rose from behind the boulder. Three riders were angling into the crease, heading straight for him. They all saw him at once — eyes widening, arms sawing back on their reins, one man yelling something unintelligible that he didn't finish before he was rolling off the rump of his mouse brown mare with a hole in his throat.

Yakima ejected the spent shell, raised the Yellowboy once more.

Boom! Boom!

One of the remaining two twisted backward as a slug plunked through his right lung. The other man gritted his teeth against the bullet that had just torn into his left shoulder, and raised his Spencer repeater. Yakima winced as the Spencer barked, the bullet hammering into the boulder to the half-breed's left.

Yakima rammed another round into the Yellowboy's smoking breech, pressed the stock against his shoulder, drew a quick bead on the man's chest, and fired just as the man worked his own cocking lever.

The man jerked as though he'd been slapped.

He froze, then looked down at the fuzzy hole in his buckskin coat, just up from his heart. He lifted his head, gritting his teeth and yelling like a lobo as he ground his spurs into the grulla's flanks. Horse and rider bounded toward Yakima as the man weakly raised his rifle and narrowed one eye as he tried to plant his sights on his target.

The Spencer exploded but not before Yakima had stepped to his right. The slug whined off over the bowl-shaped valley. Yakima blew the man off the mare's back with another bullet to the side of the man's head. As the man piled up in the snowy brush with a clipped grunt and ringing spurs and lay still, the horse whinnied and dug its front hooves into the ground.

It stopped dead, gave Yakima a hard glare, and shook its head so hard that it nearly tore out of its bridle.

Yakima looked around the indignant horse. The man he'd lung-shot lay belly down, head up, writhing in pain, foamy blood spewing from his mouth and into the brittle weeds. He was finished; no need to waste another round.

Yakima swung his head around again, seeing nothing but vacant prairie all around. Deep lines of incredulity cut into his dark forehead. Where were his other pursuers? As the mare backed away from Yakima, snorting her disapproval before turning and trotting back the way she'd come, trailing her reins, Yakima heard the rumble of fast riders. He whipped around toward the canyon behind him.

A half dozen riders were moving toward him from the north along the canyon floor. They must have broken off from the men lying dead around him, each group intending to enter the canyon via separate feeder ravines.

Hearing more rumbling, he turned to see another group, roughly the same size as the other, pounding along the canyon floor from the east. Both groups were flanking him.

Quickly plucking fresh shells from his cartridge belt and slipping them through the Yellowboy's loading gate, Yakima whistled loudly. It took only about ten seconds for the white-socked black, who'd also seen the riders heading toward it, to gallop up out of the feeder ravine behind Yakima and stand nearby, craning its neck to peer warily into the canyon where the riders were shouting, a couple snapping off desperate, furious shots.

Yakima's breaking into the lodge virtually under their noses and laying his pistol across the back of Ma's head had apparently piss-burned them good. The half-breed couldn't help grinning at that, jade eyes flashing in the steely light angling down from the low clouds with thin, lighter patches here and there.

His enjoyment was short-lived. He was outnumbered nearly fifteen to one, and he was at least three miles from the assistance of the Gatling gun. Wolf was a deep-bottomed horse, inured to snow but not to cold, especially not for long, and he'd already been ridden far and hard. How much farther could he go?

Yakima leaped into the saddle without aid of a stirrup and gave the stallion its stubborn head, dashing off along the crest of the rim, heading straight north and sweeping past the group of riders galloping from that direction along the canyon floor. A couple of the Coyote Ridge riders saw him, pointing and calling out, and Yakima put his head down and touched Wolf's flanks with his moccasin heels. The horse leaned forward and stretched its stride.

Yakima could hear the Coyote Ridge killers yelling and shouting in confusion, turned his head to see part of the group that had now become one heading on up an eroded crease in the steep ridge. Yakima found another crease, turned Wolf into it, and horse and rider galloped down the declivity, across the broad bowl, leaping a three-foot-wide creek that twisted through the center of the bowl, then shot up another wing of the canyon, heading due south.

He followed this wing of the canyon into the broken country along the broad Missouri's west side, pillars and massive boxes of sandstone rising around him. Bluffs capped with cedar impeded his way, and he had to take narrow cuts around them, heading ever nearer to the line of rocky hills in which he'd concealed the Gatling gun.

He'd traveled a half hour from where he'd left the Coyote Ridge riders milling in confusion, when he felt Wolf weaken beneath him. The stallion's stride grew short, and it began to stumble, heavy lungs working too hard and sounding like the chugging of an underpowered train. The stallion's fierce heart was pounding like a sledge.

Yakima reined in and swung down from the saddle. They were at the bottom of an aspen- and cedar-stippled slope. He looked up through the aspens, recognized the rocky ridge at the top. That wasn't the ridge where he'd concealed the big gun, but the other was just beyond.

He glanced behind at the Coyote Ridge riders loping toward him and about three hundred yards back and closing fast. They'd had no problem tracking him through the snow. If he tried to push Wolf up the slope, he'd lose his horse. And he'd gain nothing. He and the stallion had been through too much together for Yakima to abuse the beast that way. He had little chance without him, but he wouldn't kill him.

Quickly, he stripped the tack from the animal's steaming back. Blowing hard, sweat glistening on his heaving, sweat-frothed sides, Wolf watched Yakima with an exhausted, puzzled cast to his gaze. The half-breed dropped the tack on the ground beside a boulder, met the horse's incredulous brown gaze.

"Go on, boy. If I make it, I'll whistle." He slapped the horse's rump. "Git!"

Wolf lurched forward and trotted off, continuing to glance behind in bewilderment. Yakima swung toward the slope, shouldered his rifle, and began climbing, following a game trail that angled into the aspens while meandering around rocky outcrops. Behind one such outcrop and about fifty yards into the trees, Yakima stopped and hunkered down behind a lightning-split cottonwood.

He was breathing hard. His mouth tasted like copper, and his legs ached from the slippery climb. Despite the cold air, sweat bathed his forehead. He still had a good hundred yards to go through the pines, and even following the game path, it would be a stiff go.

He looked down the slope and across the rolling prairie.

The Coyote Ridge riders were within a hundred yards now, riding between a hat-shaped butte and a miniature mesa with a top like a broken table and spilling white-powdered black lignite down its eroded sides. They'd seen him climbing afoot, and they were making a beeline, spread out and whipping their horses with rein ends.

Yakima racked a shell into the Winchester's chamber. They might be ready for another ambush, but it was worth a try. He had to buy himself some time to rest up before continuing on over this ridge and climbing the one beyond it. It wouldn't hurt to thin their ranks a little, either.

As he hunkered low on one knee, slowly regaining his breath, he knew deep down that he'd likely outsmarted himself with his ploy at Ma Lassiter's cabin. Too many things had had to happen just right for that to work, and the only thing that had worked so far was that he'd managed to stay just far enough ahead, at the expense of his horse that was already blown when he'd reached the ranch headquarters, to still be breathing. He'd likely die with that quitclaim deed still in his pocket, doing Aubrey Coffin little good.

It had seemed like a good idea at the time. . . .

The riders were within twenty yards of the bottom of the slope, directly below Yakima. The half-breed caressed the Winchester's trigger, taking deep, hopeful breaths.

The riders stopped. They all looked up the slope. They couldn't see Yakima through the trees, and with a fine snow coming down to obscure him further, there was no way they could see him crouched beside a broken branch of the lightning-felled cottonwood. He could hear their voices, see their heads swinging around as they discussed the situation. They seemed cautious, hesitant.

"Come on," Yakima grated out through clenched teeth, his cheek pressed against the Yellowboy's stock. "Come on up the hill, fellers. The half-breed's likely already to the top and hightailing it down the other side."

The riders milled on mounts so tired, snouts bathed in frozen vapor, that several were sagging nearly to their knees.

Finally, the lead rider — a tall, mustached

man in a beaver coat and cream Stetson tied to his head with a green muffler — moved his mouth and jerked his head at the slope. Two men of the group moved forward and put their horses up the hill.

The others waited, watching on their enervated mounts. They sniffed and wiped their noses and spat to one side and shifted their rifles in their hands, resting the barrels on their shoulders.

The two scouts continued up the slope, their horses lunging forward, digging their shod hooves into the frozen, weed-covered turf.

"Shit."

Yakima jerked his breath-iced scarf down from over his mouth and scowled down the octagonal barrel of his Yellowboy. He'd hoped to take more than just two. And he'd hoped to send the others wheeling and riding on back down the hill, buying himself more time to run up and over the ridge.

The scout riders moved toward him, meandering through the trees. Cautious. Expectant. They each carried a Winchester, barrel high. They rode about twenty yards apart as they came up through the trees.

When one was ten yards from Yakima's position, the half-breed slammed a bullet through his brisket and sent his horse buck-kicking back down the slope. The other wheeled toward Yakima, and then he was dead, too, and rolling downhill before piling up against a chokecherry patch. His horse ran off along the wooded shoulder of the slope.

Yakima spat another curse through gritted teeth as he racked another shell into the Winchester's chamber and looked downhill through his wafting powder smoke. The riders were spreading out along the bottom of the hill, shouting excitedly as they put their mounts up the steep incline.

"Get around him," the tall, mustached man shouted loudly. "Get around that son of a bitch, and cut him off from the top!"

No, this wasn't going well at all.

Yakima turned and did all he could do.

He ran like hell.

Chapter 25

Aubrey lifted her head from the pillow with a gasp. "Yakima!"

She blinked, heart pounding. The sheets of June Trevelyan's bed were damp from Aubrey's cold sweat. Footsteps sounded beyond the blanket curtain over the door, and June swept the curtain aside as she poked her head into the room.

"What on earth?" the teacher said, cheeks flushed. "You frightened me." Hand splayed on her chest, she stepped cautiously into the room, as though afraid she'd find a bobcat waiting for her under the bed. "A dream?"

Aubrey sat up, wincing at the clawing pain across her back, and looked out the window to her left that showed a day much like the day before and which would show similar days all winter long: cold and gray. She nodded, staring as the dream faded like smoke on the wind but with a few fragments lingering like sticky cobwebs. "I dreamt she was running him down. Her and her men."

June moved up to the bed and placed her hands on Aubrey's shoulders, gently shoving her back down to the bed. "You rest easy. There's nothing you can do for him. If he's crazy enough to go up against Ma Lassiter and that passel of wolves of hers, he's crazy enough to die alone."

There was a tightness in the teacher's voice, an especially bitter anger.

"No."

Aubrey sat up and flung the bedcovers off her. She winced again. Her back was on fire, but over the past couple of days she'd regained some strength. Probably not enough for what she had in mind to do, but she welcomed the steely determination flooding her. It was better than the fury and self-pity she'd been entertaining for the past forty-eight hours — her rage at what Ma Lassiter had done to her while lamenting the burning of her farm and the general wretchedness of her life.

"Aubrey, this is crazy," June said, standing back against the dresser. "You can't go anywhere in your condition. It's cold — damn near ten degrees."

"I'm feeling better." Aubrey turned to June. "Do you have some clothes I can wear? Tough clothes. Clothes for riding?"

When June just stared at her stubbornly, arms crossed on her chest, Aubrey said softly, "I'm going out there, June. It'd be best if I went dressed — don't you think? And a gun of some kind wouldn't hurt, neither."

June sighed and shook her head in disgust. Wheeling, she left the room and came back with some rough outdoor clothes — men's denims, long-handles, a heavy cotton camisole, and a wool work shirt — which she tossed onto the bed.

"I'll find you some boots," she said as she left the room once more, the blanket jostling into place behind her.

Fifteen minutes later, Aubrey was dressed and staggering a little as she left the bedroom. She felt as though she'd taken a couple of shots of powerful whiskey, as the room was twisting and turning around her.

"You're pale," June said, placing a hand on the farm woman's forehead. "And you still have a fever."

Aubrey brushed her hand away. "I feel fine."

"Have some coffee and oatmeal."

"No." Aubrey lifted a wool-lined leather coat off an arm of a parlor chair. A heavy scarf and a knit wool cap were draped over it. "I can borrow these?"

June nodded but her mouth corners were turned down in mute reproof. "You have to have something to eat. To fight the fever with."

Aubrey pulled the coat on. "All right — I'll take a bite." She wasn't hungry — in fact, her belly rebelled at the thought of food hitting it — but she'd need fortification for the ride ahead of her.

Wearing the coat but leaving it unbuttoned, she sat down at the kitchen table. June scooped up a bowl of oatmeal and raisins, sweetened it with honey from a crock, and set it before Aubrey with a small tin pitcher of milk. Audrey picked up her spoon and began forcing the meal down her throat, following every few swallows with coffee.

"Thank you for this," Aubrey said, spooning more meal into her mouth. It was settling into her stomach without making her sick. In fact, she could feel it giving her strength and somewhat taming the burning in her bandaged back.

"You shouldn't do this," June said, sagging into a chair across from Aubrey. "He isn't worth it. No man is worth dying for."

"He saved my life."

June sighed and lowered her eyes to the

oilcloth-covered table. "He won't stay. You won't be able to depend on him."

"I didn't ask him to stay. I don't intend to depend on him." Aubrey looked over a spoonful of oatmeal at June. "Where's the sheriff?"

"Likely the same place your Indian went," June said.

The reason for June's bitterness was clear to Aubrey then. She continued to eat in silence.

"None of you will be back," June said fatefully, when Aubrey dropped her spoon into her half-empty bowl. June looked out a window, and her chest rose and fell in a long, dreadful sigh. "And I'll be here all winter . . . alone."

"Some things have to be done." Aubrey set her hand on one of June's. June looked at it, then at Aubrey, who stood then and began buttoning her coat. "Do you have a gun?"

"There's an old pistol in my desk in the main room." June canted her head toward the door. "Rance gave it to me to fend off troublemakers, if any came calling. You can take it. There's a half-full box of shells with it. I've never fired it, don't even know if it *will* shoot."

"Thanks." Aubrey turned to the door,

stopped, and turned back to the teacher who sat with her elbows on the table, cradling her chin in her interlocked hands. "I'll be back, June."

The teacher did not look up at her.

Aubrey pulled the knit cap down on her head, looped the scarf around her neck, and went out.

Yakima ran until he thought his thighs would splinter and the gray bones would slice through his kneecaps.

He didn't dare look behind and risk tripping over a branch or a rock. He didn't have to look behind or around him. He could hear the Coyote Ridge riders thundering up the slope about a hundred yards behind him and closing gradually from both sides. A couple on his left were angling toward him, hoping to cut him off before he gained the ridge, but trees and boulders were slowing their horses' progress.

The killers whooped and hollered like wolves knowing they had an old bull buff trapped in a box canyon.

Yakima powered on up the ridge, not bothering to slant but heading straight on up toward the gray sky opening above the ridgeline. He ran through a gap in the trees where there were few fallen branches or other obstacles.

Behind, guns popped. Bullets hammered into tree boles around him, chewing up the frozen ground above, behind, and to each side of him. One clipped his left heel, and he grimaced as he sucked air and continued running, trying not to let the burn slow him any.

Finally, ten feet from the ridgeline, he whipped around, bringing the Yellowboy to bear. There were several riders all around him, spaced yards apart, some moving around behind trees or boulders. Yakima picked out one and fired. He picked out another and fired. He fired two more times and emptied three out of four saddles, which wasn't bad under the circumstances.

A gun popped from along the slope to his right. He felt the bullet cut across the top of his arm, tearing wool stuffing from his coat. As he felt the warmth of his blood dribble out across his arm, he wheeled and continued running up and over the crest of the slope. He wanted desperately to stop again and catch his breath, but there was no time. He'd waylaid his pursuers with those four rounds and three more killings, but they wouldn't stop for long.

He could hear Ma Lassiter's hoarse voice shouting orders, like the most bullying of army drill sergeants.

As he plunged down the slope, negotiating snow-dusted slide rock, he could see the Gatling's lair at the crest of the opposite ridge that resembled a dinosaur spine with winter-naked oaks, ash, and aspens forming a ragged strip from about two-thirds up the ridge to its rocky crest. He couldn't see the gun itself, because it was tucked back into a niche in the rocks and screened by branches and the spindly shrubs around it, but he remembered his markers. It was between a large aspen with a broken, hanging branch, and a wagon-sized, jagged-edged boulder standing on a thin stony stem that looked so insubstantial that it could crack loose and release the rock at the smallest nudge.

Yakima gained the bottom of the ridge, wheezing, his legs feeling like jelly.

Turning his head from one side to the other, he saw the Coyote Ridge riders galloping over the ridge behind him, whooping and hollering and making a game of it. A couple of horses, their lungs no doubt exploding from being pushed so hard in the cold air, went down and rolled, their riders leaping free, then returning to the dying mounts to retrieve their rifles.

The horseless riders then continued at dead runs, yowling. This was no doubt the most fun they'd had all fall, and it would have to tide them over the winter.

Yakima triggered two more shots to keep the riders a few yards behind him, and continued running up the opposite slope. He was directly beneath the Gatling's nest. He was running hard, but his legs had turned to wood, the muscles giving out. Each lunging stride was like moving through quicksand. He grunted, pushing off his left knee with his left hand, and off his right knee with the Yellowboy's butt, hoisting himself up the slope as much as running up it.

He was fifty yards from the gun's nest when one of the several bullets sizzling through the air around him was stopped by the back of his left thigh. At first it felt like the sharp, angry nip of a horsefly. One stride later, it felt like a blow from a smithy's hammer delivered by one powerful fist.

That knee buckled, hit the ground. Yakima crumpled over it, cursing and groaning and trying desperately to turn and make a little more of a fight of it before the angels started singing him home. Three men were clomping up the slope right behind him in an arrow-point formation, their horses blown, half-frozen blood slinging from their nostrils, but still lunging.

Yakima raised the Yellowboy. The lead rider triggered a shot with a Colt revolver and missed Yakima's left cheek by a whisker.

The half-breed dropped the cocking lever, then rammed it up to rack a shell, but it stopped suddenly with that metallic, tooth-gnashing grating sound that could only mean a jam. The lead rider grinned, yellow teeth showing beneath a salt-and-pepper mustache with upswept ends. He narrowed a smug eye as he stared down his Colt's barrel.

Yakima could no longer hear the rattle of hooves for the harps being strummed for him in heaven. Angels or no, he automatically reached for the Colt, knowing he'd likely be in heaven or wherever he was going before he could get the piece even half out of its holster.

Then a black spot, like a mud splatter, appeared in the forehead of the man grinning down at him. The Colt in his hand made a sound like a rock slammed against an empty barrel.

Yakima winced, closing his eyes, but when he looked up again the grinning man was on the ground and his horse was bucking straight out in front of the half-breed. The horse's angry whinny was drowned with a sound like a railroad dray of ore rolling down a steep hill.

Yak-yak-yak-yak-yak-yak-yak! The other two men were spotted with dark red and thrown off their own pitching mounts. The Gatling gun paused, and Yakima could hear the canister's squawk atop its swivel, and then the yakking returned once more, a handful of .45 slugs drilling the ground before three more men riding in from Yakima's left before the shooter got a better read and sent more slugs hurling through chests, faces, and shoulders.

Sudden silence save for dying men's groans and horses' screams and the thuds of retreating hooves.

The gun's swivel squawked.

Yakima lay flat against the slope, keeping his head down beneath the lead storm.

Yak-yak-yak-yak-yak-yak-yak-yak-yak!

Two more horseback riders, then two men on foot, and then a contingent of four who'd turned to flee hit the ground or fell with their horses pitching, rolling, screaming, and sending blood splashing like thrown paint across the white and tawny hillside.

When the gun's caterwauling stopped, men and horses lay sprawled. A few horses had survived the fusillade and were galloping off down the crease at the bottom of the slope, angling north and the hell away from here. Below Yakima about thirty yards, one man heaved himself to hands and knees and reached for a carbine.

Yakima slipped his Colt from its holster, squinting down the revolver's barrel at the man's ear, and fired. The man slumped sideways with a grunt. Holding the smoking pistol out in front of him, Yakima looked around. None of the other slouched or twisted figures was moving.

None appeared stumpy and bulky enough to be Ma Lassiter.

Where the hell was the old bitch?

From upslope, Yakima heard the Gatling swivel again, and turned to see Sheriff Rance Hagan step out from the rocks and begin moving downhill, the ragged hem of his blanket coat jostling about his patched trouser knees. Hagan tossed a scarf end over a shoulder and pulled one glove on, then the other one.

He stopped just above the half-breed, who'd gotten busy wrapping a bandanna around his leg. Judging by the way the blood was oozing instead of pumping, no artery had been severed. There were two holes, front and back, which meant the slug had gone clean through.

A flesh wound. The wound in his arm continued to bleed, but it was even less severe than the one in his leg.

Maybe he'd live.

Yakima glanced up at the frosty, mustached face of the sheriff staring grimly down at him. "Figured you wouldn't want no part of this."

"Who said I did?"

Chapter 26

Aubrey shrugged down deeper into the coat June had given her, and kept the horse she'd rented from a livery barn in town along the wagon trail that cut through low country as it meandered toward the Coyote Ridge headquarters.

She'd never been to the headquarters, of course — she'd had no reason to — but everyone in the county seemed to know where it was without ever actually getting specific directions. Or they knew which trail would take you there. There was only one.

As she rode, grimacing against the cold that chewed at the deep abrasions on her back with every stride of the horse she held at spanking trots interspersed with lopes that she endured for about four minutes at a time, she wondered if Yakima was alive. If he was, she hoped there was something she could do to keep him alive. Barring that, she hoped she could find a way to kill Ma

Lassiter.

If ever there was a woman who needed killing, it was Ma.

Aubrey no longer cared about herself. She could live or die — it was all the same. She had nothing now. No cabin. No barn. No animals. Ma had taken everything away from her. She'd likely taken Yakima, as well.

Aubrey had no illusions that Yakima was hers — as June had insinuated, no such man ever belonged to any woman — but she was sure that she loved him and knew that even if they weren't together, the world would be a better place for her, knowing that he was in it somewhere.

She gigged the horse into a gallop and, chewing her lower lip, held the mount at a lope for nearly half a mile. When she pulled back on the reins, swooning in the saddle as a wave of weakness and nausea nearly overcame her, she spied movement off the trail to her right. A rider was moving down out of a crease in the eastern hills that abutted the Missouri. The crease was filled with snow, and the horse was having a tough time of it. It was lunging forward, lifting its front hooves high. The heavy way it moved said it had been ridden hard.

It was nearly blown.

Aubrey stopped her rented livery mount

and stared through the gray light. A fine snow threaded the air, obscuring the bulky figure astraddle the horse. Horse and rider were half a mile away, crossing the brushy line of the west fork of Hatchet Creek, so it was impossible to identify the person, but Aubrey felt her heart chug to life.

She continued to stare hopefully as the distant rider stopped on a slight rise where a large, lone cottonwood stood, stretching its lifeless limbs toward the low sky. The rider sagged in Aubrey's direction, and appeared to half fall, half crawl down from the saddle as a high-crowned hat tumbled off the rider's shoulder. It took nearly a full minute, but finally the figure dropped to hands and knees and crawled over to the tree. It twisted around heavily, put its back to the cottonwood bole, stretched its legs out in front of it, and sat there, still and quiet.

The horse stood a few yards away, hooves splayed, head and tail hanging.

The snow continued to dart around like white grain before Aubrey's puzzled, hopeful eyes.

"Come on," she urged the horse, pressing her boots to its flanks.

She put the horse off the trail's right side and started on a direct course toward the cottonwood. The horse near the tree turned its head toward her, gave a feeble swish of its tail when Aubrey's mount whinnied a greeting, then dropped its weary head once more. The bulky figure leaning against the tree did not move. Soon, the figure took on the distinguishing characteristics — round body, stubby legs, gray-brown hair wisping out from a knotted scarf — of Ma Lassiter. The eager expectation that Aubrey had felt earlier dissipated, replaced with worry.

No — don't be dead, she silently urged. *Don't die on me, you bitch. I want to be the one to kill you.*

Her blood made a rushing sound in her ears, like water in a long windmill pipe. She stopped the livery horse near Ma's near-dead claybank and swung down with a grunt as her tight back cried out in anger at the too-swift movement. She pulled her pistol out of her coat pocket and walked over to where the woman sat back against the tree, legs with their fur boots spread wide and extending straight out from the woman's hips.

The gray-brown eyes were open. Strands of hair slid across the woman's broad, pale forehead above them. She did not blink, and Aubrey felt a rock drop in her stomach when she decided the woman was dead.

Her heart surged once more, however, when Ma's chest rose, and the lids came slowly down over her eyes and rose again. She seemed to be staring right through Aubrey's belly as the farm woman stopped near the woman's feet.

"All dead." The woman's voice was like a demon's whisper from a haunted dream. "Every damn one of my men. Dead. Blown out of their saddles by that wretched Gatling gun." She shook her scarf-swathed head slightly. "Wherever the hell that cannon came from, I sure don't know. But it sure cleaned me out."

Aubrey pondered this. Gatling gun. Yakima had told her that the posse had taken a Gatling gun after him in Cottonwood Canyon, south of Wild Rose. Had he and Sheriff Hagan taken their turn with the gun? Could it be possible that all of Ma's men were, like she'd said, actually dead?

Could Yakima be alive?

"The man you were after," Aubrey said, hearing a quaver in her voice. "Is he alive?"

Ma continued to stare right through Aubrey as she shook her head again. "All dead. Every last one . . ."

Aubrey crouched and rammed the back of her hand against the woman's fleshy left cheek. It was like smacking a stout bag of suet hanging in a cellar. The woman's head moved only slightly, but her eyes didn't flicker.

"Did you hear me, you old hag? Is Yakima Henry alive?"

The woman's thick, chapped lips moved as she wheezed, "What in hell am I gonna do now? Come spring, the Fury riders will be runnin' wild on Coyote Ridge graze. Nesters, Injuns. . . ."

Aubrey stepped back with a frustrated groan and lifted the pistol. She held the heavy piece in both hands and ratcheted back the hammer.

"I'm gonna kill you. For taking the whip to me and burning my place, I should hang you, but I'd never get your fat ass up high enough. A bullet will have to do." Aubrey gritted her teeth and narrowed an eye as she planted the pistol's bead on the woman's pale forehead. She sobbed, lips quivering, as she yelled, "Are you ready to die, ready to join that yellow-livered cur of a son of yours, you worthless piece of filth?"

"Ah, don't do her any favors." Yakima's voice . . . as though from another world.

Aubrey whipped around. Seven riders rode slowly, ploddingly up the grade behind her, the other two horses turning to watch the newcomers. Yakima and Sheriff Hagan rode ahead of the other five. The half-breed rode somewhat slouched in the saddle, his dark-red face deep-lined and yellow around the eyes. Hagan was leading a packhorse that carried something under burlap on its back.

The Gatling gun.

Behind the gun were five Fury riders. She could tell by the brands on their horses.

Aubrey sucked a breath as she lowered her pistol. Her heart swelled, and she fought to swallow her emotion as Yakima and Hagan drew rein before her. Yakima stared down at her, and she returned the stare, her heart growing larger and larger in her chest and her eyes feeling wet.

"I thought she'd killed you."

"She gave it a good shot." Yakima canted his head toward the sheriff. "The law dog saved my bacon. And here I never trusted badge toters."

"No reason to start now," Hagan snorted. He glanced at Ma, who stared vacantly somewhere off between the horses and into the hazy light stitched with white. "She's finished. She can't do any more to you, Mrs. Coffin."

Emil and Emmett Fury rode up around Hagan to stare hatefully down at their old enemy, Ma Lassiter. "Christ!" Emil Fury said under his breath, spitting the word out disdainfully and wrinkling his broad nose.

Aubrey sucked a shaky breath. "I came out here to kill her."

"No need." Yakima moved his right arm stiffly, and snarled a curse as he reached into his coat. He pulled a folded leaf of paper, the corners of which the breeze crinkled. As he held it out over his horse's left wither toward Aubrey, the pellets of snow ticked against it. "For you."

Aubrey shoved her pistol into her coat pocket, came over, and took the paper from Yakima. She opened it, read it. Yakima watched her face. Small lines of perplexity dug into the skin above the bridge of her nose. She must have read the note several times, because it was a good while before she lowered it and lifted her gaze to the half-breed's once more.

"She signed her ranch over to you. It's yours if you want it."

"Why would she sign something like this?"

Yakima's mouth corners lifted a tired smile. "She didn't have much choice."

Hagan spat to one side. "I reckon it wouldn't hold up in a court of law if it was contested . . . unless it was witnessed by a county sheriff, say." He narrowed an eye at Aubrey. "I aim to put my John Hancock to it as witness, Mrs. Coffin. As far as I'm concerned — as far as this county is concerned — the Coyote Ridge Ranch is now yours."

"If you want it," Yakima said. "It's a big chunk of land."

"And, as you know," Hagan added, glancing at the Furys, "it comes with an enemy. A rather large, hump-necked spread just east of here."

"Nah, it don't." Emil Fury was still staring down at Ma Lassiter. "She made us out to be three times as big as we are." He looked at Aubrey. "Truth to tell, we got more graze than we got cattle. Too tough to run 'em up here, with Injuns and rustlers and drought. We cut back several years ago. Fewer cattle means we need fewer men to nurse 'em. And that's just fine with me. If you want the Lassiter spread, Mrs. Coffin, you'll get no trouble from us. We don't want it. Maybe . . . I don't know . . . if you need help we could make an arrangement. You know — share grazing and water rights."

Emmett said, "Our war was with her and her dry-gulching pistoleros. We never cared about her graze."

Aubrey shuttled her puzzled gaze between the two Furys, and then between Yakima and the sheriff, as though they were speaking a language foreign to her. So much was happening.

"I reckon the war's over, then," Yakima said.

Aubrey turned to regard Ma Lassiter. "What about her?"

Cousin Pat Anderson had ridden up beside Emil Fury. He slid his ivory-gripped .45 from its holster and rocked the hammer back. "I'll take care of her right now."

Emil Fury shoved his cousin's gun away. "Like the breed said, don't do her any favors, Pat. She's done been taken care of. Look at her. Like a gut-shot cur."

"I'll take her to town," Hagan said. "Have June check her out. Whatever happens, she's washed up. She *should* go to jail, but I don't reckon there's much point in that. You won't have to worry about her anymore, Mrs. Coffin. I got a feelin' if she makes it through the winter, which is unlikely, she'll spend the last of her years in Cavanaugh's Boardinghouse."

Aubrey shook her head and looked around before carefully folding the note and stuffing it down into her coat pocket, behind the pistol. "I'll have to think about this."

"In the meantime," Hagan said, "you'd best take the breed here to shelter. He took a couple bullets and could do with some tending."

"Yakima," Aubrey said, moving toward him and putting an administering hand on his thigh. "Oh, Yakima . . . why?"

The half-breed tried another tired smile, and just barely made it. He was sleepy. Oh, so very, very . . . sleepy. " 'Cause, at the time," he grunted, "there wasn't anyone else to do it." He slid his eyes toward the sheriff, then back to Aubrey. "And you deserved at least that much."

His eyelids fluttered. He sagged forward and sideways, barely caught himself by the saddle horn before he would have tumbled out of the saddle.

"Better take him home, Mrs. Coffin," Hagan advised. "I'll see about Ma."

"Home?"

"Coyote Ridge. It's the nearest shelter. Less than a mile from here."

Aubrey nodded slowly, suddenly comprehending all that had happened, was happening.

"Yes." Quickly, vengeance thoughts of Ma Lassiter drifting away on the wind, Aubrey mounted her rented horse. "Yes, come on, Yakima. Let's go home."

Yakima grunted and held tight to his saddle horn as, only half-conscious, he felt himself being led along through the chill breeze with the falling snow nipping his windburned cheeks. He didn't know how much time had passed when he woke in a big bed under many quilts with a warm, umber fire snapping and crackling nearby, in a vast fieldstone hearth. He no longer cared about time.

He smelled pine smoke and the wild musk of animal hides, the cherry fragrance of perfume.

He managed the strength to engulf the naked woman curled beside him in his arms, and slept again.

He could sleep a long time like this, he thought.

All winter.

ABOUT THE AUTHOR

Frank Leslie is the pseudonym of an acclaimed Western novelist who has written more than fifty novels and a comic book series. He divides his time between Colorado and Arizona, exploring the West in his pickup and travel trailer.

The employees of Thorndike Press hope you have enjoyed this Large Print book. All our Thorndike, Wheeler, and Kennebec Large Print titles are designed for easy reading, and all our books are made to last. Other Thorndike Press Large Print books are available at your library, through selected bookstores, or directly from us.

For information about titles, please call:
(800) 223-1244

or visit our Web site at:
http://gale.cengage.com/thorndike

To share your comments, please write:
Publisher
Thorndike Press
10 Water St., Suite 310
Waterville, ME 04901